MATADOR

D1601371

RAY BANKS
MATADOR

THOMAS & MERCER

Text copyright © 2013 Ray Banks
Originally released as a Kindle Serial, November 2012

Published by Thomas & Mercer
P.O. Box 400818
Las Vegas, NV 89140

ISBN-13: 9781611099348
ISBN-10: 161109934X
Library of Congress Control Number: 2012920570

To the *indultados*

Episode One

PASÉILLO

The first thing he heard, rising above the white noise of fourteen thousand people chattering, was the opening bars of a brassy paso doble. It echoed down the corridor to the *patio de caballos*, where they waited, mute and smoking. The grasping heat of the afternoon had faded; the light in the plaza had turned golden with age, and it was chilly in the shade of the stone corridor. He shivered as the two *alguaciles* returned to the mouth of the passage. Their ceremonial lap of the plaza was complete. It was time to leave.

He moved forward with the others. At the gate, he toed a cross in the sand as mirror to his hand before he turned and saluted his companions with the words, "May God divide the luck."

Then he stepped into the ring with his right foot forward. Aristocratic in bearing, blood thicker and richer than any of the thousands gathered to watch. He could smell them all. The odors were intrusive; they closed the throat. Tobacco, perfume, aftershave, hair oil, wine and whiskey, blood and bull; each jostled for attention, the breeze dictating priority as he crossed the plaza.

All eyes on him and his sparkling suit of lights. These people hadn't paid their hundred euros to see some *pueblo becerrada* where they could toss a clown in front of a calf and the crowd would still wave white for both ears. They'd paid to see something special, something different. As a result, they were a tough crowd. They wouldn't allow their *toreros* to cut ears unless they'd been thoroughly moved, unless something both spectacular and spiritual had taken place in front of them.

He was the senior man. To his right were the junior and middle matadors. Behind them walked their respective *cuadrillas*: three trios of *banderilleros*—he would place his own *banderillas*, but the three men would assist in other ways—and behind them, the mounted picadors, their horses half-blinkered and swaddled with padding. After them came the reserves, the wise monkeys, and the maintenance teams, and finally, the bells on their harnesses tinkling through the music, the mules that would have the honor of dragging the carcass from the plaza.

They saluted the president, asked for permission to begin, which was promptly granted. The president dropped the gate key to one of the alguaciles, who then passed it to one of the maintenance team. His banderilleros made a move to their capes, but he waved them off. As senior man, he had the first and fourth bulls, and he meant to start strong.

He'd already decided. The first pass would be his and his alone.

He walked out into the circle of sand with his capote. Something hot rolled around inside him. Sweat formed at the back of his neck. He let the capote unfurl, revealing a stiff, bright circle of magenta and yellow, as he approached the *toril*, the gate that joined the pens to the plaza. It was through this gate that the bull would enter the ring. Approaching it meant daggers from his manager, because both men knew what was about to happen.

Sacrilege, a desecration of classical form, a vulgar display for the *sol* seats. What the hell did he think he was playing at? He wasn't some *tremendista*, he was a real torero, capable of poetry without cheap theatrics.

The old man knew about bulls and how to play them, but nothing about the people who came to watch them die. It had been decades since the old man had stepped out in front of a crowd of this size, if ever, and even longer since he'd been under this kind of pressure to perform. Times changed, *toreo* changed with them, and what the old man might have called vulgar was merely a showboat move that was guaranteed to catch and hold the attention of fourteen thousand people. They'd come here to see drama and duende, not surgery, and he intended to give them their money's worth.

A matador was not supposed to die on his knees; the opening gambit he had in mind invited such a death. There were many things that could go wrong, and they all rushed through his head as he moved to his knees. If the bull's eyesight wasn't good enough, if its vision didn't adjust in time, if he didn't twitch out the *capote* in time, if the bull didn't see that twitch, if a freak breeze rattled the cape back in front of his face, then the best he could hope for was the kind of disfigurement that could end a career. On his knees, he was open to a three-inch-diameter horn to the face, throat, or upper chest, and it would be impossible to roll away once hooked.

He signaled to the attendant.

The attendant threw open an inner gate, which crashed against the concrete wall, echoing through the guts of the plaza like a gunshot.

His heartbeat thickened in his chest. He breathed deeply through his nose, his sinuses still frozen from the Afrin. Fear, or something very much like it, tumbled in his stomach.

More bangs from deep inside the tunnel that led to the pens and corrals beyond. The outer gate stood open now. All he saw was a hole, black and endless. He heard men yelling from far away.

They were calling to the bull, taunting it, providing a quick, short-burst target, bringing it out.

And then came the other noise, rumbling and rolling like thunder.

Something monstrous, something primal.

Coming closer.

Sand blew up into his right eye. He wanted to blink, brush it away, but he didn't dare move. The grain was a rock. His right eye filled with water. He saw the attendants slamming the sides of the tunnel with their hands. He felt his banderilleros shift behind the barriers, clutching their capes, prepared for the worst.

That rumbling, louder now, wilder, punctuated with a snorting, rasping breath.

Then the explosion of negative space, a half-ton of muscle and bone, its hide jet black and glistening, spindly legs a blur.

He twitched the capote. The bull wheeled and kicked dust.

Another twitch and the bull surged forward.

He held his breath. It was his one concession to absolute terror.

For a split second there was nothing but a shuddering darkness. The stench of the bull was raw and powerful, a punch of testosterone that became a dry kiss as the horn dragged across his cheek.

For that split second his eyes were closed and the grain of sand was forgotten in one moment of singular, fleeting peace.

And when he opened them again, a roar filled his ears, golden light filled his eyes, and there was nothing left to do but prepare for the kill.

TERCIO DE VARAS

One

First there was the darkness, oppressive and eternal, and then the silence.

The dead man tried to scream, and the darkness filled his mouth and throat, pushing the scream back to his lungs. His chest burned. The rest of him was rigid and electric. He tried to scream again but instead of sound, ground glass vibrated and scratched the inside of his throat until it was raw.

He couldn't see. He thought his eyes were closed, but he wasn't sure. There was an enormous pressure on his face and head; its insistence promised to crack his skull. His fingers tensed and something soft moved between them, catching at the nerves like pins and needles. He curled his hands into claws. As he did, he felt a shift of pressure against his hip, and more space opened between his side and his hand. He tried to twist, pushing out as hard as his could with tingling palms and then found himself turning around. He moved his head backward as if coming up for air, and there was an explosion in his skull, a white flash of pain that froze him.

It was okay, he told himself.

Pain was good.

Pain meant he was alive.

And pain was good, but movement was better. Movement meant survival.

He pushed forward with his body. The strain on his chest forced the last dregs of air from his lungs in one final scream.

Which he heard this time. The noise staggered out of him in fits and starts. He whooped as he sucked in breath and roared as he exhaled. Solid matter, gritty and thick, bullied past his tongue and teeth and fell as mud from his open mouth.

Once the spin in his head settled into a slow, sickening revolution, he opened his eyes. He was partially upright, one arm out and stiff, his fingers splayed. He dug in and pulled his other arm up, then pulled himself upright.

There was a sound, a rattle. Sounded like a snake. He froze again before he realized that the sound came from his own chest. He cleared his throat, forced a cough and spat to one side, wiping his mouth on the back of one dirty hand.

With the fresh air came the taste of salt and metal on his tongue. The darkness around him was blue tinged and softer than before.

The dead man blinked. He stared at the mound of dirt where his lap should have been. It took him a moment to realize that he was still half-buried, his legs numb from inactivity and the weight of the soil. He would dig himself out, but first he needed to get his lungs used to breathing air instead of dirt.

He looked up. Stars winked at him. He felt a chill.

It was night, late, and the dead man was alive.

Life came with its problems, though. With breathing came fresh pain. Not just the pulsing raw ache in his fingers, but a sharper dig in his left side, just under the ribs, of something that had punctured the skin and not quite healed. And as he turned, his head flared, pounding now and wet to the touch. He coughed again, which turned the pain up a notch.

The wounds were fresh and they were serious, which meant he needed to get moving.

The dead man hauled himself out of the earth in stages. First his thighs, then down to his knees, and then finally rolling over to one side to expose his shins and feet, twisting out of the ground like a well-plucked weed. He massaged the blood back into his thighs and kicked away the surplus dirt, then went to his hands and knees. He reached out for support and found a rock wall, which provided him with a sturdy guide as he slowly rose to his feet. When he was upright, the dead man leaned against the wall and looked at his feet. His shoes held a shine and about a kilogram of dirt. He shook his shoes out over the hole he'd made and then brushed dirt from his jacket, suddenly aware of how he was dressed. He wore a dark suit, what must have been a white shirt at some point, and both were expensive, judging by the feel of the cloth. Under one flap of his jacket he saw a wide, dark stain that stuck his shirt to his left side. He tugged at the shirt a little, and a fresh blade of pain slipped between his ribs, making him suck his next breath and abandon further exploration. He leaned against the rock wall and waited for the pain to subside.

Conjugating: *I will die, I am dying, I have* died.

He opened his eyes. His vision blurred for a moment, then focused, and as it did the salt taste in his mouth became the smell of the sea carried on a chill breeze. He thought he heard it too, even though he knew it was probably just the rush of air around his ears. He was high up; he knew that. He could feel it. He also knew that at this altitude a breeze could easily turn into a gust without warning, and so he held on to the rock until he felt he could trust his legs.

He looked down at the hole. The churned earth looked like an unmade bed. Something pale caught his eye.

A hand.

He dumbly checked his own hands to make sure they were still attached, then made a brief, indecisive move back toward the grave before he caught himself. It didn't matter who the other dead man was. He wouldn't have any answers.

He leaned back against the rock and focused on what he guessed was the horizon. Somewhere in the darkness below he saw a sprinkling of lights. They were far away and soft, and they didn't move. Beyond that, in some distant place that he knew he'd never reach, he saw more lights, some of them moving, some of them blinking. That was a town, maybe even a city, and if there was a town, there'd be people and maybe even a hospital.

The dead man felt along the rock, gingerly putting one foot in front of the other, not quite trusting his balance. He followed the rock until it dropped into a path. Breathing through his mouth, all his concentration on his feet, he pushed away from the wall and began to walk unaided. His toes felt knotted, his legs flickered with cramps. The pain was less than it had been, and he managed it with the kind of dull acceptance that came from knowing he'd suffered much worse.

He didn't remember when. He didn't remember anything.

A rock slipped under his instep. His ankle turned. He dropped. The ground whipped out from under him and left him with a sharp incline that he took on his backside. He turned onto his good side and threw out a hand. Something sturdy filled his palm.

He hung on until everything stopped.

The dead man lay where he'd fallen for a moment. Then he turned onto his back, stared at the stars and took stock.

His ankle ached, but he didn't think it was broken. His side hurt again. His head thumped. He told himself that the pain would eventually subside and, in a few minutes, it did. He pulled himself up to a sitting position and then upright. His bad ankle took his weight.

Good. He could continue.

The dead man pushed on without thinking. It was the only way to find the energy to move. If he stopped and asked himself where he was going or why he was moving at all, he wouldn't have an answer beyond the lizard-brained instinct that told him to get off this mountain and get some medical attention.

So he continued, taking it one step at a time, slow and careful, making sure his footing was secure before he put any weight on it. The last few meters of the mountain were rocky and the hardest to navigate. A fall here could snap his neck or break his leg. He'd already escaped one grave and was in no hurry to throw himself into another, so he took his time, double-checking every step, kicking loose stones out of the way before he committed. When he finally reached flat land, his legs quivered as if they missed the constant stress of an incline, and it was a few minutes before he was confident enough to turn and look at the mountain.

The rock was negative. Pure darkness. It looked as if someone had torn a huge jagged chunk out of the landscape. He hugged himself against the cold and smiled at the mountain, then laughed at it. Then something stung his eyes and throat and he had to look away, turning his attention to the lights in the distance.

It was a village, a *pueblo*. It was small, frigid and country dark apart from the main drag, which appeared to be the only street that sported lights. He followed them like a plane coming in to land, touching the walls of the low-slung buildings with the tips of his fingers as he went. The buildings looked like miniature homes that had been abandoned a long time ago.

He needed a telephone. There was a number in his head, an emergency number—112—and he knew that if he dialed that number, someone would send an ambulance, and he'd soon find out if the lights he'd seen from the mountain were within driving distance. But there were no phones on the main street, and there was nothing in the village square but a stone plinth, which was scuffed and cracked, as if whatever statue had called it home had been violently removed. This was a place of united aggression, or it had been once.

The dead man leaned against one of the streetlamps. His stomach rolled. A cold sweat broke out across his forehead, stinging the wound near his temple. He didn't dare brush at it in case it stoked the fire in his head. When he looked up at the sky again, he thought he saw his breath appear in a single plume before him.

The place was dead, its streetlights flowers by a tombstone. The village may have had phones and people to use them once upon a time, but now it was nothing more than a collection of empty buildings and an electricity bill that would never be paid. There was nothing to see, nobody to help, and he knew that he would never make it to the other lights. He lowered his head and stared at the stone by his shoe.

This was it. This was the end. The other lights were too far.

A dull sound nagged at his mind. It sounded like a bell, but more of a metallic thunk than a ring. It was constant, rhythmic, and irritating. He looked up and saw a shape emerge from the darkness on the far side of the village square. The shape changed from loose shadow to the idea of an animal, which then became the idea of a cow, which then became the real beast, which was then followed by others, a small, undulating herd apparently intent on forward motion.

The dead man blinked, but the sluggish river of cow kept flowing. He could smell them now, that heady musk of hair and manure. It sparked memories, but they were fleeting, violent, and it hurt his head too much to focus on them.

Memories didn't matter anyway. The past was never as important as the present.

A man appeared at the rear of the herd. He had the look of a somnambulant scarecrow and seemed to glide behind the cows, his gaze fixed somewhere simultaneously far away and deep inside. The dead man pushed himself from the streetlamp and took a few steps toward the scarecrow, one hand stretched out in front of him. He tried to speak, but his voice tore at his throat. When he forced a noise it sounded more like splintering wood than a human being, but it caught the scarecrow's attention, startling him out of his early morning stupor. The dead man held out his other hand. He tried to call for help. The scarecrow recoiled as he approached, and the dead man bumped into one of the cows as it passed. The cow made a distressed lowing sound and gave him one wild eye as it jerked away. The dead man grabbed at the cow, suddenly unsteady. His fingers dragged across its hide, and then he lost his balance. The dead man yelled and tumbled to the ground. Dirt flew up into his face, causing him to blink and cough.

When his vision cleared a second later, he saw blood on the sand. He heard the sound of panicked cattle and smelled the fear in the air.

And for a split second, he saw what looked like a couple of frames of sunlight before the world crashed to black.

Two

"Ah, thank God you're alive."

Gracias a Dios.

A man's voice, speaking Spanish somewhere in the dark.

The dead man understood Spanish. He *was* Spanish. At least he thought he was.

An ammonia smell tugged at the hair in his nose. Other smells: antiseptic, some kind of chemical floral smell, wet wool. He opened his eyes and let out a grunt. It was too bright in here. When he tried to turn away from the glare, he felt hands grab at him. The hands were small but strong fingered.

"No, you shouldn't move. Settle back here, please. Settle down. That's right."

The dead man waved a hand in front of his face. "The lights."

"The lights? Yes, sorry, of course." The hands disappeared. "Stay there."

The dead man did as he was told. Something slid under his head. He heard a switch, a tut of frustration, the stutter of striplights, and then finally another click of a switch. He opened his eyes, shielding them with his hand.

It was darker now.

"How's that?"

He removed his hand. The striplights behind him were still on, but he could focus without pain. "Thank you."

His hands touched metal as he attempted to sit up.

"Here, let me help you with that."

The hands on him again, easing him upright, steadying him as he moved his legs over the side of what looked like a waist-high stainless steel table. Something moved in his peripheral vision—a small white pillow—and then dropped to the floor. His side burned. When he moved, it felt swollen with what he hoped were bandages. He touched his side. No increase in pain. He breathed out and reached up to touch his temple, bracing himself for the jolt, but again he touched bandages. "Don't worry, I dressed both wounds and gave you a shot of something nice and strong. You shouldn't feel anything for another couple of hours at least." The voice belonged to a small man with a round head that was shiny where it wasn't laced with black, stringy hair. He looked older than he sounded, and he had the scrubbed complexion and exaggerated stoop of a child mimicking his grandfather. He attempted to push his spectacles up to his eyes, but they refused to budge from the end of his nose, so he raised his head to inspect the dead man. "I did my best, Señor, but I have to say, this kind of wound—it's not exactly something I come across on a daily basis. How are you feeling?"

"Alive."

"Good." He smiled, showing a large gap between his front two teeth, and gestured at the dead man's side. "That one, that was relatively straightforward, you know? Just a graze, really. Straight in and out, through and through, yes? I mean, you'll scar, of course, but it only required cleaning and dressing, so it should be fine to heal by itself."

The dead man touched his shirt. "The blood…"

"Yes, well, they *do* bleed. All wounds do, but…" He glanced behind him and lowered his voice. "One of *those* wounds, you know, sometimes it's the best thing for them to do. They bleed, they clean, you see? And you might not think it, but you were actually pretty lucky." He pointed at the man's chest. "A little higher, it could have nicked a lung, perhaps even your heart." He looked at the man's head now. "Of course, I say *lucky*..."

"What happened?"

"I don't know what to tell you, Señor Fulano—"

"Who?"

"Ah, sorry." Another smile, this one sheepish. "I've been calling you that in my head. It's just I didn't find any identification."

The dead man saw his jacket slung over the back of a chair on the other side of the room. He frowned and the movement tugged at the bandages on his head.

"It is...*el fulano de tal,* yes? Juan Doe. And so I called you Señor Fulano. Sorry, it's silly. What's your real name?"

He shook his head. "Where am I?"

"You don't remember, of course. That's understandable. You're in my surgery. Luis brought you in."

"Luis?"

"Our local cowboy. You took a nosedive into his dairy herd."

He didn't remember, but his head thumped what he assumed was a confirmation. "He thought you were a drunk and, well, I'd suppose he'd know. He looks at one in the mirror every morning." A flicker of concern. "Don't tell him I said that. Anyway, he said you came out of nowhere. You were shouting at him and waving your arms like you were upset about something. Then you went under the hooves. I have to say, you're fortunate that you did. Luis took one look at the blood and thought his herd was responsible. If he'd known the truth, I think he would've left you where you lay. He thought you were dead. *I* thought you were dead."

"Are you a doctor?"

A chuckle danced in his throat. "Sort of. One mammal is much like another."

The dead man nodded. "Thank you. I don't know what I owe you—"

"Owe me? Good God, what do you take me for?"

"I didn't mean any disrespect."

"It's my duty to help my fellow man if he's in need, isn't it?"

"I don't know. I suppose so."

"You suppose so. You *know* so." He smiled again, showing more teeth and a twinkle that said he wasn't quite the Christian he pretended to be. "Besides, I already went through your pockets, remember? They're all empty."

"Are they?"

"What happened?"

"I don't know."

"Were you robbed?"

"I don't remember."

"I see." The vet's gaze flickered up to the head wound. "Listen, I have to tell you, if a man is brought to me with bullet wounds, Señor, it's difficult for me to believe that he came about them honestly. You get shot once, I can believe it's an accident. *Twice*, though...Do you see what I'm saying?"

"Yes."

"It looks like someone tried to finish the job."

The dead man squinted at him. "Maybe."

"But I shouldn't ask questions, should I? Not if I don't want to know the answers." He waved it off. "I'll stay out of it. I did my work. You should probably go."

He was about to answer when he heard the door open behind him.

A woman's voice: "Paco, what are you doing?"

"Nothing, Mama."

"Who ith thith man?"

The dead man didn't turn—the lights in the other half of the surgery were still too bright for him—but he could picture the owner of the voice clearly enough. She was elderly, small and dumpy, probably dressed in the pueblo pensioner uniform of mourning black. Once you hit a certain age, death was a constant companion, and he had no doubt it was the smell of death that had brought her into the room.

He remembered the type of woman, but he couldn't remember anything else?

"Excuse me." The vet hurried away, his shirttails flapping from the back of his crumpled trousers. His bare feet made slapping sounds as he jogged across the tiles. The old lady started talking to him, but he ushered her out of the room before she managed to finish her first word. The dead man heard the door close, and then it was quiet in the room apart from the low, lazy buzz of the fluorescent tubes.

An innocent man wouldn't get shot twice. That was the assumption, and it was a fair one to make, one that the dead man would've made himself were he not already convinced that he was the victim rather than the aggressor. After all, he didn't feel as if he'd been punished; he felt as if he'd been abused.

He shook his head. That feeling could have been anything. He couldn't remember his own name, for Christ's sake. How the hell was he supposed to remember what kind of man he was? He was hurt, so he was bound to feel delicate, bound to tell himself he was the victim. That thought could have come from anywhere. It could have been a figment of his imagination, a subconscious extrapolation of the available evidence, or even a fragment of a cold-stored memory that hadn't been completely blown out of his head when they leveled the pistol and fired for the second time.

There.

Wait.

A pistol. Small, sleek, and black. Almost part of the hand that gripped it, the final few inches of one long, shadowed arm.

He blinked. The sun was in his eyes. He was in pain because they'd already shot him once. He was lying on his back somewhere soft.

His head throbbed. He closed one eye. He pushed on the memory, but he couldn't hold it, couldn't force it any further before it broke and tumbled into nothing.

His head hurt more now. He held it with both hands and stared at his feet until the pain eased, watching his silhouette rock slightly on the polished white tiles. When he felt a little better, he dropped from the table and looked for his reflection. He found himself in one of the glass-paneled medicine cabinets. The bandage around his head wasn't as large as it felt, but it was still bulky enough to be the focus of a first glance. He touched his face, saw and felt the stubble on his cheeks and chin. It felt rough and alien. He opened his mouth. His teeth were healthy and straight. He looked at his hands. The fingers were bloody and raw at the tips, but his fingernails were neatly trimmed.

Manicured.

Almost as if he'd been tidied up for burial. He frowned, feeling the tension on his forehead and the pain somewhere inside.

The door opened. The old woman's voice entered the room. "But what ith he *doing* here, Paco?"

"Please, Mama. Your teeth."

"For why should I put in my teeth? For *him*?" She made a spitting sound. "Never."

The dead man turned slowly, letting his eyes adjust to the brightness on the other side of the room. A small, round woman in a black woolen cardigan and nightdress bustled toward him. Her gray hair was pinned tightly to her head and her face resembled a balled-up brown paper bag. When she spoke, she showed wet gums. "You *thee*? Look at the way he'th looking at me. Like he wanth to *kill* me."

"He doesn't want to kill you. I'm sorry, Señor."

"Why are you apologithing?"

"Just let me handle it, Mama, okay?"

She let out a sharp gust of wind in her son's general direction. "*Handle* it. You can handle nothing." She waddled closer and peered up at the dead man, her eyes like nuggets of coal. Her upper lip curled to reveal more gum. "Thith one I know." She flicked at his shirt. "He'th from the thity. Look at what he'th wearing. I know you. *Bandido*. Criminal."

"Mama, please—"

"Who brought him here?"

"Nobody brought him."

"He appeared by magic? Who brought him?"

"Luis."

"*Ay*." She threw up her hands. "The *borracho*. Did *he* do thith?"

"No."

"Really?"

"He just found him."

"Then why are you taking care of hith problemth?"

"I'm not."

"Paco." She prodded her son sharply in the chest with one bony finger. "Don't let people bully you."

The dead man cleared his throat. "Excuse me."

Paco and his mother regarded him with the same mild surprise, as if they'd forgotten he was in the room.

"I'm sorry. Really. I know it's late. I was just about to go. Thank you again, Señor."

"No." The mother hustled back in front of the dead man, moving her mouth as if she was trying to chew her tongue out. "You're thtaying right where you are." She scanned him from hairline to shoes and then back up. She nipped some dirt from his sleeve and crumbled it between her fingers. "You came from the mountainth."

"Yes."

She brushed the dirt away. "Then you are a criminal. They bury their own up there. I know. I have lived here long enough to know. I'm not thtupid. I have eyeth. I can thee. I know what happenth up there. The men with their exthpenthive carth and their *gunth*." She stared at his temple now. "You're one of them. A nothing. A criminal. You belong in jail."

"Wait—"

She was already across the room. Paco made a move after her, but she slammed the door as she left. He stood looking at it. He let out a deep breath. "My mother isn't very Christian. I apologize."

"No need."

"Are you a criminal?"

"No."

"Are you sure?"

He thought about it. "No, I'm not."

Paco left the room and closed the door behind him. The dead man retrieved his jacket and went through the pockets. Just as Paco had said, they were all empty. No wallet, no identification, no keys, no loose change. Whoever it was that had buried him had made sure they'd cleaned him out first. He dipped his fingers into the top breast pocket. It was sewn partly closed, but some of the stitches had come away. Wedged in the bottom of the pocket was a small piece of paper. He nipped it between two fingers and brought it out.

A ticket for the Plaza de Toros de Marbella. The corrida on Sunday, May 27, 2012. He turned it over. There was what looked like a phone number written on the back of the ticket, but no name.

The dead man looked at the ticket for a long time, back and front, but he didn't remember attending the corrida, writing the number, or meeting anyone who could have done it for him.

The door opened again. The old woman stood smiling at him with every single one of her false teeth. It wasn't pleasant, wasn't friendly—this was a smile of triumph. And behind her, starting to edge past, was a policeman. He was broad in both shoulders and waist and carried himself like a rented mule.

The mother jabbed a finger at the dead man. "That's him. That's the man I was telling you about."

The policeman's holster was open. Whatever the old woman had said, it wasn't flattering. The policeman raised one hand in a calming gesture that had the exact opposite effect. "Would you mind coming with us, Señor? We have some questions for you."

"Am I under arrest?"

"No, but it would be better if you came along, don't you think? The lady would like to get to bed, and you've imposed enough for one night."

The dead man nodded. He had nowhere else to be. He shrugged into his jacket and then allowed the policeman to escort him off the premises and into the back of the waiting car.

Three

"You are a piece of work, my friend. You really are."

The detective was a wiry man with a heavily pocked face that was mostly forehead. His only compromise to style was a patterned tie, which hung like a noose around his neck. When he moved, which was often, there were ripples thanks to a nervous tremor in his hands. It was obvious that the detective didn't find much to interest him normally, but he *was* interested in the dead man. To him, the dead man was a question to be answered, and so he'd made him call the number on the back of the corrida ticket while he watched. When the number appeared to ring out, the detective brought him back to the hot, smelly box that they called an interview room. Then he'd sat down and asked more questions, some of them new, some of them the same, and all of them were met with the same old refrain of "I don't know" and "I can't remember."

After three hours, the detective stopped asking questions and started talking about himself instead: "I'm not from here. I don't know many people who are. Most people born here leave pretty quickly, as far as I know. Can't say I blame them." The detective sniffed and wiped his nose. "No, I'm from Seville originally. Started working there. Las Tres Mil, you know it?"

"No."

"Gypsy town. Baptism of fire." He looked at the table and tapped it with one finger. "Then I moved down to Benalmádena, worked there for five years." Another sniff. He looked irritated. "So I've been around. Just so you know. And I've seen it all, or close to it. I've seen gypsies going at each other with razors, I've seen pasty Anglo baby-dealers sticking each other on street corners, and here I've seen Russian gangs decimate each other over nothing, and you know what I learned?"

The dead man shook his head.

"I learned that it doesn't matter where you were raised, how brown you are, what kind of bad luck you've had; if you're a criminal, then you're a criminal. You know what defines a criminal?"

"Someone who commits a crime?"

"Someone who gets *caught*." He opened his hands, sat back in his chair. "Crime only really exists when it's charged and prosecuted. Before then, it's a social transgression."

The dead man nodded.

"And criminals get caught because they're stupid. Or they're greedy, which is a kind of stupidity. And because they're so stupid, they don't *know* they're stupid. And this is why they keep trying and why they keep getting caught, do you understand?"

"I think so."

"Good. I'm glad you understand because this is relevant to you. I want you to know that you can stay as silent as you want for as long as you want. That's your choice. But if you keep quiet, you're going to end up back in those mountains, whether they cart you off to Alhaurín or bury you...*again*."

The dead man looked at the table.

"Listen, I know you think it's all 'us against them,' but it really isn't. Not all the time, anyway. Not now." The detective's voice was softer now. He leaned forward. "I'm just trying to help you. Let's say I believe you. For the sake of argument, let's just say that head wound really did knock the sense out of you and you can't remember a damned thing. You're blank up there. The trouble is, though, just because you forget *them*, it doesn't mean they forgot *you*. Do you see what I mean?"

"Them?"

"The people who shot you."

"I don't know. I don't remember."

He threw up a hand, a grin on his face. "Of course you don't."

"I really don't, Detective. I've told you. I've tried—"

"But you can speak, you can walk, you can use a phone, which makes me think that your long-term memory's absolutely fine. You've followed this conversation without any trouble, you know where you are and what's happening, so your short-term memory's fine too. So what is it, everything in the middle? Trying to find some filling for your sandwich? What am I supposed to do with you?"

"I don't know."

"What a surprise. Of course you don't know. You don't know *anything*, do you? Especially when it's inconvenient." The detective pushed back his chair. It scraped against the floor. He stood and looked at his watch. "Tell you what, let's play to your strengths, shall we? We'll forget this chat ever happened. I mean, my conscience is clear. My duty of care has been carried out. So we'll just call it a night, and I'll get one of the officers to give you directions to the hospital. What do you say?"

"I'm free to go?"

"Of course you are. What am I going to charge you with, possession of *one* bullet? If you're telling the truth, then you're a liability. I don't need someone fucking up my morning by dying in custody. And if you *are* lying to me, I already gave you the opportunity to talk and you didn't take it. So, off you go." He was at the door now. "Godspeed."

The detective called for one of the uniforms, who escorted the dead man to the front desk, where the wide policeman who'd brought him into town scribbled directions to the hospital on the back of a badly drawn map.

The policeman watched him leave, and when the dead man headed in the opposite direction, nobody stopped him.

He didn't want to go to the hospital. His head hurt, but he wasn't scared about it anymore. If he hadn't died yet, he probably had a few more hours. Besides, he didn't relish the idea of more questions, not when he had plenty of his own.

The Plaza de Toros was marked on the map, and he headed for it. When he arrived, he stood and stared at the building, hoping that a jolt of familiarity would knock loose a memory or two. It was a large, sandy-looking structure, a strange mix of ancient and modern, but if it didn't have large corrida posters hanging on the outside wall, the dead man wouldn't have recognized it as a plaza.

So if the ticket itself wasn't important, then it must have been the number written on the back.

There was a café-bar across the street, Casa de Verónica. It was open. The place looked as if someone had taken a job lot of dining furniture and thrown it into a garage. A bar stretched up one wall. A stick insect with hollow eyes and a mop of black hair stood behind it, watching the television in the far corner. When he approached the bar, he smelled coffee and heard the low strains of pop flamenco. He took a stool and looked at the corrida posters on the wall behind him. There was only one customer, a man in a gray suit and an open-necked white shirt, something shining around his neck. What remained of his hair was swept up into a style that belonged in an old movie about teenage gangs. He was reading a newspaper, and when he looked up, the dead man turned back to the bar.

The stick insect had a badge on his chest that read FREDDY. The dead man ordered a glass of water. When Freddy left, he took the ticket from his pocket and set it down on the bar in front of him. He stared at the number, willing it to mean something, or at least suggest the first few syllables of a name. He needed help, but he wasn't sure if the number belonged to someone who could provide it. The police *had* to protect, they had a duty of care, and the dead man had tried to be as truthful as possible. Out here, it was different. Out here, admitting his memory loss would be an admission of weakness, and the vultures would be sure to circle if he said anything.

Freddy put down a glass of water in front of him. The dead man drank. He wiped his mouth and thanked the barman, who looked over the dead man's shoulder and then retreated up the bar, where he brought out a telephone from under the counter and turned his back on the room as he dialed.

The television above the barman showed the date. Sunday, June 3. A week later than the date on the ticket. So he was at the plaza last week, or he knew people who were. And if there were others, then there was a chance they would attend this week's corrida, too. Okay, so it wasn't exactly a sure thing, but it was a possibility, and a possibility was better than nothing.

But first he had to find out who they were. He caught Freddy's attention. The barman had just finished his call. "Could I use your phone?"

Freddy looked suspicious. "There's a pay phone in the back."

"I don't have any change. Please, it's important."

The barman appeared to think about it, then beckoned him over to the other end of the bar. The dead man slipped from his stool. He glanced behind him at the man in the gray suit, who was staring at him. He turned away and continued to the phone.

"Don't take long."

"Thank you." The dead man dialed the number on the back of the ticket. It rang again. A ringing tone was a good sign. Or a bad sign, if this was his own number he was calling. He looked back at the ticket. Surely his own number would look familiar to him? "Hello?"

The voice hurt his head. It was scratchy with tobacco.

"Raf, is that you?"

He caught the name like a nail to the temple. Freddy was staring at him now. The voice at the other end kept saying the name. It was *his* name, he was positive of it. "Hello."

"Raf, my God, it *is* you. What's the matter? What happened?"

"I don't know."

"Did you want to talk?"

"I think so."

"Where are you?"

He blinked. The name of the café had disappeared from his head. He lowered the phone. "Excuse me, what's the name of this place?"

Freddy frowned as if he'd been asked a trick question. "Casa de Verónica."

He told the voice on the other end of the phone. He didn't dare ask the man's name, just in case it had same effect on him as his own.

"Okay, stay there. I'll be over as soon as I can."

The dead man disconnected. The barman scooped up the phone and set it back behind the bar. "You okay?"

"Yes. Thank you."

But he wasn't. He was sick, confused, and in pain, and generally about as far from okay as it was possible to get and still manage to breathe.

And even the breathing came hard now.

"Your toilets?"

The barman pointed off to one side.

"Thank you."

Four

The toilets were cool and coldly lit. The dead man still heard the music from the bar, but it sounded as if it were being piped through water. He approached the sinks and saw a corpse walking toward him in the mirrors. His jacket was dirty. When he opened it, he saw the dried yellow sweat stains and brown blood-stains on his shirt. The bandages were fat and tight to his head, and yet a brown mark told him he'd been bleeding despite the dressing.

He ducked to the basin and washed his face, careful to avoid the bandage.

When he straightened up, he saw how sick he really looked. That was why the barman and the man in the gray suit had stared at him. That and the bandages. He peeled back a little of the tape that held them in place.

The vet had done a thorough job, but there was still a gap between the gauze and his skin, where the blood had managed to break through. He unwound the bandages and dropped them into the sink. Then he peeled back the gauze a little. It made a sticky sound, revealing a small wound that didn't look as serious as it felt. A hole, no bigger than a one-cent piece but black as tar inside. There was some smudged blood around it, and the skin was pale and pruned under the dressing; the combination made the wound look like a cheap special effect.

He reattached the gauze and replaced the tape, smoothing it to his head. Without the bandages, it looked less like a bullet wound, more like a nasty bump. That was better. He needed to blend, at least for the time being. If it started bleeding again, he'd think about bandages, but until then this would have to do.

He looked at himself again. Said his name.

"Raf."

Short for Rafael.

It was definitely his name. He could feel it. It fit.

As if to confirm, he heard it again, but this time it was someone else speaking, punctuated by the slow creak of the toilet door as it swung shut.

Rafael saw the man in the gray suit. The man in the gray suit watched him. He broke into a crooked grin. "You know, I *thought* that was you. You ignoring me, Raf?"

"No."

"Rough morning?"

"Yes."

"Rough night too by the look of it. What happened?"

Rafael watched him. "Long story."

"You spent the money yet?"

"What money?"

The man's grin widened, almost split his face in two. "You forget already?"

"No."

"First payment's due tomorrow."

"Payment?"

He tapped his head. "You need to remember that."

"Okay."

"You sure?"

"Yes."

"Okay, good. Because I've heard things, Raf." He started walking toward Rafael, ambling almost. The man looked at the floor. "I

mean, you know me, I like to keep on top of local current affairs."
He made a mouth out of his left hand and flapped it. His other hand
dipped into his jacket pocket. "Talk to people, you know, ask them
what's going on, like why is Rafael Ortega coming to *me* for money,
right? Like you don't have enough anymore, you need to weather
my vig? I mean, to me that's a sad state of affairs, you know? The
people I deal with, I'm not going to lie to you, they're pretty desperate. And I'll tell you, you looked pretty scruffy the other day, and
you know me, I don't like to ask questions just to be nosy, but *now*?
Jesus, you look like you've kissed rock bottom with an open mouth.
So what's the score, Raf? What made *you* desperate?"

"I'm not."

"Then why did you come to me?"

Rafael looked at the door to the bar. The man in the gray suit
moved into his line of sight, blocking his exit. Rafael swallowed
and pushed away from the basins. "I don't know. I don't remember."

"Because there's people telling me that you borrowed from me
because you think I'm a fucking idiot. Because you plan to take my
money and run, and that I'm too stupid to see it."

"I wouldn't do that. I don't think you're a fucking idiot." Rafael
moved into the middle of the room, circling round the man in the
gray suit. If he could get a clear run to the door, he might be able
to get out of there clean. "I don't think you're stupid. You know I
wouldn't do that."

"Where you going, Raf?"

"Outside."

The man came closer. His hand came out of his jacket pocket
holding a small switchblade, blade gleaming. "Where's my
money?"

"You said tomorrow."

The man put a flat hand in the middle of Rafael's chest and
shoved him backward. The floor was slippery. Rafael threw out
a hand, grabbed on to one of the stall dividers and caught his

balance. The man held the knife lightly in his hand, out to one side so it glinted only in Rafael's peripheral vision.

"I don't have any money."

"Then what's going to happen tomorrow?"

"I don't know."

"That's not fucking good enough, is it?"

"Please."

"Please?" There was a flicker of disgust, and then the man in the gray suit grabbed Rafael and threw him up against the back wall. Rafael's head smacked against the tile and then went loose on his shoulders. He thought he was about to lose his footing, but the man hoisted him up and showed him the knife up close. "The fuck you saying please for, Raf?"

He pulled open Rafael's jacket, rifled through his empty pockets. When he saw the blood on his shirt he pulled back, his face creasing.

"Jesus Christ."

Rafael launched forward, slammed his shoulder into the man's chest and then stumbled toward the exit. He heard the man recover and turn on the tile, a squeaking noise as he slipped. Rafael pulled on the toilet door and barged through. He heard the man close behind him as he spilled out into the café. He felt a hand on his jacket, pulling on it. As he jerked his jacket free, he tumbled into an empty table, and then the man with the knife was on top of him.

But only for a moment. The next, the man in the gray suit was gone, lifted up and thrown across at the bar. "The fuck d'you think you're doing, Javier?"

The voice belonged to another man. He was younger than the pair of them, taller, dressed in jeans and a white shirt, but both were designer, and Rafael got the whiff of gigolo from him. Javier leaned where he'd been thrown. The knife dangled from his right hand. He stared at the newcomer. "None of your business."

"He's my friend. I'd say it was my fucking business."

"Yeah, he's your friend. You help him to cheat me?"

"Nobody's cheating you."

"He owes me six grand, Sancho."

"So?"

"So check his pockets, he's broke. He owes me tomorrow. Where the fuck is he getting the money from?"

"You'll find out tomorrow, won't you?"

Javier moved from the bar. Sancho stepped up between them.

"You want to do this, Javier?"

Javier looked at Rafael. He moved the knife in his hand. Then he looked back at Sancho. "You bring him back here tomorrow."

Sancho smiled. "Of course I will."

"You make sure you do."

Sancho signaled for Rafael to follow as he backed away from Javier and headed for the door. When Rafael got close, he grabbed his arm and pushed him on ahead.

"Tomorrow, Sancho. I fucking mean it."

And then they were gone.

Five

Hayley snatched Aiden's DS because she wanted to play her girl's game on it—something about makeup or ponies or fashion—and Aiden hadn't finished with his, so he was building up to a double-lunged whinge that wouldn't stop until she either gave it back or Tony belted the kid. And as much as he wanted to preempt the little bastard—at nine years old, he was turning into a slack-arsed little whiner—he couldn't, not with Lisa in the car. Both the kids were calling on her to adjudicate, knowing full well that Tony didn't give the first fuck about their situation, but Lisa was too busy touching up her slap in the pull-down mirror to give her kids much more than a filthy look. "Hayley, give him his game back."

"It's my turn."

"It'll be your turn on the way back. The whole way, all right? Give him his game."

Tony watched his daughter's face tighten in the rearview mirror. Two years older than Aiden, already picking up her mother's facial expressions when she was pissed off. Hayley did as she was told. As soon as the game was safely back with Aiden, she bunched up one fist and jabbed her little brother just below the shoulder. He opened his mouth and screamed, and then he made a move to batter her back. Lisa twisted in her seat and shouted at the pair of them. They shouted back. Tony tried to keep the car on the right side of the road. His head was banging. They called the N-340 "the road of death" on account of all the accidents. Tony wondered if they were really accidents, if it wasn't just family men like him who'd heard their kids get lippy once too often and decided to plow into oncoming traffic rather than listen to yet another fucking screeching match in the backseat.

Lisa grabbed the DS from where it had fallen on the backseat, snapped it closed and then slung it onto the dashboard. "There. Nobody gets it."

The kids moaned, but Lisa cut them short with a look. They traveled in silence for a minute or so, and then Tony heard a helicopter. He glanced up at the sky through the windscreen. Couldn't see it anywhere, but he knew what it meant depending on which direction it was going. If it was headed out to Málaga, then it was probably a hospital chopper. Otherwise, it was Guardia Civil or the SVA.

He saw it. Black-and-white markings, one of those spotlights hanging from its belly. Going at some speed too. Which meant someone's day just went to shit. He hoped it wasn't his.

"What you looking at?"

He sat back in his seat. "Nothing."

Lisa kept looking at him, then shook her head and carried on applying her lipstick. Only time she talked to him this morning was to score points, or provoke him into a situation where he'd look stupid. *What you looking at, a fucking helicopter? What's the matter with you? You a fucking kid or what?* That kind of shit. She still had the hump with him on account of Tony having to drive down to the Rock yesterday afternoon on business. Apparently he was spending too much time away and he should spend more time with the kids, which translated to him as *she* wanted to spend more time gassing with her mates down that grotty fucking salon. He knew better than to say that, though, otherwise the hump would escalate to full-blown hissy fit. So he kept schtum, let her carry on ignoring him and the sulking kids, and enjoyed the closest he'd come in months to peace and quiet at home.

They continued that way until he pulled into the supermarket car park. Sunday morning, time for the family big shop, and Lisa was adamant they shopped at one of these out-of-town places that looked like a warehouse even though there was an Iceland in Fuengirola. The kids made a run for the trolleys. Tony chirped the alarm, then pulled out a wedge.

Lisa wrinkled her nose. "Serious?"

"No cards. Not yet."

"Still?"

"It's the way it has to be. You don't know what they're watching." He peeled off some notes and handed them to Lisa. "I'm going to get some breakfast."

"Ah, right. You just leave me to do everything."

"It's business, babes."

But she was already off across the car park, sliding large sunglasses onto her face, her arse swinging in the leggings. She shouted at Hayley to bring a trolley over; Hayley did, Aiden riding on the back of it as it clattered over the pocked tarmac. He watched the three of them head into the supermarket, the automatic doors sealing them inside, and then he crossed the road to Fiona's, where Lawrence and Max were sat at one of the outside tables. Lawrence was a case study for gout and male-pattern baldness and was busy shoving what looked like a full English slapped between two slices of white bread into his mouth. Max sat opposite, watching him with clinical distaste, a cigarette between two long fingers. He was the one who saw Tony first. "How you keeping, Tone?"

"Not so bad, Max. Not so bad." He took a seat at the table, nodded at Lawrence, who nodded back and splattered brown sauce onto the plate. The smell of fried eggs from the sandwich made Tony's gut quiver in a cold way. He pulled out his dago Bensons and sparked one, which seemed to put it right.

"Come on, Tony, it's bad enough with that one. I'm fucking eating here."

Max raised his eyebrows. "Is that what you're doing?" He blew smoke at Lawrence. "From the noises, I wasn't sure."

"Fuck's that supposed to mean?"

Fiona emerged from the café, and Tony smiled at her as he ordered black coffee, two sugars. Fiona was large in the arse and nowhere else, which meant she waddled everywhere. Lawrence watched her leave and then shoved the rest of the sandwich into his gob. He wiped his hands on a paper towel and nodded at Tony. "You look like shit."

"Thanks."

"On the nest, was it?"

Tony shook his head. "Fucking Rock, mate."

"When?"

"Last night. Ollie had us out there since yesterday. Had to drive back this morning. I've not been to bed yet."

"You wrapping or what?" Max smoked the last of his cigarette and killed it in the tinfoil ashtray.

"Do I smell like I've been wrapping?"

"Lost my sense of smell a long time ago, Tony." Max gestured at Lawrence. "With good fucking reason, might I add."

"No, it was straight supervision."

Lawrence nodded. "Got to watch them darkies."

"Thieving bastards to a boy." Tony smiled again when Fiona emerged with his coffee. "Ta, love."

As soon as she left, Max pulled a hip flask. "Nip?"

"Nah, mate, I'll be out like a fucking light. Besides, I've got her doing the big shop. Don't need the fucking earache."

"Please yourself." Max glugged what smelled like brandy into his latte and gave it a quick stir before he slipped the hip flask back into his side pocket. "You see the Customs bird?"

"Nothing to do with us, is it?"

"Nah, it's going up the Blanca. Nothing happening down here anymore, is there?"

"That's what I thought."

"Ollie's wanting it quiet. Nobody does nothing. Pain in the arse."

Lawrence smiled. "It's like a holiday."

"Yeah, except you don't get paid."

"You might not."

"Fucking hell, yeah." Max was grinning now, showing yellow teeth. "Listen, Lawrence, tell Tony about your new best mate. You heard about this, Tone?"

"No."

"Tell him about it."

"Who, Bruce?"

"Yeah, Bruce. Wait until you hear this. This is fucking mental, this."

"Who's Bruce?"

"He's a writer. Author." Lawrence rubbed the back of his neck. "Books an' that."

"Fucking mug, more like. He's going to make our Lawrence a star, mate. *Danny Dyer's Deadliest Men*: *Fucking Fat-Arse Special*."

"Bruce Parr." Lawrence adopted a posher accent than his usual. "He's actually researching a book—nonfiction, of course— on the expat community on the Costas. I have been helping the gentleman with his inquiries for a small fee."

Tony sipped his coffee. It was strong. "You tell the truth this time?"

"Now, Anthony, whatever the fuck do you mean by that remark?"

"I mean you confessed to topping Charlie Wilson the last time someone gave you an ear, mate. You were telling him all about the fucking flowers in his back garden and everything…"

"I did not."

Max was laughing. "Yeah, you did, Lawrence. I was there when you said it."

"Then the pair of you need your fucking ears scooshed out. I may have hinted that I was acquainted with Charlie Wilson, and the young man may have inferred that I was somehow involved with Charlie's untimely demise—God rest his soul—and he may have written something to that effect in his book, but I never said nothing outright, and I was never quoted by name, so any evidence you purport to have, gentlemen, is hearsay and inadmissible."

"All right, what'd you tell this one, then?"

Max nodded at Lawrence. "He only tried to sell him a fucking gun, didn't he?"

"You what?"

Lawrence held up one hand. "Not exactly."

"He called it a shooter."

"Fucking Ray Winstone over here." Tony laughed. "You slaaaag."

"He wanted to know what he could get, and I told him. That's all I did. I never said I could get him a gun, I just said, y'know, give us a week and I'll see what I can do."

"How much?"

"Why, Tone, you in the market?"

"Just curious about the going rate."

"Revolver'll cost you fifteen hundred euro, a grand up front."

"Fucking hell." Tony exchanged a look of disbelief with Max. "What did he say?"

"He said thank you."

"What, he paid up, did he?"

"What d'you think? No, he didn't pay up. He didn't want a fucking gun, did he? What's he going to do with a fucking gun?"

"I don't get it. Why'd he ask then?"

"Because he's a psycho, isn't he?" Max lit another cigarette. "They're all psychos, that true crime lot. Vicariously living in the danger zone, know what I mean?"

"What if he comes back with the money?"

"I don't know."

"Here." Max pointed at Lawrence. "I got my granddad's Webley you can sell him."

"What's he going to do with a fucking Webley?"

"Shoot Germans, same as my granddad."

Lawrence shook his head. "He won't be back. He's a tourist."

Fiona returned and removed Lawrence's plate. He ordered another tea, Max another coffee. Tony put a hand over his cup. Fiona was heading back to the café when she turned at the sound of an approaching engine. A Mazda rolled into the car park across the road.

Max squinted at the driver. "That your Jason, Tone?"

"Looks like it."

Jason slammed the car door and jogged across the road. He was pale and frowning, the youngest of them, and apparently still not used to the way his arms and legs worked. He was a handy lad to have around, but right now he looked like ball-ache personified.

"All right, Tone?" His voice was cracked with worry, and he didn't want to show it to the other two. He nodded at Lawrence and Max, who returned their own variations. "Listen, can I have a word?"

Tony raised his eyebrows. "If you'll excuse me, gentlemen, my young colleague would like a word." He got up and followed Jason back across the road to the car. "This new, is it?"

"Been trying to call you."

"I was at the Rock."

"All night?"

"Yes, all night. What's up?"

Jason looked over at the café as if Lawrence and Max were eavesdropping. "We got a rabbit, Tone."

"You what?"

"A rabbit." He looked at Tony directly now, showing bloodshot eyes. "Police picked him up last night."

"You're having a laugh, aren't you?"

Jason shook his head. "I got the call. They called."

"Then *they're* having a laugh. You're talking about from the other day, right?"

"I don't know what to tell you. I tried to call you, but your mobile was switched off."

"I was on a drop, wasn't I? Fucking hell…" Tony rubbed his face. Too knackered for this. He thought about it for a few seconds. "Hold on, which one?"

Jason stared at him, and he knew exactly which one.

"You are fucking—" He turned his back to Jason. He wanted to scream. Across the road, Lawrence was watching him. He smiled at the pair of them and turned back to Jason, his voice low. "I shot him *twice*."

"I know."

"You saw."

"I saw, yeah. I don't know what to tell you."

Tony rubbed his face again, then his mouth. "He's walking around, is he?"

Jason nodded.

Tony breathed out. He smoked the rest of his Benson in a single drag and dropped it under one shoe. "All right, where is he?"

"Local police picked him up."

"Ours?"

"It was our man who called, yeah."

"And you told him we were on our way."

"Yeah, but I've had to find you since."

"Okay, just forget about that. Let's just…" He gestured to the Mazda and pulled out his mobile. He turned it on. Right enough, five missed calls. He called Lisa on his way round to the passenger side. "It's me."

She was straight in there, no fucking about: "No."

"Babes—"

"You tell them no."

"I'm needed."

"They can get someone else."

"No, they can't."

"They can—"

"Look, I'll speak to you later, all right?"

She started to reply, but he killed the call after the first syllable. He left the car keys in the wheel arch and then returned to the Mazda. He leaned against the roof of the car and closed his eyes for a moment. He hadn't even managed to finish his fucking coffee. He pinched the bridge of his nose and breathed out.

"You all right?"

"Yeah." He got into the Mazda. "Come on, son. Let's just get this over with, eh?"

Six

"Jesus Christ, Raf, what were you thinking?"

"I don't think I was. Not something I'm used to doing."

"What?"

Rafael waved a hand at his head and tried a half smile. "I don't…It's difficult."

"All right, well, we can talk about it on the way." Sancho hustled Rafael toward a white Land Rover, one hand pressed against his back. He glanced over his shoulder and pointed at the car. "Go on, get in."

Rafael went round to the passenger side, saw two large dents in the door. He stopped. Looked up to see Sancho watching him. He tugged on the buckled door and got in the car. Sancho ducked into the driver's side and slammed his door shut.

"What happened to your door?"

"What happened to *you*?" Sancho started the engine. It rumbled. "Look at the state of you."

"I was robbed."

Sancho looked in his mirrors, then pulled the Land Rover away from the curb. "Who robbed you?"

"I don't remember." Rafael secured his seat belt and wondered if he owed Sancho money too. There was a quiver in his chest. He didn't know what to do.

"You look like a dead man walking." Sancho grabbed some French cigarettes from the dashboard and held the pack out to Rafael, who shook his head. "When did you give up?"

"Yesterday, I suppose."

"You suppose. You feeling all right?" Sancho stuck a cigarette between his lips. It had a white filter. He lit the cigarette and smoke billowed from his mouth. "You sick or anything?"

"No."

"Where've you been?"

"Around."

"That's funny. I remember looking there, and I didn't see you." Sancho cracked the side window and pulled into traffic. Fresh air mingled with smoke. The smell made Rafael tired. "Been looking for you, Raf." He glanced across. "You haven't been home."

Rafael stayed quiet.

"What, you don't trust me?"

"I'd like to go home now."

Sancho laughed and flicked ash out the window. "I don't think that's a very good idea, amigo. I think we better get you cleaned up first."

"I was supposed to meet someone."

"Javier?"

"No. The man on the phone."

"Who?"

"I don't know his name."

Sancho frowned at him. "You're not making much sense."

"I know. I'm sorry." Rafael touched his head. It ached, but it was a dull pain. Give it a few more minutes and he'd forget it like he'd forgotten everything else.

"They hurt you?"

Rafael nodded. He was warm. He opened the window and sucked in the cold air.

"What happened?"

Rafael's eyes were closed. He listened to the rush of wind around his head. "I don't know."

"They robbed you?"

He pointed to his head. "They shot me."

"Jesus, are you all right?"

"I'm okay." Rafael opened his eyes. They were on a main road. He looked around. "I'm just a bit...fuzzy. I'll be fine. I was supposed to meet someone."

"The man on the phone, you said, yeah. What did he sound like?"

"Old. He called me Raf."

Sancho nodded, his face tightening for an instant. "Okay."

"You know him?"

"I have an idea."

"Who is he?"

"Doesn't matter. Trust me, he's not the guy you want helping you out. You're better off with me. Listen, do me a favor and get my phone out of the glove compartment, would you?"

Rafael poked at the glove compartment until he found the catch and then popped it open. Inside was a map, a bottle of water, a bag of chewy sweets, a mobile phone, and a small, silver semiautomatic pistol. Rafael stared at the gun.

"It's okay, you can have a sweet if you want."

Rafael retrieved the phone and handed it to Sancho, then slapped the compartment closed. "I'm not hungry."

"Please yourself." Sancho watched his speed and thumbed a text as he drove.

"Where are we going?"

"Somewhere safe. You need to get your head down, and I need to make a few phone calls, find out what the fuck's going on."

"I want to go home, Sancho."

Sancho raised his eyebrows but didn't look at him. "Oh, really?"

"Why not?"

"I think that knock on the head's more serious than it looks." He finished his text and tucked the phone into his jeans pocket. "Can't imagine why you'd want to walk back into that house otherwise." He laughed, and when he saw Rafael wasn't joining in, he cleared his throat. "Besides, you obviously need medical attention, and you need it as soon as possible. Let me get that sorted first, make sure you're not going to snuff it before we sort out what's been going on. I wouldn't want to bring Daddy home just to have him drop down dead five minutes after I leave. I don't need that kind of hassle."

"Daddy?"

Sancho didn't say anything, and Rafael didn't push. "Daddy" meant family. He didn't remember any family.

"Here." Sancho nodded at the windscreen.

According to the sign on the lightbox, the place was called Whiskies. It was a squat concrete box that had been painted white about twenty years ago and left to peel. Both windows on the front of the building were barred, and the front door had a wrought-iron gate attached to it. There were two large truck cabs parked outside, and a smattering of vans and small cars. Sancho pulled in between a Fiat and a Renault and killed the engine.

Inside, the place was dim and red. A tiny reception area led through to a main room that looked like the inside of a heart. A ruddy gloom played across purple carpet. The room was littered with chairs and tables in a rough cabaret layout. A small, raised stage area backed by long tinsel tassels stood empty in the corner, above it an old, black speaker that was playing dance tunes at a low volume. On the far wall facing the door was a short bar, the kind old rich men have in their basements. Behind the bar, a top-less girl with long blonde hair that looked too thick to be real stood by a line of name-brand whiskey bottles and a small beer fridge. She was smiling at Sancho. The smile appeared genuine. Sancho went over to talk to her. Rafael stayed where he was.

There were two customers, and both looked as if they drove long haul for a living. One was asleep in the darkest corner of the room, his head back, mouth open. His low, grinding snore provided an industrial underscore to the music. The other man was less drunk, but his face had the scarlet starburst of long-term alcoholism. A dark-skinned woman wriggled and giggled on his lap. She touched his jowl and leaned in to whisper something into his hairy ear, and he made a moaning noise that was halfway between ejaculation and heart attack, which made her giggle again.

He tried not to watch. He looked at the floor.

Sancho returned to his side. "We're on."

"What?"

"Come on. I know the owner. He's an Arab, but he's all right. He's got a room sorted for you."

The topless girl had disappeared from behind the bar. She reappeared in a doorway off to their left. Yellow light leaked into the room. Sancho led the way, and the pair of them followed the girl into a corridor that was stuffy with perfume. Rafael coughed. It hurt his side.

"You should be all right here, just as long as you don't get hands on with the girls." Sancho looked at him, holding his side. "Which isn't going to be a problem, is it?"

"No."

"I didn't think so."

Sancho grinned, and there was something about it that stopped Rafael in his tracks. He'd been in places like this before, seen that kind of grin in that kind of light with this kind of perfume in the air.

He'd been here before.

Sancho saw the look on his face and the grin disappeared. "You okay?"

"Yes."

"Come on, then." He put a hand on Rafael's arm and let him fall in behind the girl. "You should keep to your room for the time being.

The girls will look after you until I can get a doctor. In fact, you carry on following Amber there, and I'll see about getting you one now."

Sancho broke off and wandered back up the corridor, digging his phone out of his pocket. Amber led Rafael to an open door. A white girl with mousy hair and thin lips, skinny in the hip, was busy throwing what passed for clothes into a Lidl bag. She was wearing a sheer negligee and not much else, and she could have been anything from thirteen to thirty-five.

"This is you." Amber's accent was oddly inflected. She wasn't Spanish.

The mousy girl looked up. Her blue eyes were red rimmed and her nostrils were pink. It was the only color in her face. She nodded quickly at him as if she knew that she was already supposed to be gone and sped up her packing. She gathered up a couple of plastic bags along with the Lidl bag she'd just filled and then hurried out of the room, squeezing between Rafael and Sancho, who had just reappeared at his side.

Sancho watched the girl as she struggled down the corridor. "I've seen worse. She's not Russian, is she, Amber?"

"No, love."

"Because you know what we say about Russian girls."

"A shitstorm waiting to happen."

"That's right."

The room was small, pink, and airless. It smelled of patchouli, baby oil, and cigarettes. A filter smoldered in the heart-shaped ashtray on the bedside table.

"Here." Sancho threw his cigarettes at Rafael, who caught them and made a move to throw them back, but Sancho raised a hand. "Give it time. I don't want you suddenly remembering you smoke and be stuck without them. You don't want them, don't have them, but keep them just in case."

Rafael put the cigarettes on the bedside table. He ground out the filter and wrinkled his nose at the smell. "Thanks. For helping me at the café. For all this."

"It's okay."

"How did you know I was there?"

"Freddy called me."

"Freddy." Rafael turned the name over in his head. He remembered Freddy. The barman. "Well, thank him too if you see him."

"No problem. Listen, get some sleep. I'll be back with a doctor in a couple of hours, okay?"

"Okay."

After Sancho left, closing the door behind him, Rafael pulled the sheets over the bed and then lay down on top of it. He listened to the music that rolled against the wall, something with a steady, almost metronomic, beat. The sink in the far corner of the room had a leaking tap. He watched the water drip but didn't hear it.

He had a family. The way Sancho had talked about it, though, they were probably a thing of the past. Maybe this place was the cause of it. Sancho was obviously a regular here, and he'd treated Rafael with the kind of familiarity that came with a long-term friendship, so it was plausible that Whiskies was one of those places they went to after a few drinks, just like the two truck drivers out there.

Which meant that Rafael was the kind of man who paid good money to fuck strangers.

He was also the kind of man who racked up debts he didn't intend to pay. Rafael Ortega, the surname provided by Javier, who'd been this close to cutting him open before Sancho stepped in. He'd been easily cowed, which meant that Sancho had either beaten Javier senseless at one point, or he didn't need to. Rafael guessed the latter. There was something about the way Sancho appeared to work that made him think the man had contacts everywhere. What were his first impressions again? Gigolo. That still felt correct somehow.

And so that was Rafael too. The man whose breathing had become shallow and whose hands now twitched in his lap like dying fish. The man who'd thought of himself as a victim of a robbery only a few hours earlier and who'd now turned into the kind of flashy bastard who stiffed low-level loan sharks and hung around with hookers. He stared at his hands. The fingers were long, the nails manicured. He looked at the cigarettes on the table, then picked one out of the pack and lit it.

He took a couple of baby puffs, the way nonsmoking actors did on the television. Then he took a lungful and told himself that if he coughed or if the smoke caught him like a fist in the throat, then it would mean everything that Sancho had told him was a lie, that he wasn't the Rafael he knew, that there was a chance he really had been a victim—an innocent man, a good man—and that it would all turn out fine in the end.

He let the smoke out of his chest slowly, and there wasn't so much as an itch in the back of his throat.

Rafael exhaled the rest through his nostrils. So he was that man. He leaned back against the headboard and let his eyes lose their focus. He gazed through half lids at the small dressing table and mirror that stood behind the door. The mirror caught the pink bulb in the bedside lamp and showed the cigarette burning between his fingers. He watched the smoke rise from the end in the reflection, then looked at the chair that stood in front of the dressing table. It looked too small, too fragile, and too ornate to be in this room. Its presence made the room seem sick.

He took another drag on the cigarette. Still no catch. He closed his eyes a little more.

Something shone in his peripheral vision. His head thumped. He turned his attention to the back of the chair and thought he saw something draped over the back, shining red and gold, sparkling as if it were made entirely of light.

It was so pretty, it hurt his head to look at it. He put the cigarette in the nub of the ashtray and closed his eyes.

Within seconds, he was dead to the world.

Episode Two

Seven

The police station was all concrete, tile, and steel, and the outside facade needed a good fucking hose down. Across the road was a scooter dealership, a car upholstery service, and a café with tables outside, and the road wasn't that wide, so when Tony spoke, he had to keep his voice down. He didn't exactly relish the idea of discussing this right outside the fucking *comisaría de policía*, but he didn't have much choice, seeing as this squat brown turd of a man wouldn't shift.

"All right, Manuel, there's a couple of things we need to go over. First is, when he came in all bashed up and that, and when you put him in a cell, why the fuck didn't you call us then?"

The copper pulled a face like a bad De Niro impression. Tony shifted his weight to the other foot, felt the tension in the back of his neck. He had to stoop to maintain eye contact with this fucker, who was about a foot shorter than any normal bloke. It was annoying, even more so than the way this bastard spoke English, just like the rest of the fucking Spaniards, all mock earnestness and no contractions, like he was some kind of fucking robot.

"Well?"

Another shrug. "Señor, we did not expect to have one of your amigos in our custody. If we had known, we would have telephoned immediately."

"And then what happened? You let him go?"

"That was not my decision."

"All right then, whose fucking *day-siggy-on* was it?"

The policeman bristled. "The detective, Señor."

"What detective?"

"The detective who questioned your man."

Tony heard Jason sigh behind him. Heard him mutter, "Fuck's sake…"

"He was interviewed?"

"Sí."

"What'd he say?"

A third shrug made Tony want to break one of the copper's shoulders. "I do not know. I was not present."

"And it was the detective that let him go?"

"Yes. He said your man should go to the hospital."

"When was that?"

"Eight, Señor."

"You what? That's two fucking…" He controlled the flash of rage and straightened up. Two hours ago; the rabbit could be in France by now. "All right, so did you see him go to the hospital?"

"No." The policeman looked to his left, then his right, then pointed up toward a patchwork of apartments. "He went that way."

"You sure?"

"That is the way he went."

"Right." Tony headed back to the Mazda. "Thanks for fuck all."

"*De nada.*"

Jason fell into step beside him. "You should've given him a dig."

"Shut up."

"I'm serious. He was taking the piss."

"He's a copper."

"Since when did that mean anything?"

"Since we had agreements." He got in the Mazda.

Jason got behind the wheel. He was still looking at the copper. "Where are we going?"

"Here, listen, don't be fucking stupid, all right?"

"What? I wasn't—"

"Save it for the rabbit." Tony nodded in the direction the policeman had indicated. "*Vamos.*"

Jason started the engine. The Mazda cruised up the Avenida de Arias de Velasco, past the apartments, more cafés and bike shops, a petrol station, and various buildings that looked like the upper decks of a cruise ship dropped onto land. When they came to the large intersection, Tony had a brain wave. "Turn left here."

"Can't turn left, I'll have to go round."

"Then go round."

A few minutes later, they were at the Plaza de Toros. The place was surrounded by apartment blocks, and this early in the day the car park was deserted. When he saw the Casa de Verónica open for business, he told Jason to stop the car.

Tony led the way into the café. A skinny lad with black hair stood looking worried behind the bar. Tony ordered a couple of San Miguels. That was the only good thing about Spain apart from the weather—if you were English, you could get a beer any time you wanted.

When it came time to pay, he noted the name badge. "Freddy, you wouldn't happen to have seen a man come in here with a head wound, would you?"

"Sorry?" Pretending his English wasn't that good. Tony gazed at him and waited. The fucker was a barman in Marbella. His English was fine.

"Head wound. *Dolores de cabeza.*"

The barman frowned. "*Migrañas?*"

"Don't be fucking smart, Freddy. You know what I mean."

Freddy paused, his lips twitching, apparently giving it some thought when he was really just prepping his mouth for the lie. "Ah, no, Señor. I am sorry."

Tony nodded as if that was just fine, don't worry about it, he was only making conversation. Freddy smiled and retreated, didn't seem to realize that his lie was confirmation enough.

This was the place. They shot the matador in the head; only stood to reason that he'd come back to a place he knew. Tony turned in his seat and surveyed the rest of the bar. There were a few customers. A middle-aged woman sat with a small terrier at her feet. She wore what looked like a floral-patterned tent and sunglasses and was reading a glossy magazine with lots of suntanned, smiling faces in it. Over in the corner, a man in a gray suit was busy talking to another man, who was broad and old. When the older man saw him looking, he said something to the man in the gray suit. Both stopped talking and looked at Tony.

Tony went back to his beer.

"What d'you think we should do?"

Tony kept his voice low. "He was here. Two old lads in the corner saw him."

Jason started to turn. Tony put a hand on him.

"Come on, Jase, be clever, will you? You'll see them in a minute. They're not going anywhere. Drink your drink."

"What if they don't know anything?"

"They know something. We just need to give them a little time to get soft again."

"And what if they don't cooperate?"

"Those two grew up with Franco, mate. They're used to doing what they're told." Tony drank some more of his beer. It was starting to make him slow upstairs, but it took the edge off. Normally he would have waited another half hour or so, let them fall back into their conversation and feel secure again. You got more out of people with surprise than intimidation. But the beer and lack of sleep were beginning to catch up with him, so he took another sip and nodded to Jason. "All right, come on, then. Let's make some new friends."

They walked over to the corner. Tony put his beer down on the table and pulled up a chair. Jason sat to Tony's right. They had the two old men boxed. The man in the gray suit said something in Spanish to the other one and gestured to Tony and Jason like *I told you.*

Tony smiled and pointed at the man in the gray suit. "You look familiar."

The man stammered something in Spanish, sounded as if he was playing dumb.

Tony nodded at the older man. "You speak English?"

The older man nodded. The man in the gray suit shut up.

"What's your name?"

"Alejandro."

"What about him?"

"Javier."

Javier glared. The name was as familiar as the face. He was known, but Tony couldn't quite put his finger on why. He addressed Alejandro instead. "I'm looking for a fella, came in here this morning, probably wearing a dark suit."

"Sorry, Señor. I have not seen him."

"You didn't let me finish, mate. You see, he has this head wound." He turned to Javier and pointed at his temple with one gun-shaped hand. "About here. *Entiendes?*"

Javier nodded. Alejandro remained still and said nothing.

"You see him?"

Alejandro shook his head. "I arrived here only a few minutes ago, Señor."

"What about you, Javier?" Javier looked at his companion. "Don't bother looking at him, mate. He's not going to help you. He arrived only a few minutes ago, apparently."

Javier opened his mouth and then closed it again. Yeah, he'd seen him, which was why he was all set to rabbit, and why it was time for a little financial sedative. Tony pulled his second roll and peeled off a couple of fifties. He put the notes on the table. They were pristine and snide, which was why he kept them on the other clip. No sense in bribing people with kosher cash, was there? And it was much easier than sending the kids out to buy Cokes in order to break the notes.

Javier focused on the money. He was the kind of man who showed what he was thinking without saying it. "I saw—"

"He saw nothing."

"That's not what he said."

Alejandro raised his chin. "He is trying to take your money."

"Well, he's not taking nothing until I hear what he has to say for himself."

"I saw him." Javier looked directly at Tony now.

Alejandro frowned. "Why do you want this man?"

"You didn't see him, mate. You're not involved."

"I am interested."

"Interested doesn't mean entitled, though, does it? So how about you shut up and let your friend speak?" Tony waited for a response and was ready to smack the old bastard if he got one. He didn't, so he nodded at Javier. "On you go, son."

"His name is Rafael Ortega. He owes me money. He is supposed to meet me here tomorrow, but I do not think he will. I saw him here this morning, Señor."

Tony's mobile vibrated in his pocket. He ignored it. "Nothing I didn't already know. You'll have to do better than that." Alejandro stood up, pushing the table. The leg smacked into Tony's leg. "Where d'you think you're going?"

"I have done nothing wrong. You said that I am not involved. I want to leave."

Jason put on his best bouncer face. "You're going nowhere, mate. Sit down."

Tony smiled and pulled out his mobile. There was a text message from the *GQ* dago. Been awhile since that prick had texted. He opened the message. "It's all right." He looked up at Alejandro. "We're going anyway." He stood and took a step away from the table before he turned and pointed at the cash. "Buy yourself something nice, eh?"

Jason was frowning as they left the café. "Did I do something wrong?"

"Nah, mate. Everything's fine. Just caught a break for once."

Another buzz in his pocket. This time the mobile was ringing. Tony answered it immediately. "Just got your text, mate. Thanks for that."

"What text?"

Oh, for fuck's... "Sorry, Ollie. Thought you were someone else."

Jason grimaced, and they stopped by the Mazda.

"You found your rabbit yet?"

"On it, Ollie." Jason ducked his glare by getting into the car. "Just about to pick him up now."

"When you do, bring him up the ranch."

"I thought you wanted this taken care of."

"I did. But now I want to see him."

"Okay."

"It wasn't a request, Tony."

The phone went dead in his hand. Tony waited for a moment, then slipped the phone back into his pocket and got into the Mazda, slamming the door behind him.

Jason looked sheepish. "I couldn't get hold of you."

"You don't do that, Jase."

"I'm sorry—"

Tony pointed the phone at him. "You can't get me, you try Lawrence, or you try Max or Liam or one of that lot. You don't go to the fucking gaffer. That's me—that's *us*—in the shit now." He rubbed his nose and shoved the phone back into his jeans pocket. "He only wants to see him at the fucking ranch, doesn't he?"

"Why?"

"I don't know, do I? I don't need to know. Ours is not to reason why. All I do know is we could've sorted this nice and easy if you hadn't flapped your fucking mouth." He slapped the dashboard. "Come on, get going."

"Where?"

"He's in a *whiskería*."

Jason looked blank. The sight of him broke Tony's filthy mood. He smiled. "You don't know what a whiskería is, do you?"

"No."

He shook his head. "No whores in Benalmádena? Fucking hell, no wonder you lads spent so much time stabbing each other. Come on, get on the motorway, I'll give you directions from there."

Eight

The crash at the door jerked Rafael awake, but he was slow to rise. Two men entered. A young one in a T-shirt, slim and short haired. The other one was older, alcohol fat and sweating through a polo shirt. The older man was smiling.

"Oy-oy. Buenas días, Señor Slugabed. Up and at 'em."

Hands on him now, dragging him to his feet. He broke the thick blanket of smoke that hung over the bed and coughed. He closed his eyes. Someone slapped him, and he blinked the world back into focus.

"Think this fucker's still in siesta mode. Jason, be a good lad and turn on the tap over there, will you?"

Rafael raised his head and saw the younger one—his name was Jason, he remembered that—head over to the sink as the other one shoved him forward. Rafael tried to resist, bending over until the older man grabbed him by the hair and ran him toward the sink.

"Mind his head, Tone."

Rafael resisted. The older man—*Tone? Tony?*—put his fist in Rafael's gut, which doubled him up and unlocked his knees. Cold water hit him like an ice storm and ripped what little breath remained in his lungs. He tried to pull away, but Tony held him tight. He couldn't breathe. The pain in his gut throbbed like follow-up blows. He choked, gurgled. Water ran up his nose, forcing its way into his sinuses, rushing his head. They were drowning him. Bubbling through the water, he heard laughter, heard Tony say something he couldn't make out, and then he felt the pressure on his back and neck whip away and his support vanished with it.

Rafael dropped to his knees and spewed water onto the carpet. He sucked breath, the air rushing over his vocal cords in a moan. He blinked, couldn't stop himself from slithering to the floor.

"And there he is, sitting on his arse again. Lazy bastard."

A sharp kick in Rafael's side. He looked up. Tony looked familiar, and the familiarity made Rafael's head hurt.

"Come on, old son. Haven't got all fucking day, have we? Got to see the gaffer."

Jason pulled Rafael to his feet. "Fucking deadweight."

Rafael coughed again and either water or vomit rose in his throat before he swallowed it back. He looked at Tony. "Who are you?"

Tony laughed. "You hear this?"

"I don't remember."

"Shut up, you dozy twat." He grabbed Rafael's other arm, and the pair of them dragged him to the door. Tony pulled it open and led the way. There was the sickly sweet smell of perfume. Rafael swallowed again. It hurt. Everything hurt. Tony pushed open a fire door, and the sudden sunshine was a belt across the eyes.

They shoved Rafael up against the side of a car and pulled his hands behind his back. He heard the creak and snap of tape as they bound his wrists together, before they pushed him into the back of the car. The leather upholstery was cold against his cheek. The two men got in the front. Jason drove them farther into the countryside, where the roads and pylons were the only sign of man. They listened to flamenco on the radio. A strummed guitar and a heel-kicked floor. The singer wailed his life away in an empty room. It was a lonely, painful sound, and it fell on four tone-deaf ears.

"I love all this kind of shit." Tony shifted his weight in the passenger seat. "Like all that Gipsy Kings and that. Smashing."

Rafael stayed quiet. They were speaking English, and he could understand it, knew he could speak it too.

The car bounced along a dirt road. Rafael struggled to get himself upright in the backseat. He looked out of the window. They were in the middle of nowhere, blasted scrubland all around them. He could see the mountains in the distance, looming like giant tombstones. Then, up ahead, the whitewashed buildings of a ranch, and a worn sign that read GANADO BRAVO. The car turned into a long dirt-and-gravel driveway and then crawled up toward a set of low-slung gates set into a wire fence. There was a man at the gate. He wore sunglasses, a short-sleeved shirt and white chinos. He would've looked like a tourist if it hadn't been for radio on his hip and the small machine gun in his hand. The car slowed to a stop, and Jason buzzed down the window.

"You all right, Chris?"

Chris lowered the sunglasses and peered in at Rafael. "That him, is it?"

"Yeah."

"Doesn't look like much."

Tony smiled, but there was no humor. "Fuck off, Chris, eh?"

"No offense."

"Just open the fucking gate."

"Ollie's up at the corral waiting for you." Chris stepped back from the car and went over to the gate.

Jason looked at Tony. "The corral?"

"Must be playing with his bulls." Tony glanced in the rearview mirror. "You like bulls, don't you?"

He didn't answer.

The car continued up past the main house and then on toward a series of corrals out in the countryside and, beyond them, he saw the black specks of what could have been a herd of bulls. The sight of them made something spasm in his chest. He was cold.

Jason pulled the car in next to a white Land Rover. It was only when they dragged Rafael out of the car that he saw the two dents in the Land Rover's passenger-side door. His legs felt watery. A breeze whipped sand into his face, and he lowered his head, blinking, letting Tone guide him. When he could see again, he looked up and saw the makeshift bullring over on his left. It was a practice ring for calves, and it hadn't been used for decades, judging by the state of the barriers, which were splintered and rotten.

Up ahead a group of six men had gathered on a viewing platform over a double pen. As Tony pushed him forward, the man in the middle turned. He was dressed like the old-fashioned Englishman abroad—white shirt, linen trousers—and when the wind made the light material flutter, it did so against a boxer's body. He was heavily tanned, and his black hair was combed away from his face, which was obscured by large sunglasses. He smiled at Rafael and showed teeth that were too white to be real. In among the other men, Rafael saw Sancho, who was busy trying to ignore him.

Tony shoved Rafael forward a few steps. "As you wanted, Ollie."

Ollie removed his sunglasses as he stepped down from the platform. "So you're the bloke who won't stay dead."

Rafael kept quiet.

Ollie frowned at Tony. "Can he understand what I'm saying?"

Rafael nodded. "I speak English."

"I learn it from a booook." There was laughter on the viewing platform.

Ollie glanced behind him, and the laughter descended into coughing. Back to Rafael, and he was all smiles again. "You know why you're here?"

"Because I did not stay dead."

"That's partly it." He cocked his head, regarding Rafael through narrowed eyes. "To be honest, I don't really remember you."

"That makes two of us."

A frown, showing lines in Ollie's forehead. "You being funny?"

"Why did you want me dead?"

Ollie looked confused for a moment, the frown deepening, and then he burst out laughing. The other men on the platform followed suit. "You *are* being funny. Fucking Michael McIntyre."

"No."

"No?"

"I do not remember."

Ollie looked at Tony. "Really?"

"He said something like that before, but it's bollocks."

"It is not." Sancho came down from the platform. "I do not think he remembers anything."

"Huh." Ollie stuck out his chin and tapped it. "If that's the case, then that throws up an interesting dilemma, doesn't it? Because if you don't remember what you did, then how can we punish you properly?" Another tap, then he nodded and moved away from Rafael, back toward the viewing platform. "What I should probably do is take that as a sign to leave well enough alone. I mean, on a basic level, the fact that you're standing there breathing this good country air means I can't trust these two to do what I tell them."

"Come on, Ollie." Tony sounded indignant. "I shot him in the *head*."

"And then we buried him."

"I don't care." Ollie stopped, frowning. "I told you to kill him. I don't care how you go about it. I care about the result. And here we are." He pointed at Rafael and smiled. "Which means you're cleverer than you look. Certainly cleverer than these two. Or you're a good actor. And if you can play dead, I'm pretty sure you can play forgetful."

Sancho dropped his cigarette and ground it into the sand. "He is not acting, Señor Graham."

"I don't recall asking you anything." Ollie jerked his chin at Rafael. "What do you remember?"

Rafael swallowed. His arms felt dead. There were more men looking at him now. Chris had appeared from somewhere, and there was another man, slim and dressed in an expensive suit. There was a fat man in a bowling shirt with stains down the front. A skinny man leaning against the railing of the viewing platform. Sancho. Tony and Jason. And then the gaffer himself, the one they called Ollie or Señor Graham. He cleared his throat. "My name is Rafael Ortega. I owe a man named Javier some money, and I am supposed to pay him some of it tomorrow. I think I was robbed. I know I was shot twice. From what you said, I think that one of these men shot me. That is all I remember."

"What about Palmer?"

"Palmer?"

"Tell me about him."

"I do not know any Palmer."

Ollie approached him and studied his face. "You don't remember a fella by the name of Gavin Palmer."

Rafael shook his head. The name meant something to Ollie, obviously, but it was the first time Rafael had even heard it. And from the look on Ollie's face, he knew it.

"Okay." Ollie smiled at him, gestured for him to follow. "Got something to show you."

Tony guided him over to the side of the bullring. Ollie pointed across at the pens. There was a huge black bull standing motionless in one of them.

"See him?"

"Yes."

"You know what he is?"

"A bull."

"You know what kind?"

He saw the brand on the bull. An *A* with a half halo. One word swam into Rafael's head. He said it without comprehension. "Miura."

"Spot on. Not exactly kosher, mind. The Miura brothers don't know we've got one of their rejects, but it's not like I'm going to put him in the plaza, is it? They wouldn't have him. He's too old and too fucking cunning, which makes him good breeding stock. See, I'm building something here, Rafael. A new dynasty. A man can only own so many bars and restaurants before he loses interest, know what I mean? This place, it's like tapping a fucking artery. Get right into the heart of the country and take it over. I've been talking with the men in the know, and I know what we should be looking for now. Your impresarios want the short legs and long necks, they can have 'em, but they won't get 'em from here. I mean, if you're going to stage a bullfight, it better *be* one, know what I mean? If the only thing getting damaged is some poof's reputation, then it doesn't exactly make for riveting viewing. You stick a bull like Tyson over there in the ring, you could pull in some big fucking numbers."

Rafael nodded. He couldn't find the breath to speak.

"Miuras killed more matadors in a hundred and fifty years than any other breed. That's a hell of a record. I read somewhere there was one in 1879. It took twenty-four fucking jabs from one of those spears you lads have. When you usually do how many?"

He said it without thinking. "Three."

"Three." Ollie nodded. "There was an escaped half breed up north. Police didn't have the bottle to try and capture it, so they did what dago coppers always fucking do and they brought out the guns. Thirty rounds before it went down. That's a tough bastard. What do you think?"

"I do not know."

"You do not know. Yeah, you don't remember, do you?" Ollie turned and gestured to someone behind Rafael. Rafael started to turn, but Ollie jabbed him in the head. "All gone from there, isn't it? You don't remember Palmer. You don't remember why Tony and Jason over there took you up to the mountains. You don't remember me. You're just one big fucking empty space, aren't you?"

"I do not—"

He felt his wrists pop free. Someone had cut the tape. He looked behind him and saw the other men congregating. The fat man approached with a brown canvas bag which—on Ollie's nod—he threw into the bullring. It fell open, and Rafael could see a scrap of red.

Ollie put his arm around Rafael's shoulders. "Bulls are herd animals, Rafael. They like to stick together. I've found that it's the ones that break away that make the better fighters. The ones that charge without thought. The ones that attack everything without hesitation. But the trouble is, like they say, a bull is like a melon. You can't tell if he's sweet or not until you open him up."

The arm disappeared from his shoulders, and hands appeared at Rafael's back. He struggled but felt his feet leave the ground, and three of the men—Tony was there, so was the fat man and the one who'd been smoking before—carried him toward the bullring and tipped him over the barrier. He hit the ground hard, throwing up a cloud of sand. He saw into the bag now.

The red cape, the *muleta*. The shine of a sword blade reflecting the weak afternoon light.

He heard the barrage of bolts as they shot back, the screech of a gate, and the sudden stench of bull filled the damp air.

Ollie appeared at the viewing platform. He cupped his hands over his mouth. "All yours, matador!"

And Rafael stood staring at the Miura.

Nine

Matador. He was a matador.

Rafael crawled to the brown bag, took out the muleta and sword, and let the cape unfurl little by little as he moved out of the bull's immediate line of sight. He felt the tremor in his sword hand and adjusted his grip. It was too light. No good for a killing blow, but it might be good enough to work the cape, and there were certain movements that felt natural to him.

He was a matador. That was what Ollie had shouted, and it felt correct. He swallowed, throat dry and scratched. He tried to regulate his breathing, slow it down so he could breathe through his nose and ignore both the tension in his chest as well as the slow, painful pulse in his temple. His heartbeat echoed in his ears. He could feel blood, warm and viscous, as it moved down by the edge of his eye.

The fear was normal. It was normal to be frightened when you were confronted with a half-ton animal that wanted to kill you. But if he was a matador, then he should be able to control that fear.

Think.

This wasn't a working ring. He remembered that the barriers that surrounded the ring were broken down and only partially standing. Which meant that there was nowhere to hide. So he had two choices. He could go over the side or he could kill the bull. If he went over the side, he would be caught by one of the men who'd now gathered ringside to watch, and he would either be thrown back to the bull or shot on the spot. If he somehow managed to kill the bull with a practice sword, then he'd no doubt be shot anyway, because it would mean he'd been lying to Ollie.

They expected him to die, and they were watching closely to make sure it happened. Up on the viewing platform, the best seat in the house, Ollie stood like the president.

Rafael turned back to the bull. The bull did the same, shifting its back legs. It had seen him, but it didn't appear to know what he was just yet. Rafael angled his body sideways, the muleta held out to his right, the sword guiding it.

He moved the cape, just a little, almost imperceptibly. A test of the bull's eyesight. If the Miura was a reject, he might not be able to see very well.

Nothing.

Good. It meant the tremor in his sword hand wouldn't give him away.

Another shake, a little more vigorous this time. The bull lifted its head in one short, violent thrust, the horns pointed skyward.

The bull's eyes were good but not brilliant. There was a slight bias in the raise of its head toward the right. Its skin shuddered over its muscles as if tugged by wires, a rush of violence surging through it. It moved a few steps forward. A nervous reaction, but also the recognition of Rafael as a threat, and a reaction made worse by the sudden cheer that went up from the audience. The Miura broke concentration from the cape and bolted for the side of the ring, charging for one of the louder men, who pushed away from the ringside quick enough to draw laughter, a round of applause, and a few sarcastic olés.

Rafael breathed out through his nose. It felt blocked. He swallowed and moved the cape once more as the bull wandered back toward the center of the ring. Another movement, and the bull's head followed a split second later. It moved hooves against sand in a parody of a dancing heavyweight, its legs too quick and dainty for the bulk of its body, and then it turned toward Rafael.

There it was, that freezing fist that grabbed at his heart, that primal terror. Crosshairs etched across him. To that Miura, he was the most abhorrent creature ever to walk the face of the earth and had become the sole focus of the bull's animal wrath. That look, combined with the musk in the air and the adrenaline in Rafael's bloodstream, further distilled his options to a bitter few.

Fight or flight.

Or another option. Both?

Yes, maybe. But not yet.

He forced himself to shift the cape, switching the bull's hatred from man to muleta, and another shake prompted the bull into an explosive charge. Rafael felt a sudden rush of wind, the rumble under his feet, and suddenly the bull was on him. He whipped the cape out of the way, stumbling backward as the bull careered toward one of the barriers and prompted another exodus from ringside, which further provoked it. The bull collided hard with the barrier, hooked once and then backed away, snorting its displeasure at connecting with wood rather than flesh.

He couldn't wear down this bull by himself. In the plaza, he would've had assistants to pic and place their banderillas. By the final third, the bull's head would be down. It would be bleeding. It would be slow. It would be mortal.

Rafael moved around the ring. The space around him seemed to close in with every step. Panic grabbed at him again—he was boxed in, couldn't move. This wasn't a proper plaza. There wasn't enough room to see how the bull moved. He felt a breeze against his face and glanced up at the sky, with its thick, gray-bellied clouds. Something told him to kick sand onto his cape, but it wouldn't stick. His hands started trembling. He let out a low grunt of frustration that pricked the bull's ears and sent it rocketing back in his direction. Rafael dug in, held firm with the cape, watching the bull's arc, and then tried to switch out of the way. The smell was eye-watering, the shaking under his feet immense, and then he felt the horn scrape his leg. He heard the ripping of cloth, felt the ice on his skin, then warmth, and he shook the muleta with a panicked flourish that stopped the Miura short and caused someone to shout "Olé!" from the sidelines.

Rafael staggered back out of the bull's line of sight, something warm and wet running down his leg. His suit trousers were torn just below the crotch, the material hanging open to reveal a gash across the top of his thigh.

He looked up, saw the Miura turn, trying to get a fix on his position. It shook its head and wandered back to its safe spot.

Rafael breathed in through his nose then out through the mouth, huffing his breath into a call that started to punctuate the shake of the muleta—*ha ha ha*. The bull reacted immediately, bursting into a stiff-legged gallop. Just before it reached Rafael, it chopped with its right horn, flicking it up and through the whipped cape as Rafael backed away. The bull wheeled and hooked farther right, snatching the cape out of Rafael's hand as the left horn jabbed into his jacket. Rafael felt the jerk at his side pocket, twisted out of the Miura's path. He felt the pull of stitches in his side and then the raw power of the bull as it wrenched his jacket open. Rafael shook the jacket from his shoulders, left it hanging off the bull's left horn. It shook its head, trying to free itself of the irritation.

He had to get out of there. Had to take the chance. He bolted for the side of the ring. The bull followed and caught Rafael high on the hip, hooking once and then, unable to sustain the momentum, letting him drop. Rafael hit the ground and rolled, leaving a trail of blood in the sand. He struggled to one knee, and the fierce bolt of pain that hit him as he leaned on his bad thigh almost put him back down.

The Miura turned.

Rafael saw the cape on the ground a few meters away and made a move for it just as the bull charged again. He grabbed the muleta and rolled, felt one of the back hooves kick him off to one side before he came to a stop. Rafael got to his feet and staggered back a few steps before he turned and sprinted for the edge of the ring once more. The Miura caught the movement and charged. He caped once, doubled the bull, and felt his thigh brushing the beast as it passed, smearing its hide with his blood. He snapped the cape up over the Miura's horns while its back was turned and then ran for the barriers. He saw the fat man reach for something in the back of his jeans and threw the muleta at him just as he heard the thunder of hooves behind him.

Then he stopped dead. Denied the Miura its target. Watched the bull follow the cape instead.

The bull careened into the side of the bullring and straight into the barrier, which splintered and broke in front of the fat man. There was a gunshot, a scream. Rafael looked over his shoulder, saw the bull break loose, and ran for the opposite side of the ring, stopping only to grab the sword. He threw himself over the barrier and into Sancho as he ran past, pulling him to the ground. Rafael scrambled to his feet and put the sword to Sancho's throat; it was sharp enough at the point to draw blood. He heard the screams of the fat man, the shouts from the other men, and felt nothing but the agony in his legs and side and the trembling in his hand as he tried to keep from thrusting the sword through Sancho's larynx.

"Get up."

Sancho got up. Rafael ducked behind him and dragged him back over toward the Land Rover.

"Keys."

Sancho fumbled in his pockets. He was trying to say something, but Rafael couldn't hear it over the shouts by the bullring.

"Just give me the fucking car keys."

Sancho pressed keys into Rafael's free hand. Rafael looked behind him and saw the Land Rover a couple of meters away. Eyes front, and he saw Ollie's men look in his direction. They all had guns in their hands. Other men were over by the fallen fat man. There was blood on the sand—lots of it. Then they started shooting at the bull, which was wandering beyond the ring now. It bellowed at the sudden pain and charged each man it saw.

Thirty shots to bring him down.

Rafael shoved Sancho forward, not waiting to watch him lose his balance, and limped quickly toward the Land Rover. He threw himself down behind the steering wheel as an explosion took out both the driver's-side mirror and Rafael's hearing. He ducked down, twisted the key in the ignition, and leaned on the accelerator. The car lurched forward and growled as it picked up speed. Another brief tattoo of bullets rattled across the bodywork, and Rafael felt a sudden breeze by his head. He stayed tense and out of sight, let the Land Rover roar in first gear until the gunshots faded to pops in the near distance. Then he pulled himself upright, threw the gear stick into second, then third. The Land Rover jumped from countryside to dirt road.

There, up ahead, was the wire fence that separated the ranch from the rest of the world. He floored it. The Land Rover barreled through, the wire whipping against the side of the car, the collision putting a slight swerve into the car's trajectory until Rafael managed to wrestle it back.

There was a real road in the distance. He glanced in the rearview mirror. The ranch looked as if it were miles away now. The whitewashed buildings had almost faded into the landscape.

Once he hit the real road, he eased up on the accelerator.

It was only then that the adrenaline leeched from his system, only then that he felt the ice in his legs, and only then that he saw the blood that covered the inside of the car.

Ten

Alejandro was half-drunk by the time he arrived at the Plaza de Toros. He made it to his seat in time to see the poster attraction, an old hand in his midthirties by the name of Alonso Hernandez, take on his second bull of the corrida.

A few short capes to the bull, and then the picadors rode out. Hernandez promptly retreated behind the barriers to spend his second *tercio de varas* talking shit with his banderilleros. Everyone else in the crowd was busy watching the picadors, but Alejandro didn't need to see the blood to know they were twisting. Instead, he watched the torero, who stood with his back to the ring.

It was a stupid move, and even though he didn't say it out loud, he hoped that it would come back to bite him. The whole point of the picadors was to let the torero see the bull charge from a distance, from one side of the ring to the other. Not taking note of these charges meant that Hernandez would have no measure of the bull's speed, aggression, stamina, and, most importantly, intelligence. If you knew the bull's velocity, if you took the time to study your bull, then you would be able to adapt accordingly. You would know how to use the cape and lure, how the bull saw and what provoked it at what distance. You would know the bull better than it knew itself, would be able to predict its next move, and you would be able to maintain clarity and purity of form. A torero who achieved that would cut ears on a regular basis and make a lasting impression. A torero who ignored those observations, whether through an attack of ego or simple inexperience, would underestimate his *toro* and take a horn to the belly as his reward.

At least that was the way it was supposed to work. Like many of the others, Hernandez was content to let his picadors and banderilleros grind the bull to nothing before he deigned to approach his *faena*. To Alejandro, it was a sign of disrespect to both bull and audience—not that the latter would understand, especially today. The assembled crowd were all expats and socialites, more concerned with atmosphere and showing themselves off than anything else. One of the English in front asked his Spanish friend if he should say olé yet. The Spaniard shook his head.

And that was it, wasn't it? You shouldn't need to ask permission. It wasn't a word that was supposed to pass through the brain at all. It was a spontaneous reaction to a work of art. The level of ignorance on display made Alejandro sick to his stomach.

He removed the cigarette from between his lips and rammed a fist against his mouth as a rattling, sticky cough shook his lungs. There were a few glances—*who was that old man distracting them from the corrida with his reminders of sickness and death?*—and he waved them away, irritated. Once he managed to catch his breath, he replaced the cigarette between his lips, reopened his notebook, and breathed smoke through his nostrils at the handwritten notes and the small spots of blood that covered the page like errant punctuation.

A cheer went up around him. He saw the bull bleeding and already struggling to breathe. One of the mounted picadors had struck too deep. But the bull wheeled and charged at the opposite horse. Only a real fighting bull would charge knowing that it would bring further pain. It was a shame that it wouldn't get a chance to prove itself with a proper torero.

Alejandro wiped his lips and swallowed the bad taste in his mouth. He was sweating. He told himself it was a reaction to sitting in the cheap seats, even though the sun hadn't touched the concrete on this side of the plaza for at least an hour. He flipped the page in his notebook, tapped pen on pad. Next to him, a loud-mouthed *villamelón* screamed obscenities at the picadors. He was dark skinned and gypsy featured. His shirt was open three buttons from the throat and he wore a gold chain. His hands were stubby and nicotine stained, and so were his teeth. "Where's your bull, Hernandez? You killed it already!"

The villamelón turned and looked at Alejandro. He smiled, showing those small teeth. Alejandro stared at the blank page. He barely saw it. He wasn't going to write anything. He shouldn't have come. He should've been somewhere else.

Rafael was in trouble. He'd known that the moment he turned up at the Casa de Verónica and seen Javier stationed in the corner of the café with a coffee and a liqueur. Javier was a scalper for the plaza and a part-time loan shark who frequented the bars and cafés exuding the kind of authority that a man can only bestow upon himself. And when he saw Alejandro come in, his smile told him what the mouth confirmed: "Your boy was in."

What he heard after that was even worse, that Javier had been all set to make an example of "your boy" when Sancho Rios turned up. "And don't think I don't know who fucking called him, Freddy." Alejandro tried to get more information out of him, but then the two English had turned up, and that was the end of their conversation. By the time they left, Javier had tried to sell Raf to the English, but Alejandro got the feeling that Sancho had beaten him to the punch. Which meant that Raf was in trouble, and Alejandro had failed him again.

He blinked the smoke out of his eyes. Looked down and found he'd scribbled on the blank page. It was gibberish.

The last time he'd seen Raf was Monday gone in a café well away from his usual haunts. It was a tumbledown place, small and dirty, the kind of place that served good tapas if you didn't think about the kitchen too much. A panicked phone call brought

Alejandro there. He arrived first, took a corner table and a small cup of coffee. He didn't have much hope for the meeting. They hadn't parted amicably, thanks to that last-minute replacement job in Seville where he'd pulled two *manso* bulls. They'd been skittish, shy, and difficult to draw, and the crowd naturally put the blame on Raf, whose own desperate need to stoke some kind of reaction— because silence was worse than jeers—almost resulted in the kind of nasty *cornada* that would have ended the corrida one bull early.

And then Raf did the worst thing possible. He dismissed it as *mala suerte*.

"Mala suerte?" It was the last-chance utterance of a loser. Raf knew damn well that luck had little to do with either success or failure, and a good torero—a *professional* torero—was one who owned chance and who could mold *suerte* to his own ends. And he did that by studying the bloodlines and the breeders. He watched and he learned and he paid attention both to the bulls and himself. If a torero slipped in a wet patch of sand, then he hadn't bothered to watch his footing. If his muleta blew up during a pass, then he hadn't scuffed enough dirt to weigh it down. There was no such thing as mala suerte other than as a euphemism for arrogance or inexperience. To blame your mistakes on mala suerte was to close your eyes to yourself, and if you couldn't deal with criticism, then you were nothing more than a café maestro and liable to remain that way for the rest of your life.

Alejandro told Raf all this in front of his cuadrilla after the corrida. Raf responded with a punch to the mouth that split Alejandro's lip and broke their working relationship. He knew there were other corridas after that—the contractual obligation to Ernesto Brava needed to be fulfilled—but Raf suffered without his *apoderado*. Then there were rumors that Raf dropped out of the business altogether, that he'd taken up with that rat-faced lothario who used to provide him with girls. Alejandro told himself he didn't care, and yet a week earlier he'd gone to that grimy café to talk to him.

The door squeaked, and a gust of warm air followed Raf into the place. He was heavier than he used to be, and it manifested itself in a puffy face and noticeable tire around his midriff. It was a drinker's weight to go with the smell that came off him. He wore a black suit and a white shirt, and it looked as if he'd slept in both. As he approached, Raf appeared to read his mind and closed his jacket.

"Get you something?"

Raf sat down opposite. He leaned slightly over the table. "I'm fine."

"Good to see you."

"You too."

"You working?"

"Kind of."

"Haven't seen you at the Plaza."

He shook his head. "Are you still training?"

"Not really."

"What does that mean?"

"It means not really." Alejandro sipped his coffee. It was bitter. "I haven't found anyone worth the time and money. Too much of a commitment to make with someone who isn't going to go all the way. You know."

"Yes." Raf straightened in his seat and glanced over his shoulder, then turned his gaze to the table. "I'm sorry about the way things ended."

"So am I."

"It was unfair to you."

"I know."

Raf tapped the table and worked his mouth for a few seconds before he spoke again. "I was thinking maybe I should get back into the business."

"Really?"

"Not here, but maybe over in Mexico or South America, somewhere like that."

"The money's no good there."

"The work is."

"You never wanted to do that before."

"Well, you know, things change." He looked up at Alejandro. "Do you think you could arrange something like that?"

Alejandro looked back, searched for the remnants of the old Rafael, but saw nothing worth protecting. "I don't think so. You've been out too long."

"A year, and you know I can—"

"Two years. At least. You'd need training."

"You could train me."

"Why?"

"You said you weren't busy." He blinked. He didn't understand. "I apologized, Al."

"You regretted the way it ended. You didn't apologize."

Raf frowned, his lips tight. "Okay, I should've known."

Gone was the boy with the ramrod spine, replaced by a crumpled thirtysomething whose confidence had curdled into sloppy desperation.

"What happened?"

Raf shook his head. He stared through the table.

"If you don't tell me, I can't help you."

"I already asked you for help."

"You asked me to be your apoderado again. Which would mean me financing you and moving halfway across the world."

"You don't have to. It was just an idea." He tapped one finger on the table, and then the others joined it in an irritated dance. "But I need to go, and I can't do it without your help."

"I don't have any money, Raf."

A flash of rage or embarrassment masquerading as indignation. "I didn't ask for that, did I? Did I ask you for money?"

"Not yet."

"Then…" He pushed away from the table. "It doesn't matter. I'll think of something else."

"Wait a minute." Alejandro fished around for something to write on, and the first thing that came to hand was his corrida ticket. He wrote his number on the back and held it out to Raf. "Here. You want to talk about this when you're sober, you know where to get me."

"Fuck off." Raf shook his head, biting back his embarrassment. "I'm sorry. I shouldn't…I told you what I need, Al."

"No, you told me what you want."

Raf snatched the ticket and stuffed it into his top pocket. "You're a fucking bone in the throat, you know that?"

Alejandro nodded. He knew. And maybe he should've been easier on the boy, but at the time he thought he'd done the right thing.

Now, with the pressure of a couple of thousand bodies around him and the taste of blood on his tongue, he knew he hadn't. Raf had been looking for an open door, maybe the only one left, and Alejandro had slammed it shut. He sucked on the filter of his Fortuna and realized there was no cigarette attached to it anymore. He dropped it underfoot. He should have followed the English, should have done something to find Raf. But he didn't, because he was too old and too scared.

Another cheer went up. The bull, blood glistening on its back, charged into its third pic. A strong hit. The horse leaned back as the picador struck too close to one of the larger wounds and then twisted. The crowd should've been up in arms; the president should have called it. If Alejandro had seen the twist from the cheap seats then there must have been others. The bull disengaged and moved off to one side, its head swaying on its shoulders. The torero performed a half-hearted *quite* and Hernandez called for one more pic.

Alejandro got to his feet and screamed at the president to call time on the tercio. The villamelón next to him did the same, and suddenly Alejandro felt ridiculous. He turned and shoved his way down the *tendido*, desperate to leave. He trod on feet, kicked legs and personal belongings out of the way. He heard the crowd shout their appreciation of the fourth pic as he took the stairs to the street.

He was surrounded by animals. And the only one with any dignity or intelligence was about to be slaughtered.

Episode Three

TERCIO DE BANDERILLAS

Eleven

It was dark, it was warm. The air around him felt close and heavy.

Rafael heard the sound of birds somewhere far off, coming closer, as he regained consciousness. He didn't move, just concentrated on breathing, listening to the birds, picturing tiny cartoon vultures circling around his head. Once he was sure he could breathe without thinking about it, he opened his eyes in a rapid blink that strobed the world for a moment before he settled into a stare.

It was gloomy outside. Shadows moved, the dance of branches against a gray sky. A rising smell accompanied his ability to focus—the stench of blood, sweat, and old meat—and it swiftly became unbearable. He put one hand to his nose. The movement made him dizzy. Something bubbled up his throat. He closed his eyes and swallowed the liquid back. It left a dead taste in his mouth.

The birds continued.

He opened his eyes again, took it slower this time. The smell remained, but he breathed through his mouth. He was in a car, and he was in the driver's seat. It was gray outside, so that meant he'd probably been here for some time. He didn't remember arriving.

He didn't remember much. He tried to move, but his legs were stuck to the seat. There was pain—his head, his side, his leg, a bruised ache high on one hip. He looked down, saw the rip in his suit trousers, hoped that there weren't any other wounds. He put one hand on the driver's door and pushed, but he was too weak, his arm like a length of rope. He slumped against the door and when he exhaled, something like a sob attached itself to the breath and startled him. He blinked, felt his eyes closing again. He straightened up, head spinning.

His breathing slowed, and it became more comfortable to breathe through his nose. His head felt loose.

And then he collided with something hard. He let out a yelp and jerked back. Looked down at the steering wheel as if it had reared up and smacked him as he felt the new nip of a split top lip.

No.

Rafael threw his weight against the driver's door, scrabbled at the handle until his fingers caught, curled, and pulled. He leaned on the door, tumbled out of the car with a sickening rip as his legs peeled from the seat. He hit the ground hard. His entire body burned on impact. He opened his mouth and let another low moan spill out over his tongue when he pressed his forehead into the cool dirt. He tried to focus on the breeze that danced through the hair at the back of his head.

Waiting out the pain. Letting the air get to him. Nothing, not even pain, lasts forever.

And then, slowly, the pain subsided into a manageable ache.

Rafael turned himself over, a brief jab in the leg telling him that his thigh had yet to scab over. He put a hand out, felt for the driver's door and used it as a guide as he pulled himself to his feet. Once upright, he favored his good leg and leaned against the side of what looked like a white Land Rover. There was tape on his wrists. He tore it off, balled it and tossed it to one side.

He looked at the grass by his feet. His voice was hoarse. "What's your name?"

He thought about it. Nothing came.

"What's your name?"

His head felt stuffed to bursting. His name was in there somewhere, in among all the barbed wire. He just had to find it.

"Tell me. What's your name?"

Rafael.

That was it. He didn't remember his surname, but he knew his first name, and that was the most important thing right now. And he knew that if he just focused, he'd remember what had brought him here. Maybe he'd even work out where he was.

It looked like the car had left the road at some point and bounced down into this field, where a gnarled dead tree had stopped it. It wasn't a crash—from what he could see the front of the car was okay—but there was some damage to the side of the car. Holes. The car engine wasn't running, so he guessed he'd either turned it off before he blacked out or it had stalled while he was under. He wiped his nose on the back of one bloody hand, then looked down at his leg. It glistened where it hadn't crusted over.

He'd been hurt. A lot. And yet he had the feeling that his injuries were the least of his worries.

There were people after him. He remembered men running toward him. He remembered guns. That explained the holes in the car, perhaps even the leg wound—he wasn't sure. His heart fluttered like a trapped bird. If there were people after him, there was a good chance they'd be coming to finish the job. If that was the case, and he didn't know how long he'd been here, then it was time to leave. He just didn't know where to go.

He turned back to the driver's door and saw the blood all over the seat. It had dried now, but there was still enough of it showing in the half light to throw water into Rafael's legs and a roll into his stomach.

It was okay. It was his blood, but he was still alive. That was why he was weak.

Just blood loss. It would be fine.

He leaned against the car and looked at the ground.

Still functioning. He'd made it this far. Disgust was a natural reaction, but it wouldn't help him now. Neither would puking. He needed to straighten up and get out of here. Now.

He swallowed, pushed away from the car, then turned and eased himself into the driver's seat. He didn't want to pull the door shut just yet, wanted to keep the air coming in. He placed his hands on the steering wheel and looked at everything in the car, trying to remember what all the buttons were for.

Blank.

A small voice in the back of his head told him to go to sleep.

No. Focus. He couldn't go to sleep. Something demanded his attention here. He didn't know what it was.

Come on, Rafael. Come on, Raf.

He put both hands to his head, closed his eyes. Focused. Tried to remember. Tried to picture the car interior. The glove compartment button. The radio. The air-conditioning or the heater. The cigarette lighter. The gear stick. The steering wheel. The steering column. Small levers on it. One of them operated the lights...

The ignition.

He opened his eyes and there it was, right in front of him, the key in position. He turned it.

Nothing.

He tried again.

Still nothing.

Didn't matter. The important thing was that he remembered. He tried the button for the windows, but they didn't work, either. The whole car was dead.

That was okay. There were other options. A quick glance in the rearview mirror told him he was dirty and bloody, but he knew he could walk. And if he could do that, then he could make it back to the main road.

And then what?

A name sat in the corner of his mind: Alejandro. He knew it belonged to an older man, but Rafael couldn't remember the face beyond a few sketched lines. The man's voice was rough. Vowels cracked in his mouth. He couldn't hear what the man was saying, but he knew it was important.

His foot found the accelerator pedal. He pressed down. His other foot found the brake. He pressed down on that, too.

Alejandro. Remember the name. Turn it over. Connect it to something. Another word. Another word that sounds a bit like the name, perhaps...

Apoderado.

A connection. Alejandro was an apoderado. He was a man with a plan. He was a trainer. He was a cantankerous old bone in the throat who used to force Rafael's mind and body into a painful position, stretching his muscles and stiffening his back as he bent his mind with talk of classical...something.

Toreo. The bulls.

Yes. What it was, what it wasn't, what it could be. The sun beating down on his face. Rafael's throat dried at the memory of it.

The birds started again. The noise came from somewhere in the car. A small light caught his eye, over on the dashboard on the passenger side. He shifted in his seat and stretched for whatever it was.

A mobile phone. It was ringing.

The display showed a number without a name. The number seemed familiar. He connected the call. "Hello?"

"Raf? Is that you?"

That voice. He knew that voice. He'd spoken to the owner of that voice before. Recently. Today?

And the name became obvious. "Alejandro?"

"Yes, it's me. Where are you?"

His hand trembled. He put his other hand up to steady the phone. "I don't know. It's dark."

"Where's Sancho?"

"I don't know who that is."

"You answered his phone."

If this was Sancho's phone, then it was probably Sancho's car, too. Something small and hungry gnawed at his stomach lining. "I don't know where he is. I'm in a car."

"His car?"

"A white car. A Land Rover. I don't know who it belongs to. There are holes in the side." He looked out of the open door. "I'm in a field. I don't know where."

"I don't suppose you have a GPS or anything, do you?"

"What's a GPS?"

"Like a small screen. An electronic map. It should be somewhere on the dashboard if you have one."

"No, there's nothing like that."

"Okay. Can you drive?"

"The car won't start."

"Can you walk?"

"Yes." He got out of the car. He saw the two troughs that ran away from the car. "There's a trail. I can follow it back to the road."

"Good idea. Stay on the phone."

"Okay."

"How are you? Did they hurt you?"

He knew about "they."

"I don't know." He laughed a little, but there was no humor in it. "I am hurt, yes, but I don't know where. It hurts all over. There was blood all over the inside of the car."

"Take it slowly, then."

He felt drunk. "They tried to kill me."

"The English?"

"Yes." And he blinked through some more recent memories as if he were flicking through a book, speaking as he remembered. "They woke me up and took me out to a *ganadería*, and then they put me in the ring."

"A bullring?"

"Yes."

"With a bull?"

"He said it was a Miura."

"Who said?"

"The man in the white shirt. He wore sunglasses. They called him the gaffer. Do you know what that means?"

"It means boss. Did he have a name?"

"Yes, but I can't remember. They knew me. They called me by my name. They called me Rafael." He stopped. "Wait, hang on."

He removed the phone from his ear and blinked his eyes back into focus. He breathed out, feeling sick. Alejandro was talking, but he couldn't hear what he was saying. Sweat ran down the back of his collar. When he looked up, he saw lights moving up ahead. The main road.

He put the phone back to his ear and heard "Okay?"

"I see the road."

"Good. You sure you're okay?"

"Just got a bit dizzy. I'm okay now."

"Slow down. You're almost there. Don't rush it now."

It was farther away than "almost there." It almost became "too far." By the time Rafael reached the road, his legs trembled with the effort and he could barely focus on his own feet. He climbed the steep slope up to the road and then lay down for a moment, letting the exhaust-tainted breeze wash over him. It was only the chill that kept him awake now. Alejandro's voice had taken on the distant quality of a radio in another room.

And there it was, even more distant now: "Raf, stay with me, boy."

He put the phone back to his ear. "Yes."

"Look around. See if there's a sign anywhere."

Rafael struggled upright and did as he was told. His bad leg had stiffened and his walk became a limp that meant he could only take three steps before he had to rest. He moved away from the road as two headlights sped his way, edging over as far as he could before he braced himself against the buffet of wind as the car charged past, throwing light on the road as it went. The headlights caught something large and square by the side of the road about ten meters away. It was blank on Rafael's side.

"There's a sign."

He heard movement at the other end, as if Alejandro was getting ready to leave. "As soon as you can read it, you need to tell me what it says."

Rafael hobbled to the sign, put his hand on it. The metal was freezing to the touch. He held on as he shuffled round and then backed off a couple of steps to read it. "Junta de Andalucía. A-397, KM 24."

"Okay, stay there. I'm coming to get you."

"That's what you said the last time." Rafael smiled and disconnected. He leaned his forehead against the sign. The trembling in his legs started again. He eased himself to the ground. Another car went past and made a noise like the sea.

Stay there.

As if he could go anywhere else.

Twelve

Ollie Graham wasn't happy. Then again, nobody expected him to be. The fact that he was still several notches below volcanic was a fucking blessing, actually. After all, here he was, a man very much concerned with his image who believed he had everything under control, thought his men knew their stuff, and he'd just seen his entire workforce lose their minds at the sight of a mad bull. Blood everywhere, Lawrence all buckled up and screaming because this dig in his leg was the worst pain the fat, lazy fuck had ever suffered, and meanwhile the rabbit had done one in Sancho's car. Nothing they could do about it, either—the bull had taken three full clips before it showed signs of weakness, and by that time the rabbit was offski, wasn't he?

Tony empathized, he really did. If he'd been in charge, he'd be taking it a lot worse than Ollie was. The only lucky thing was that Frank Graham never saw it, because it all happened up at the ranch instead of the villa. Not that Ollie would be able to keep it from his dear old dad, but at least he could spin it so they didn't all look like the Keystone Kops. In the meantime, Ollie had gathered Tony, Sancho, and Jason in his den, a high-ceilinged room attached to the back of the ranch. There were bookshelves that ran the length and height of the walls, but Ollie'd never read a book in his life, so they were packed with matches recorded off Sky and Setanta, plus a load of action movies. Mostly crime, a lot of kung fu, podgy Seagal, skinny Lundgren, some porn—the kind of stuff a bloke chucked into the DVD player after a night on the drink, stuff to look at rather than watch.

Ollie leaned against the back of a recliner and opened his hands. "So what's happening here, lads? What's the score? This cunt doesn't have any Russian in him, does he?"

Tony stayed quiet. So did the other two. The picture windows that were normally blacked out for movies were clear now, but it was dark outside and Tony caught a glimpse of his full-length reflection in one of them. He looked haggard, unkempt. He knew he smelled bad. Jason was the same. Sancho looked as if he'd been beaten up, his clothes all disheveled.

Ollie moved off from the recliner and came closer. "What's your plan, Tony?"

"I don't know, Ollie." Tony addressed the floor. "Finish off what we started?"

Ollie nodded, kept nodding. "How dangerous is he, d'you reckon?"

"The rabbit? Not dangerous. He's just lucky."

"What does he know?"

"I don't know. I mean, honestly, you heard him. He said he didn't remember anything."

"I know what he said."

Sancho cleared his throat before he spoke. "He was not lying."

"You think so?" Ollie looked at Sancho. His eyes glittered like diamante studs. "He remembered how to fight a fucking bull, didn't he?"

"No. He did not. I have seen him in the plaza. Even against a Miura, he would not have been injured. As Tony said, he was lucky. And he is clever. But I do not think he remembered anything more than basics."

"You know him?"

Tony nodded at Sancho. "Used to be in the bloke's entourage." He wanted to add that he was also the one who brought the bastard into the business but decided against it. Sancho was already up to his chin in shit. No point heaping more on him. Besides, he might prove useful yet.

"So you know him?"

"Yes, Señor."

"So you know what he's going to do next?"

Sancho shook his head. "He is not himself."

"I don't give a fuck. You're the one supposed to know him—"

"I *knew* him."

"So you have a think about where he's going to go and you take these two along with you. And when you find the rabbit, I want you to bury him fucking pronto, you get me? I don't care what he remembers anymore. I don't care if it's a fucking act or what, just take care of him before my dad gets a whiff, all right?" He pointed at Tony. "You're in charge."

"Yes, Ollie."

"Now get out of my fucking sight, the lot of you."

They did. Tony led the way. The three men didn't say anything to one another as they walked out through the ranch. Their footsteps echoed on the tile. They passed an indoor fountain that made Tony want to piss. Once they got outside, the smell of blood and smoke still in the air, Tony told Jason to drive and told Sancho to get in the front seat.

Sancho shook his head. "I need to go home."

"Don't we all, son? Get in the car."

Still shaking his head. "No, I cannot do this. I cannot be a part of this."

"You what?"

"I am sorry, Tony. I did not want to say anything in front of Mr. Graham—"

"So you're saying it now? You're the one supposed to know the cunt, Sancho. You're the one supposed to tell us where he's going, man."

"I do not know."

"You had an idea."

"He does not remember anything, Tony. I promise you he was telling the truth."

"I don't fucking care, and neither does Ollie. If he's supposed to be dead, then he needs to be dead, d'you understand? Doesn't matter what he fucking remembers. The time for defending the prick is *long* gone, mate. You wanted to protect him, you should've told him not to go mouthing off to customs, shouldn't you? Would've saved us all a lot of fucking work if you did. But you didn't, so he did, and so here we are." He grabbed Sancho's arm and steered him toward the Mazda. "Now get in the fucking car."

"Tony. *Señor*—"

"Don't start with your señor bollocks. Get in."

Tony pushed him into the passenger seat and then got in the back.

"Jason, pass us the Walther and the torch, will you?"

Jason opened the glove compartment and passed back the pistol and a small Maglite. Tony checked the clip. Three gone, which was fine. Still enough to put several holes in the bastard's head once they caught up with him. He flicked the torch on and then off. It worked. That was all it needed to do.

"All right. On you go."

Jason looked at him in the mirror. "Where are we going?"

Tony pointed toward the edge of the ranch. "That's the way he drove off, isn't it?"

"You sure?" Jason started the engine and pulled the Mazda away from the front of the main ranch building.

"Any other ideas?"

"I'm just thinking about my suspension."

"Fuck your suspension."

Jason let the car roll across the rocky ground, which sent a series of jolts through the backseat.

Tony stretched out, watching the scenery. "Anything we should know about this bloke that we don't already, Sancho?"

"Like what?"

"Like something you didn't tell Ollie."

"No."

Bollocks. Typical fucking Spaniard. Run his mouth off every chance he got if it was his specialist subject of *putas* or football. Put him in a real need-to-know situation, the bastard clammed up and quietly shat himself.

That was the thing with the Spanish contingent. They didn't understand the business. All they saw were the spoils—the cars, the money, the drinking. They thought it was all living *la vida loca*, all that. What they didn't realize was that this business was a fucking graft. It took work, even if you weren't working with the high-money product.

Because Ollie Graham wasn't an idiot. He knew his limits. He and the rest of them worked nothing stronger than cannabis. And yes, it was unfashionable and it was bulky, but it was still a safer proposition than cocaine. With the coke, you had to deal with those raw-arsed South Americans, all politics, buzzing heads, and military-grade weapons. Plus, you had the Spanish authorities on your back the whole fucking time. Not that they didn't care about cannabis, but it wasn't exactly a priority either, and the Moroccans might have been thieving Third World bastards, but at least it was the product they were after taking, not your life.

Still, there was work involved. There were the moonlight runs across the Strait, armed customs taking beered-up potshots at anything their light happened to hit. There were the all-night wrap and packs. Talk about your forced labor. Jesus, you'd come out of them first thing in the morning, your arms aching and your clothes stinking of puff and the coffee grounds they were packed with to throw off the dogs. Or if you were on the deliveries, you were on the long haul, up to the French border with a motorbike scouting for checkpoints. And then sweating bullets in the cab of a fruit truck, stuck in the queue for the ferries with a couple of millions worth of weed in the back, covered by twenty tons of oranges.

Not easy work. And the Spaniards like Sancho here didn't understand it because they were rarely trusted with it. Maybe the odd inter-Europe run like the rabbit used to do, or a little manual labor on the packing front. But nothing big and nothing important. So they never understood the amount of graft involved.

And that was only the beginning. You get yourself in further, get yourself trusted, you had to deal with shit like tracking rabbits in the fucking countryside. Whoever it was that said a responsible man always got the heavy workload was right as far as Tony was concerned. In this game, you were punished for being good at your job.

The Mazda bumped up onto a road. Tony looked out of the side window.

"Wait a second. Stop the car."

Jason pulled over. Tony got out of the car, clicked on his torch and shone it at the road. There were skid marks. He went back to the Mazda and pointed the way.

They were on the road for another couple of minutes before Tony saw the drop on one side of the road and the scrubland beyond. He looked out of the other side window, patted the back of Jason's seat. "Slow down."

"Why?"

"Stop the car here."

"It's a main road."

"Just stop the fucking car, will you? Jesus Christ."

Jason leaned on the wheel, brought the Mazda over to the side of the road. He looked in the mirrors and let out a sigh. "Listen, I'm on a corner here, Tone."

"So?"

"It's dangerous."

"Then stick your hazards on."

Tony got out and headed back toward the road sign they'd just passed. He glanced over his shoulder, checking for cars, but the road was dead. He reached the sign and swung the torch beam onto it.

Blood.

He turned and surveyed the countryside. Some trees, mostly scrub, difficult to see out here. He let the torch run along the road until he found some more tire marks on the tarmac.

Tony pulled the gun from his jeans. "Sancho, get over here."

Sancho approached slowly. He looked tired. Tony slapped the torch into his hand and then shoved him in the direction of the skid. Sancho turned and looked at him.

"On you go." Tony waved him toward the field. "Lead the way."

"Why me?"

"You keep a gun in your car?"

"Yes."

"Well, then."

Sancho didn't understand, and Tony wasn't going to spell it out for him. The Spaniard had to go first. Because if he kept a gun in the car, and the rabbit had the car, then there was a good chance he had the gun, too. Given his injuries, he'd be more likely to take a shot rather than run, and when he did, Tony didn't want to be the one holding the only point of light. Yeah, he'd probably miss, but Tony wasn't taking any chances. And if Sancho accidentally caught a bullet, all the better. It would save him the job of topping the arsehole later on.

They walked on through the grass, Sancho up front and Tony trying to keep to the darkness. Behind them, the Mazda's headlights moved, sweeping across the scrub as Jason pulled a U-turn on the road.

Tony tugged on Sancho's arm. "Wait."

There it was, the Land Rover. Sancho took one look at it and made a weird coughing sound. He rushed over to check the damage as Tony looked around for any sign of the rabbit. If he was here, he should've made his presence known by now. Unless he was sparked out in the grass somewhere.

Or, more likely, he was waiting for an opportunity to strike.

Sancho made a disgusted sound.

Tony hoped he'd found a dead body. "What is it?"

"Look."

The driver's door stood open. Sancho shone the torch on the driver's seat, which was sticky with blood. The rabbit was alive, but he was hurt. Tony moved away from the Land Rover and listened.

Nothing.

Maybe he wasn't here. But if he wasn't here, he couldn't have gone far, not without help.

"Sancho, I think you better start talking, mate."

Sancho turned from the car. "What?"

"Where's he gone?"

"I told you—"

"I know what you told me, but that's not worked out too well so far, has it? So you're going to have to tell me something else." He looked back at the road. Jason was still with the car. He took a deep breath. "Listen, I'm going to level with you, Sancho mate. I was down the fucking Strait last night—must've got, like, fucking two hours kip, right?—so I'm tired, I've had enough. I thought if you shot a man in the head, he wouldn't get up, but every day's a school day, eh?" He rubbed his face and sighed. "So I'm tired. I want to go home. You want to go home; you said so yourself. But we can't do that until we find this cunt, so you need to tell me everything you know, and you need tell me now."

"I do not—"

"Fuck's sake." Tony pointed the gun at him. Sancho flinched, his hands jerking up to his face as if his palms were bulletproof. "Enough with the excuses."

"Tony. *Por favor.*"

"Talk."

"*Que paso?*"

"In English. Where's he gone?"

"I keep telling you, I do not know."

"I know what you keep telling me, Sancho, because I keep fucking hearing it, don't I? Flip the record, mate. Make an educated guess."

"Tony, I am honest—"

The gun seemed extra loud out here in the dark. Sancho dropped to his knees. For a moment, Tony thought he'd shot him. Then he heard the sobs.

"One's a backfire."

Sancho was weeping, muttering in Spanish. The usual shit—mostly God talk. Tony didn't understand the rest.

"Don't make it two."

"I do not know where he is."

"You're really going to keep pushing this, aren't you?" Tony took three steps and jabbed the gun into the top of Sancho's head. "Have it your way."

He started talking then, fast and loud.

Thirteen

The taxi driver was a Moroccan who sported a roll of fat at the back of his neck that you could safely stand a wine glass on and whose mood had turned surly the moment Alejandro told him where he was going.

He wasn't happy about driving to the middle of nowhere in the middle of night, he said. It was dangerous, he said. There were friends of his, he said—good friends, good *men*—who had driven out into the hills—and yes, Señor, they had *also* been promised more money to do so—and their fare had robbed them and stabbed them or shot them and then left them for dead.

It wasn't safe.

Alejandro reminded the taxi driver that he posed no threat and punctuated that reminder with a throaty cough.

But the taxi driver, even as he was driving, remained suspicious. "Anyone with a knife, Señor, or a *gun*, yes—they can be a threat. You don't need physical strength."

"I'm not going to hurt you. I promise."

"You promise. We shall see. I have a mobile phone. I have pre-dialed, Señor." He held up the phone, showing the three numbers. "All I need to do is connect the call."

"Very clever." Whatever it took to put the taxi driver's mind at ease.

As they traveled out into the countryside, Alejandro saw the driver glance at his phone every few seconds as if expecting a blow from behind. When he told the driver to stop, he made another grab for the phone. "This is not a destination, Señor."

"Yes, it is." Alejandro got out of the car. "Wait there."

The taxi's engine revved slightly. He stopped and swapped a warning look with the driver—*stay put or else*—and then continued toward the sign.

"Raf? You here?"

He heard a sudden intake of breath and something moved in the darkness by his feet. He found Raf huddled behind the sign, half-conscious and covered in blood.

"What did they do to you?"

Raf turned his head at the sound of Alejandro's voice. He showed his teeth, but his eyes were closed. "Tired."

"Come on, let's get you out of here." Alejandro ducked under Raf's shoulder and boosted him. Took three tries, but he finally hoisted the boy upright. He told Raf that he needed to walk, and he appeared to understand, which gave Alejandro some hope. If he could follow simple commands, then there was a chance he'd make it home alive.

"No." The taxi driver had buzzed down the window. He waved one fat hand at them and tried to stop them from getting into the back of the cab without moving from his seat. "No, I'm sorry. I can't allow it."

"He's hurt."

"I can see, yes. He's bloody. Dirty. You need an ambulance, Señor."

"Shut up and help me with him."

"No, I'll call for an ambulance. That's much better." He connected the call to the emergency services.

Alejandro eased Raf into the backseat of the cab. "You okay?"

Raf nodded. Alejandro shut the door and went to the front passenger side. The driver was talking on the phone. "I don't know where we are—"

"Let's go. Now."

The driver looked at Alejandro, then realized that the bloody man was in the back of his cab. He twisted round as much as he could, his mouth open. "No, you get him out. You get him out of there right now. He's a mess. He'll mess up my seats."

"I'll pay."

"An ambulance—"

"Will be too late for him. He's not going anywhere. You want him to die in your backseat, then keep talking. You want me to pay for any cleanup and throw in a tip, then get driving."

The taxi driver considered it for a count of three, then disconnected the call, slotted the phone into its dashboard holder, and put the car into gear.

When they arrived back in Marbella, Alejandro threw money at the driver and struggled with Raf up both flights of stairs before he managed to get him inside and onto the bed. Then he slumped into a chair and watched the steady rise and fall of Raf's chest. The boy was unconscious, passed out the moment he hit something soft. Islero nudged his way into the bedroom and took the opportunity to jump onto Alejandro's lap.

He brushed the cat away. "Not now, Izzy."

Alejandro stood stiffly and went through to the living room, Islero at his heels, where he called Sanchez. Twenty minutes later, Sanchez arrived and told Alejandro to stay out of his way. Sanchez went into the bedroom and didn't come out for a very long time.

When he did finally come back into the living room, Alejandro was sitting in his usual spot, smoking and staring into space. He'd opened a bottle of Rioja and poured two glasses, but neither had been touched. Islero looked like an Ouroboros, curled and asleep on his lap.

"How is he?"

Sanchez gave him a tired look. "I have no idea. I never worked the plaza, so I don't really know how bad the leg wound is. I've cleaned him up as best I can, but I don't know what the other doctor did, so I can't be sure he wasn't an infection risk."

"What other doctor?"

"The one who dressed the other wounds." Sanchez put his case on the floor and picked up his glass of wine. "Your boy's been shot. Twice, as far as I could tell. And I don't know who was responsible for dressing the wounds in the first place, but 'doctor' is a charitable word for what he is." He sipped the wine and made an approving face. "In all honesty, Al, I don't know how he's still walking around. I'd say he needs to go to hospital as soon as possible, but I'm not even sure he'll make it through his nap."

Alejandro ground out his cigarette. "He can't go to the hospital. They'll check."

"Where did you find him?"

"Out on the A-397. They were holding him at a ganadería."

Sanchez sat on the sofa. "I don't know the area."

"You remember Hector Ramirez?"

"No."

"Probably a bit before your time. He was a good breeder. Fierce bulls with personality. The kind they don't really want anymore. Anyway, he went broke. What I heard was that some English bought him out and took over the place."

"Breeders?"

"Maybe. I don't know. I heard they weren't legitimate."

"Figures." Sanchez nodded. "There's a lot of them about."

"He said it was a Miura, but the way his mind is, it could have been a one-year-old in the ring with him, and he wouldn't have known the difference. But they were torturing him, I know that. And I know it had something to do with that boy Rios."

"Rios?"

"Sancho Rios. One of Raf's cuadrilla back in the day, though I don't remember him doing much more than play the pimp. You know the type."

"Not intimately."

"Lucky you. Not a lot you can do about it when you see it. Tell the boy his friend's a parasite, you get a cold front in response. He's his friend, right? And I'm his apoderado; I'm the the old man; I'm the one who knows what he's talking about when it comes to the bulls, but nothing else. Only thing I could do was try to tell him what was right and hope he wanted to hear it."

"He was one of yours, then."

"Yes."

"Any good?"

"Could have been the next Tomás. Smart, strong, tenacious. When he was a kid, caping a cow, and that cow tossed him, he was the only one I ever saw who kept coming back in there until he had to be removed. He didn't give up."

"What happened?"

"He gave up." Alejandro showed a thin smile. "He lost his nerve. But that wasn't him, not really. He was a different person then. The business changed him in the wrong way."

"It didn't end well?"

"No." Alejandro reached for his cigarettes. "I didn't see him for a long time. And then I talked to him a few days ago, he was in trouble, wouldn't tell me what it was. Talked about going abroad, starting again. Sounded as if he was running away from something."

"Looks like it caught up with him."

"Perhaps." Alejandro held the wine in his mouth for a moment before he swallowed. "You think he's involved with drugs?"

"I don't know. I don't think he has any in his system, and there are no signs of intravenous use."

"I meant the English."

"Possibly. I mean, we're all *this* far from that trade on a daily basis. I don't know who I'm treating half the time, but I know if it's a bullet wound, then they're probably part of something criminal. So yes, it's plausible to me that your boy was involved in criminal activity, especially if he wasn't working in the plaza, and if the English were involved, there's a good chance it was drug-related criminal activity. What did he tell you?"

"He doesn't remember."

"You believe him?"

"I think so. He's quite badly hurt, isn't he? His head, I mean."

Sanchez nodded. "If he fought a bull, even if it was just a calf, then his muscle memory and long-term are okay. Beyond that, I don't know. Of course there's damage, but I couldn't tell you what kind of amnesia, or even if it's *just* amnesia, without examining him further. Even then, I'm not a specialist. His best bet is to get to a hospital as soon as possible."

"He needs to rest."

"Listen to me, Al—"

"He's asleep. He'll be fine."

"He needs medical attention. More intensive than I can provide. And if there are people after him, then the best thing you can do is inform the authorities. If he dies overnight and you keep him here, then you'll have a hell of a lot of explaining to do. If I'm honest, he should be dead already. I don't know what's keeping him alive other than sheer force of will."

"Like I said, he's tenacious."

"And like you said, he gave up. Look, even if he doesn't die in the night, there's no telling what kind of mental state he's going to be in when he wakes up. He might not remember you. He might even think you're one of the people who hurt him."

"He won't."

"You don't know that for sure, do you?"

"And you don't want a man's death on your conscience, I understand."

"It wouldn't be the first time." Sanchez finished his wine and stood. "I dare say it won't be the last, either. I just don't want you getting into trouble for some brat you used to know."

"It's not like that." Alejandro pushed Islero from his lap. "What do I owe you?"

"Don't be silly."

"For your trouble. For dragging you out of bed."

Sanchez picked up his case and headed for the door. "I wasn't in bed. I was planning our family holiday."

"This late?"

"It's a big family. A big, fussy, complaining family. Lots of special needs."

"Well, okay. Thank you."

"Did you need a prescription?"

"No."

"The pain pills working okay for you, then?"

"They do the job."

Sanchez narrowed his eyes. "You know you should—"

"If I wanted to feel sick all the time, I'd drink that cheap red you brought back from Italy. I'll see you to the door."

Alejandro showed Sanchez out. The doctor paused as he crossed out into the hall. He looked as if he wanted to say something but then clearly thought better of it, undoubtedly realizing that anything more he had to say about hospitals would fall on deaf ears. Instead, he gave a small shake of the head and turned to leave. Alejandro watched until he'd disappeared down the stairs and heard the door to the building close. Then he shut and locked the front door before he crossed the hall.

It was dark in the bedroom. The only light in the room came from the hallway. Raf had been stripped and cleaned. He was motionless apart from his breathing. Alejandro was about to close the door when he heard the boy's voice. "Is the doctor gone?"

"Yes."

"I can't go to a hospital."

"I know."

"People die in hospitals."

Alejandro smiled. "I know."

"Thank you for helping me."

"I gave you my number, didn't I?"

"Yes."

"Well then. I'll talk to you tomorrow. Get some sleep."

Alejandro left the room, closing the door behind him. He returned to the living room and picked up his wine. Islero was curled where Sanchez had been sitting. He watched Alejandro. Over on the table, the laptop standby light glowed. The article remained unfinished. It would just have to wait. If he missed deadline then he missed deadline. Same for the one on Hernandez. It didn't really matter anyway. There were more important things to worry about.

He lit another cigarette before he realized that he'd left one smoking in the ashtray. The first drag made him cough and something scratched against the inside of his chest. He drank some wine. Islero stood and stretched. The sofa looked uncomfortable.

Sanchez was right. The people who hurt Raf would come for him once they knew he wasn't dead. It was just a matter of time.

He was a dead man walking.

"Suppose that makes two of us then, doesn't it?"

Islero blinked. Looked like an agreement.

Alejandro shooed him away and started to arrange the cushions for the long night ahead.

Fourteen

"Lisa, listen to me, all right? It's not that simple…"

But Lisa was past all that. According to her, she'd listened to enough of his shit already; he had nothing new to add; he was repeating himself, so she'd taken that as her cue to steamroll right over him.

Normally he'd steamroll right back, shout her down, but he couldn't do that on a quiet street on a Monday morning, not if he didn't want to draw attention to himself. He could hear the kids in the background. They were screaming and shouting and demanding all sorts, so it was no wonder Lisa's voice could've brought down the walls of Jericho. Tony waited until she'd bitched him out a bit more, then jumped in when she paused for breath. "This is important."

"Where are you?"

"Working."

"That's not what I asked."

"I'm in town, aren't I?"

"Which town? You're not down in Gibraltar again, are you?"

"This town. Marbella. Christ."

"You're working?"

"I told you that."

"Working all night, yeah?"

"I had to." He squinted in the morning light. It hurt his eyes. She hurt his head. "Believe me, love, it's not by choice. If it were up to me, I'd be home, wouldn't I?"

"It's a bank holiday."

"In England, I know."

"It's the Jubilee."

"Again—"

"Are you wrapping?"

"No."

"Then what?"

"It's delicate."

"How?"

"It just is." He breathed out, felt around in his pockets for his fags, but came up empty.

"You're not with a slag, are you?"

"A *slag*?" He would've laughed if he hadn't been so knackered. He tapped on the car window, pointed at the pack of Bensons on the dashboard. Jason passed them out. "The fuck are you talking about, Lisa?"

"All the rest of them have slags on the go, don't they? Going up the whiskerías and that. Don't think I don't know what you lot get up to."

Tony lit the cigarette and spoke through his first drag. "I'm not with any other woman, slag or otherwise. I'm with Jason, all right? We're working." He checked his watch. "I'll be home later."

"We're meeting Lawrence and Jill tonight. Don't forget."

He had. Lawrence hadn't said anything about it. Then again, the last time he'd seen Lawrence, the fat man had just taken a horn to the gut, so he probably had other things on his mind. "Might want to double-check with Jill on that one, love."

"Why?"

"I'll let her tell you." He looked back at the car. Sancho and Jason were talking. Or rather, Sancho was talking and Jason was listening. Sancho couldn't keep his gob shut now. Soon as he saw a gun anywhere near him, he'd yap his jaws off. As long as he was talking, he was breathing. It made Tony think that he was either full of shit or a treacherous little bastard for grassing his mate. Either way, it was all Tony could do not to get Jason to drive them up to the mountains so they could end the fucker.

For now, though, he needed to be patient. There'd be plenty of time to take care of Sancho later on.

"Tony?"

"Yes."

"You're not the job."

He laughed in spite of himself. "I know."

"I'm serious."

"I know." They'd talked about it a lot, and they'd talked about it a lot *more* in the last few months. Trouble was, he *was* his job. He was trapped by the Grahams. Wasn't like he could speak much of the local language, or that he had any marketable skills that weren't illegal. If he left the Grahams, they'd have to leave Spain, and that wasn't on anyone's fucking wish list. Just the thought of England in the winter was enough to keep him killing for a living. "This shouldn't take too long." Something fluttered in his peripheral vision. Jason was signaling to him. "Listen, I've got to get on, all right? With a bit of luck, I should be home for lunch. Kiss the kids for me."

"Okay. Take care."

"Always do."

He killed the call, then the mobile, and followed where Jason was pointing.

The broad man from the café, the one who'd given them gyp, had just rounded the corner. Alejandro, the one Sancho said was supposed to meet the rabbit. The bloke moved slowly, had trouble walking but didn't have a stick or anything. He was too proud, too determined, didn't know how weak he was.

Well, he was about to find out.

Tony crouched by the driver's side and spoke to Jason through the open window. "Wait until he goes in. Give him a minute to get himself settled." Then, to Sancho: "You're positive that's the bloke?"

"Yes."

If the rabbit contacted the old man once, then there was a good chance he'd do it again. The way Sancho told it, this Rafael Ortega was all kinds of fucked in the head thanks to the bullet that still rattled around in his skull. He could barely remember his own name, so what few memories he did have, he was probably clinging on to. Lucky for Sancho that this old bastard Garcia stuck to a routine, because otherwise they wouldn't have found him again. Sancho didn't know the old man's address, and apparently he worked from home. The only other option was to hang around the newspaper he wrote for, but that was just asking for trouble. Too many people with inquiring minds.

Alejandro walked into the café. He smiled at someone just inside the door before he disappeared.

Jason looked at Tony. "What d'you want to do?"

"Not much we can do." The smart play would be to keep the tail on him, follow him back to wherever he lived and then proceed from there. But then smart plays were for people who had plenty of time to fuck about, and Tony wasn't one of those people. He straightened up and leaned against the car. It was red hot against his back, so he moved away again. "I'm not sitting out here all fucking morning waiting for him."

Sancho leaned across the seats. "What about me?"

"You said the rabbit was in touch with him?"

"Yes."

"Anyone else he's going to talk to?"

"Maybe his family."

"They live up in Estepona, don't they?"

Sancho nodded. "But I don't think he'll go there."

"Why not?"

"I don't think he remembers them very well."

"All right." Tony didn't want to see the wife and kid—not yet. No sense in making this nastier than it had to be. An old man was one thing, a young family another. Christ, he had one of them himself. He crossed to the front passenger side and opened the door, one eye on the café to make sure he wasn't being watched. "You can fuck off home if you want."

Sancho got out of the car. He was pale and smelled bad. Tony stepped back as he squeezed past, then slammed the door and moved away from the car.

Sancho seemed reluctant to go. "If you need anything else—"

"You've done enough, mate."

He didn't know how to take that. His English wasn't as good as he thought it was, and Tony's voice was neutral. Sancho looked to Jason for a clue, but Jason followed Tony's lead, which was giving Sancho the freeze. He could fuck off home? Really? Or would he be lucky to manage three steps before they shot him down in the street?

Tony nodded at him. "On you go."

"Thank you." Sancho took his first three steps carefully. When he made it to a fourth, he burst into a jog, and a few seconds later he was gone.

Jason leaned out of the car. "You going to talk to him?"

"Give us a couple of minutes, then swing the car round front so I don't have to take him for a walk."

Jason nodded and buzzed the window. Tony felt the weight in the back of his jeans and reached back to pat his shirt, just to make sure the butt of the gun was covered. He crossed the road, looking both ways like he was supposed to, and then glanced back at Jason to make sure he was in position before he went into the café.

It was busy, most of the tables full, and the barman was moving, which meant he was rushed. Most Spanish barmen spent their time asleep on their feet, something that Tony wouldn't have minded learning how to do himself, given the circumstances. He went to the bar and ordered a Pepsi with plenty of ice, then sat with his back to the counter and surveyed the café. There was a family in the corner. A toddler owned most of the room with her little song and dance. Over here, kids were the life and soul. Tony didn't even like his own kids that much, never mind anyone else's. Next to the family was a woman in an expensive-looking outfit, a kind of linen trouser-suit thing. Older, well preserved, possibly English. Actually, no. On second glance, that kind of lemon-faced elegance could only have been French, and it became rapidly obvious to him that he was the only Brit in the place.

He sipped his Pepsi and looked up the bar. There was an older guy at the end. He was tanned like a satchel and had a gray mustache that covered his mouth. He drank his beer through it. Above the bar, the guests on a TV chat show did more screaming than talking. It resembled a bad joke or a nightmare—a female presenter in a power suit, a tearful fat woman, a priest, and a guy who could've been either a civil servant or a journalist, all stuck in the same room where giant photos of sad children gazed down at them.

"*Los niños robados.*"

Tony turned, saw Garcia sitting on the stool next to him. Garcia watched the television. He looked tired and sick. When the barman showed up, he ordered a beer.

"I don't speak Spanish, mate."

"Of course you don't. You only speak English."

"Problem with that?"

"No. Not at all." He nodded at the television. "Los niños robados—it means 'the stolen children.' That's what they're talking about up there."

"Fascinating."

"It is. During Franco's regime, the Catholics stole over three hundred thousand children from unmarried mothers. The doctors and the priests, they told these women to give up their children for

adoption, or else they were told that their child was a stillborn."
The beer arrived. Garcia smiled at the barman. "They had babies
kept in a freezer in case the mother wanted to see her dead child.
Some of them were told to kiss the baby good-bye. Some of them
were told that they should not worry, that the clergy would baptize
the child so that it would go to heaven. The doctors told them it was
good that their child had died, that a child born disfigured or with
a congenital illness..." He broke into a cough that sounded as if it
came from the soles of his feet. When he was finished, he dragged
a napkin over his lips. He swallowed some beer and cleared his
throat. "Excuse me. They were told that an ugly or sick child would
have been a burden on them, and so it was better that it was gone.
Of course, what they were really doing, these pillars of the community, these doctors and priests and nuns, was they were selling the
children into Francoist families for the price of a two-bedroom flat."

"Fucking hell, son." Tony watched the television. The tears
were in full flow up there. He sipped his Pepsi. "Got yourselves in
a right mess there, eh?"

"Sí. All because Franco did not want the *rojos* to breed. Now
we have three hundred thousand people who do not know their real
parents, who do not know who they are, and we are supposed to forget
about it. Ancient history. Stick to the *olvido*." He shook his head.
"We had a cancer as head of state for thirty-six years, Señor. You do
not forget cancer easily. You cannot. Otherwise it will wait for another
opportunity to rise." Another cough, this time less aggressive, followed by another drink of beer. "He is dead and good riddance, but
we deserve more. Every other country like ours has had its truth and
reconciliation. All we have had is amnesty and embarrassment."

Tony nodded and pretended to give a shit. Then he turned to
Garcia. "Where's the matador?"

Garcia's lips buckled into a smile, but there was no humor in
it. He considered his beer. "I am sitting next to him."

"You what?"

"Matador, Señor, is someone who kills. That is what the word means."

"And you know what I meant, so don't be a prick. Where is he?"

He turned back to the television. "What would you have done? If you had been one of these women?"

"What?"

"I think I would rather my child was dead than have him sold to the enemy."

"Maybe thirty years ago you'd have had a choice, mate." Tony drank his Pepsi until the ice knocked his teeth. "But time's got a way of making people older and weaker, and I can't be arsed with the history lessons, know what I mean? So, one last time before I lose my fucking patience: Where is he?"

Garcia didn't answer.

"Listen, I know you arranged to meet him in that café. That's why you were there. Except you didn't tell me that, did you?"

"No."

"But you've made contact since then."

Garcia shook his head.

"Then you won't mind if we go round yours and check, will you?"

Nothing from the old man, except a slight change in color.

"Yeah, you heard from him, old son. That's why you look like someone chucked flour in your face." He put a hand on the old man's arm. "Come on, upsy-daisy."

Tony pulled Garcia to his feet and looked around the room. Nobody paid them any attention. Nobody would call the police. Nobody would even remember them. Garcia turned in his grip and knocked over the glass of beer, sending a river of booze across the bar top. Tony put a hand in the middle of Garcia's back and sent him out in front, chucking a handful of paper napkins at the spill as he went.

"Nice try, Al. But nobody's going to remember you."

They never did.

Fifteen

He had been obvious in the café. An Anglo that big and stupid, that obviously foreign, would never blend into those surroundings. It was one of the few places in Marbella that charged enough for its drinks so that it didn't have to suffer the English. If any tourists happened to stumble in, they didn't stay for long, and that was just the way the regulars—Alejandro included—liked it.

This man ushering him out of the café was the dangerous one of the two. He was bigger, older, and carried himself like a man who had taken lives. But Alejandro knew better. Alejandro would have called him bovine were that not an insult to bulls, so instead he thought of this one as just another wage slave, a man who had been ground down to nothing by a thankless job. All he cared about was money, an idea confirmed by the flicker of indignation on the man's face as he paid for the Pepsi. He was a pig tottering around on his hind legs pretending to be a man.

The older one pushed him toward the kind of small car a woman would drive. Alejandro sat in the front passenger seat. The man got in behind him. The other one was behind the wheel, younger and pale. He kept his eyes on the road and pulled away almost as soon as the doors closed. It looked as if neither man had shaved, washed, or changed clothes for at least a day. The inside of the car smelled of sweat and something else, more perfumed.

French cigarettes.

The rodent Sancho had been in here at some point. That figured. Sancho sold Raf to the English, and so it stood to reason he'd do the same for Alejandro. He wondered where the rat was, or even if he was still alive.

He felt a jolt against one shoulder. The older one glared at him. "Asked you a fucking question."

"Excuse me?"

"Where d'you live?"

They didn't know? Of course they didn't. They'd braced him at the café. If they'd known where he lived, they'd be there now.

The older man leaned over the passenger seat. Alejandro saw him lift his backside from the seat long enough to pull a small gun from the back of his jeans. It was a piddly little automatic, looked like James Bond's gun. He guessed it was supposed to be intimidating, but he'd seen bigger guns in the hands of children playing in the street. He stared at it and then turned to look into the red-webbed eyes of the man holding it.

"Señor, I will not talk to a man holding a gun to my head and who is stupid enough to do so in a moving vehicle."

He lowered the gun. "Turn out your pockets."

Alejandro produced his wallet, some coins, some fluff, some keys. The man with the gun took the wallet and went through the cards. He read out Alejandro's address and the young driver nodded, turning at the next junction to double back the way they'd come. The man with the gun sat back.

They turned the corner in time to see a taxi leave. Alejandro watched it go as the young one pulled the car in and stopped. He heard the back door open and shut and saw the man with the gun approach his door.

"Get out."

Alejandro did as he was told, as slowly as he could. After a few seconds of dawdling, he felt hands on him, pulling him away from the car and then shoving him toward the front door. He stumbled a couple of steps, his ankle aching, and backed into the door. "I need my keys."

The man slapped the keys into Alejandro's hand. The metal teeth dug into his skin, and he dropped the keys. They jingled as they hit the ground. Alejandro bent over to fetch them and glanced at the column of buzzers as he straightened up.

The man shoved Alejandro into the door. "Don't fuck me about, granddad. Get it open and get inside."

Alejandro opened the door, stepped into the cool of the hall. The young one came in after them. Alejandro led them up both flights, their footsteps echoing on the stone stairs, the temperature dropping with every step. The man with the gun paused after the first flight, breathing a little heavily. He was slow to move. When they finally reached the second landing, Alejandro led them to the large red door at the end of it and stopped.

"What you waiting for?" The man's voice was quiet, almost a whisper.

There was a chance that Raf was behind the door. He'd been walking around that morning, a little stiff in the legs—especially the wounded one—but otherwise able to move and apparently lucid. They'd talked a little about the night before, but there'd been no discussion of what would happen if they came back, so there were no warnings, no special knocks that Alejandro could use. He wondered if he'd be able to warn him. He wondered if Raf would be able to move quick enough to escape. Neither seemed possible. He couldn't warn Raf, and even if he could, Raf couldn't run in his condition. It was a miracle he was still alive.

"Hey." A hand squeezed his shoulder. Something cold and hard pressed against the nape of his neck. "Open."

Alejandro put key to lock and opened the door. The man with the gun was close behind him, but he let the younger one take over as soon as they were over the threshold, and the boy pushed

Alejandro in short, sharp shoves toward the living room. The room was empty apart from Islero, who was curled in his usual place, a black bundle of fur in the only spot of sun on the floor. He opened his eyes and regarded Alejandro and the young man with something like contempt before he lowered his head and went back to sleep. The young man pushed Alejandro into the middle of the room. The other man was elsewhere, searching the apartment, which shouldn't have been as lengthy an operation as it was.

Alejandro glanced across at the table. The laptop was on. The printouts next to it had been disturbed and his notebook was gone.

"Where is he?"

Alejandro turned to see the older man standing in the doorway, bloodied bandages in one hand, the gun in the other.

"I told you. He was never here, Señor. I have had no contact with him since he telephoned me."

The man threw the bandages at him. "What's that, then?"

"I had an accident. A long time ago. I am sorry, Señor. As you can see, I am not very house proud."

"You're dirty is what you are." The younger one had a tongue after all. "Place is fucking minging, mate."

The man with the gun stepped forward. "I know he was here."

Alejandro moved away, backing toward the table, both hands up. "He was not. It is only me, Señor." He threw a wobble into his voice. "I swear. Myself and Islero. I saw him, yes. He contacted me on the telephone, as I told you. But I do not want to help someone who is trouble with the law. I told him this." The wobble tickled his throat, caused him to cough. He forced some drama into it, whooping for breath and doubling up, which soon felt more real than fake. When he removed his fist from his mouth, there was blood on it and the sight of it made him weak. That wouldn't do. He needed strength. Just one good boost and he'd be fine.

The younger one looked worried. He had a conscience, then. Something like empathy. Perhaps something to play on if he could get him alone.

The man with the gun hadn't changed his expression. "What did he say?"

"He said that there were some men after him. He said he owed money. He asked me for money, but as you can see, I do not have any. So I refused. I told him I could not help him."

"You're lying."

"No, I swear—"

"Don't fucking swear, just tell us the truth."

Alejandro brushed up against the table. He glanced down at the contents as if surprised but noted where everything was. "I *am* telling you the truth."

"Then what was all that bollocks about stolen children?" The man with the gun came closer. The smell of him made Alejandro blink. "What was the point of that?"

"A story, Señor. A figure of speech. My English—"

"She is not so good? Fuck off."

The man raised the gun. Alejandro grabbed the laptop—just the way he'd rehearsed in his mind—and swung it sideways like a baseball bat, catching the man across the side of the head. Something cracked as the man's head snapped to one side, his body twisting afterward. The gun had gone from his hand, landed somewhere on the floor. Alejandro brought the laptop down on the man's crown and watched him crumple before he tossed the computer to one side. It smashed against the far wall. He looked for the gun, but the young one was one step ahead.

"Don't." The young one held the gun up now. The muzzle trembling slightly, his eyes gleaming. "Don't fucking move. Don't."

"Calm down, young man." Alejandro put up his hands. "It is okay."

"No, it isn't. Stay there."

The older man groaned and cursed as he rolled to his knees. Blood welled up in a thin cut on his scalp. He touched it with one hand and struggled to his feet, lurching toward the sofa. Islero scampered in front of his feet and the man kicked out at him before he dropped onto the sofa. Islero bolted for the door, his claws skittering on the floorboards. The man clamped one hand to his head and leaned forward on the sofa, hissing breath though his teeth, his face a woodcut of pain. He held out his free hand to the young one. "Give us the gun."

"I've got him."

"Give us the fucking gun, Jason."

Jason looked at him, back at Alejandro, then sidestepped toward the man on the sofa. He put the gun in the man's hand and then backed away.

"Fetch us that chair over there."

Jason blinked. He looked as if he'd just woken up.

"The *chair*. The fucking chair, fetch us it." He waved the gun in Alejandro's general direction. "You, sit down."

Jason dragged the chair over and used one of its legs to knock over a pile of books before he dumped it in the middle of the floor. Alejandro, watching the gun, sat down. Jason reached for his waist and pulled off his belt, using it to bind his hands behind the back of the chair. The man with the gun slowly rose from the sofa. He looked dizzy, kept touching the wound on his head. His fingers kept showing blood. He was breathing through his mouth, showing bottom teeth. He kept adjusting his grip on the gun. "I don't know what the fuck you think you're playing at, mate, I really don't."

Alejandro watched the man. He was in a bad way. He was weak. The thought put a smile on Alejandro's face. "Did you shoot Rafael?"

The man blinked as if trying to focus. "Yes."

"Then that is what I am playing at. You could not kill Raf with your little *pistola de puta*, and so you cannot kill me. You do not have the skill or the cojones, and neither does your boyfriend."

There was a blur of movement and white lights flared in front of Alejandro's eyes. He was blind for a moment, numbed by the shock of the blow, and then as the blood came, so did the pain. One of his teeth, an incisor, hung by its torn root, suspended like a fly in a loose thread of spiderweb before it dropped into the gutter of his mouth. Alejandro let his head drop forward. He lazily regarded his lap before he spat the tooth at the floor.

"Where'd he go?" The man's voice was quiet again.

"*Me cago en la madre que te parió.*"

Another blast against the side of his head. Not as hard this time, but piling fresh pain on top of old. Alejandro saw the man, then the ceiling, and realized he'd toppled backward in his chair. Jason struggled to push him back upright. Once he was, Alejandro let his head hang loose on his neck as he felt his face begin to swell.

The man's voice came from somewhere off to his left. "He was here, yes?"

Alejandro nodded, but only slightly.

"So where is he now?"

He tasted blood from his missing tooth and split lip. He swallowed it and raised his head. He stared at the corner of the room and didn't say anything.

"Watch him."

The man passed the gun to Jason, who held it in both hands, before he marched off in the direction of the bathroom. The blood on his head was worrying him, no doubt. He needed to see how badly he was injured before he continued. And so Alejandro was left babysitting. He smiled at the boy, wondering what kind of life he'd had that had pushed him to this place. He pictured a gray, wintry, concrete home somewhere. He pictured lots of pale children running around sporting ragged tracksuits, carrying paper bundles full of chips and bottles of cheap cider. When he thought of England, he thought of puffy white people who looked like albino slugs, writhing drunkenly on a dirty, patterned carpet.

There was a crash from the kitchen. He wasn't serious about torturing Alejandro, just like he hadn't been serious about killing Raf. He was an amateur, and he was tearing the place apart looking for a clue to Raf's whereabouts.

Meanwhile, the computer lay smashed in the corner of the room, with everything they needed to know in fragments at the bottom of a broken hard drive.

Episode Four

Sixteen

There had been lots of information on Alejandro's computer, folder upon folder, all of it neatly labeled and archived, a direct contrast to the confusion of books and magazines that surrounded the old man on a daily basis. There were historical pieces about famous matadors whose names weren't familiar to Rafael, opinion pieces on the cruelty of the corrida—mostly arguing that its cruelty was only seen as such because it was out in the open, whereas subcultures like dog breeding ("animals that have suffered generations of medicated cruelty and can now no longer bear their own litters"), and factory farming ("a fighting bull has four full years in the fields before it dies; beef cattle have barely eighteen months of industrial confinement") were hidden from public scrutiny—notes on reviews that he'd since written and filed, and what amounted to a decade of electronic scrapbooks that must have been transferred from computer to computer over the years.

And one file, the one that proved the most interesting—the one named RAF.

There it was, his career, all thirteen years of it.

The story told was a romantic one: a young boy growing up on the outskirts of Fuengirola, busing tables in his uncle's café, nursing dreams of one day performing in the biggest plazas in the country. An apoderado saw the potential in him and took the boy under his wing. He trained extensively, bided his time, ignoring those who blundered on into short-lived careers, before he appeared as an old hand for his *alternativa* in Marbella at the age of twenty-two, with his second confirmation in Madrid later that year. He became popular, thanks to a clean style and classical form, and he worked hard to stay that way. At his best, he was the living embodiment of the Kenneth Tynan observation that when bullfighting was done well, it was pure minimalism: all you saw was a man standing in a ring making a bull run around after a cape. He was a traditional *figura* in the making and a stark contrast to the tremendista school of showy theatrics and plastic bravery. Even his private life was elegant. There was the marriage to a Miss Spain runner-up named Pilar Pelayo. She had been voted Miss Photogenic by the press and modeled for fashion spreads and advertisements after that, so her face was well known to the public. They had a son together, Samuel. There were no pictures of him in Alejandro's file.

Without the memories to temper it, the story read like the stuff of cheap melodrama, and so it was only logical that the rags-to-riches story would eventually become riches to rags. And that was when the press really started to take an interest, confirming that ever-present prejudice that you could take the boy out of the slum, but you could never take the slum out of the boy. There were reports of fighting behind the scenes, managerial and agency quarrels, drug use by his cuadrilla, and unfortunate affairs with other women who weren't Pilar. There were arrogant quotes from Rafael stating that he'd been worked too hard, that his apoderado took the lion's share of his recent contract with impresario Ernesto Brava, and that these women selling their stories were nobody whores. He ordered the press to confine its commentary to his performance in the plaza, which of course then took a spectacular turn for the worse. There were injuries, there were recriminations, paranoid outbursts, and then, finally— almost mercifully—his corrida clippings and cuadrilla invoices came to an abrupt halt.

That was it. Career over. The last clipping was two and a half years ago.

Nothing between then and now. He wondered what he'd been doing all this time. Whatever it was, it hadn't made the news.

Rafael went back through the invoices. They all had the same address. He picked up the notepad and copied it down. It didn't look like an office address, and he hoped it was home.

Sancho had lied to him about being his friend. It was possible that he'd also lied about his family—perhaps they weren't really estranged after all—and that he could have gone there immediately after he got out of the police station and all of this would have been over. He didn't recognize Pilar. She was pretty, yes, but there was no punch of emotion that he'd associate with seeing a loved one. He just hoped she'd be able to tell him what had happened between his last bull and his first bullet, because otherwise the only people who did know were those who wanted him dead.

So he called a taxi and got out of there as quickly as his injuries would allow. He gave the driver the address and told him to take his time. They traveled out along the coast to the west, the sun battering the inside of the taxi the whole way as beaches, palm trees, and cheap apartment blocks whipped past the window.

By the time they arrived at their destination, Rafael was sweating, not least because there was a sign outside that read EN VENTA.

The address was a large whitewashed villa. He could see the glint of glass around the back, guessed that those windows overlooked the Mediterranean and maybe on a clear day you could see right across to the Strait of Gibraltar. There was no obvious way in. The villa and its grounds were surrounded on all sides by an imposing wrought-iron fence that must have been at least three meters high. He rubbed his index finger and thumb against the bridge of his nose. The light hurt his eyes.

He told himself that he should go back to Alejandro's place. There was nothing here for him. He didn't remember the villa; he didn't remember Pilar or the boy—he couldn't even remember the boy's name, and he'd read it on a screen less than an hour ago. There was also a strong possibility that neither were living there. The place was up for sale, after all. It could have been bought already. And even if it hadn't and he got out of the cab and walked up to that gate, pressed the buzzer and his wife answered, how would he know? The last photograph he'd seen of Pilar had been taken years ago by a professional with an airbrush to hand. It was also before the child. If he didn't recognize her the first time, what possible chance would he have of recognizing her now?

And then something else crept into his mind—what if Sancho had been right? What if they had split up? According to Alejandro's clippings, Rafael had given her more than enough reasons to leave, so it wasn't beyond comprehension that the reason he didn't recognize the house was because he'd never actually lived there.

But no. The invoices had been addressed to this place. If he hadn't been living here, he wouldn't have had his bills sent to this address.

"You know you're on the meter?" The cab driver was a flabby man with a thin face. "I mean, I don't care. It's all money to me—"

Rafael got out of the car. The man's voice irritated him. He didn't have any money, hadn't thought about paying him. Someone else would have to take care of it. He looked around, didn't think he'd be able to find his way back to Alejandro's flat from here and told the driver to wait. A quick look, maybe a chat, and he could either get money from Pilar if she was here or else Alejandro would pay for it when he got back. He'd understand.

He walked to the gates and peered through the bars. There was a large stone patio that led to a side door. Beyond that, he saw palm trees, the same kind they had lining the streets of Estepona. He pictured a garden beyond that, thick green grass and the heady smell of tropical plants. No desert here. He heard a child scream, but it was a happy noise, the kind that came with a chase and ended in a giggling fit. Before he had a chance to move away from the bars, the child came screeching round the corner and then shuddered to a stop. The boy was small, thin, and blond. He wore denim dungarees and a red T-shirt with a lightning bolt on the chest. Rafael didn't know how old he was, but he looked young— younger than his son was supposed to be. The boy watched him with hooded eyes, and Rafael squinted at him, trying to see if he could recognize any of his own features in the boy's face, or even if he could recognize anything about the boy himself.

But no, this kid could have been anyone's.

Rafael opened his mouth to speak, but the boy ran back behind the villa. He shouted something that Rafael couldn't quite make out, something about a man. He moved away from the gate and looked over at the taxi driver. He'd shaken out his newspaper. He felt Rafael's stare and matched it with one of his own.

This was no good. Every second was more of Alejandro's money down the drain. This house wasn't his; the family who lived here wasn't his. He was wasting time.

"Rafael?"

A woman's voice, breaking in the middle. She cleared her throat and said his name again. She was a little older, a little thinner, and a little duller than in the photos on Alejandro's computer, but it was Pilar. If he'd expected a physical reaction—a twitch of the heart, a rush of emotion—he would've been sorely disappointed. But it was enough just to recognize her. Even if it was just a case of matching her face to a recent memory, it felt like progress.

Pilar and the kid, they hadn't moved away just yet. But they wanted to.

"Pilar." The name felt alien in his mouth. He was glad to be rid of it.

She opened the gate and looked over his shoulder. "Are you staying?"

He glanced back at the taxi driver. Was he allowed? Something ground at him, made this situation seem terribly wrong. He swallowed. "I don't know."

"Do you have any money on you?"

"No."

"What happened?"

"Nothing."

"Your head, though—"

"They shot me."

"Are they here now?"

He looked around. He hadn't thought about it. They could've been anywhere. There were hills all around him. He searched for movement in the trees. He suddenly felt blind. "I don't know."

"Then come on." She grabbed his arm and pulled him in behind the gate.

"The taxi."

She waved at the driver. He tapped on his watch. She raised her head and appeared to scan the landscape the way Rafael had. "I'll pay him in a minute. We need to get you inside."

She ushered him away from the gate, her hand tight on his forearm. He followed, staring at her the whole way. Her eyes were large and blue. Her lips had thinned a little with age but still held the echo of a fashionable pout. He recognized her as beautiful, objectively so, but unapproachable. Nothing motherly about her. Nothing wifely. He wondered if that feeling was instinct or based in some kind of memory of her.

Pilar pushed open the double doors and stood to one side. "Welcome home."

He searched her face for sarcasm, but she was blank. She nodded toward the open door and he stepped inside.

She wasn't the only blank thing around here. He stood in a vaulted hallway, marble floored, a marble-topped occasional table and umbrella stand against one wall, and steps that led to a large, light, open-plan living area in front of him. Two couches formed an L-shape by an open fireplace that was caged by a fireguard. Straight ahead, a wall of windows looked out onto the back garden. The grass was as green as he'd imagined, and short, stocky trees kept the garden private. Other than the large pieces of furniture, there were packing cases lining the bare walls, taped shut and ready to go.

Pilar closed the door. She touched his arm as she passed. "I'll get Sam."

"Don't bother."

She stopped. The light caught her face and sharpened her worry, showing up lines that he hadn't seen before. "What's the matter?"

"You're leaving."

"Sorry?"

"You put the house up for sale."

"Yes."

"Then you've made your decision. I don't need to see the boy."

"You made the decision, Raf."

He stared at her and blinked. He didn't understand.

She frowned and came closer. "You don't remember, do you?"

He thought about lying, but he didn't see how he could. And he was tired of pretending he was in control. "No."

"Then you need to sit down, okay? We need to talk."

Seventeen

Tony's hand ached. The skin was red across his knuckles and split across the second joint. He stood in Garcia's tiny kitchen, running cold water over his hand and trying to ignore the throat-closing stink of the cat litter by his feet. Jason was out in the living room, keeping an eye on the old bastard. Not that it was necessary, really. He wasn't going anywhere. Tied to a chair with his face half beaten off, he wasn't about to make Tony's day any worse. Because let's face it, it was pretty much all the way fucked already.

He removed his hand from under the tap and flexed the fingers. Never used to feel the ache this much, and certainly not this soon. Maybe he was throwing harder punches. Not like the prick didn't deserve it. He touched his scalp again. It bristled with fresh pain, but at least his fingers weren't bloody this time. The pain burrowed down into his head, and he shook a couple of pills out of the bottle that he found in the bathroom, along with a load of other little orange bottles with white labels on them. Names like oxycodone, fentanyl, hydromorphone, meperidine. Serious-sounding stuff. He swallowed two of the pills he knew—codeine, but a high dose—and ducked his mouth under the water to wash them down. It took four slurps, because the pills weren't coated and they left a rotten taste in his mouth, but they kicked in pretty fucking quickly.

Couldn't believe he'd left himself open like that. Saw the old man working his way toward the table, knew he was going for something but didn't see what it was until he'd already lamped him. Course, by that time, he didn't know what fucking year it was, never mind have the sense to get out of the way before he got hit again.

He shook his head, flexed his hand again. It still ached, looked slightly swollen. He stuck it back under the water.

A whole fucking laptop. Hadn't seen that coming. And he should have. He should've been on the ball. Maybe if he hadn't been so bloody tired, he would've been.

And how long was he going to keep blaming the fatigue, eh?

You could not kill Raf with your little pistola de puta, *and so you cannot kill me. You do not have the skill or the* cojones, *and neither does your boyfriend.*

Should've shot him in the fucking face right there and then. How was that for cojones, you dago cunt? Or shot him in the leg or something—got him screaming. See who was fucking smiling then.

But no, he couldn't shoot anyone in here without the neighbors picking up on it. Everyone in these buildings was in each other's fucking business. Shoot someone in here, you'd have some mad old bitch banging on the door, demanding to know what was going on. And the mood he was in, he'd shoot her too, and it could only escalate from there.

So he'd have one shot, maybe two, before he and Jason had to get out of there.

It was no good. In fact, it was shit. It was all shit. Because he didn't want to go back out there. That was the thing of it. He couldn't stay here, but he didn't want to carry on with this. The old man wasn't going to tell them anything, was he? He'd made that abundantly fucking clear. And judging by the amount of pain medication he was on, whatever Tony had already dished out probably hadn't put much of a dent in his buzz. Maybe if they had the time he could use the medication as a lever, keep it from him when he needed it. It would be the smart thing to do, but yet again the smart thing was the thing that demanded the most time and patience, and Tony had neither.

There were problems. They'd been fermenting for a while, nipping at him every now and then when he was sober and sensitive enough to let them, but it was situations like this when they became too obvious to ignore. Fact of the matter was, he was beginning to think he shouldn't be here. Like Lisa said, he wasn't around much for the kids, and he was starting to hate them. That wasn't right. A man shouldn't feel that way about his own family. Maybe the fucking Spaniards had a point about that. And maybe it wasn't them that was doing it to him. Maybe it was this place. Marbella, Estepona, Fuengirola, Málaga, up to the Blanca. England's fucking playground. Back in the day it was party fucking central, ramped up on the amphetamines or a touch of charlie, buzzing off the effects of a six-hour drunk. Great when he was in his twenties, a fucking treat when he was in his thirties, but his forties looked like they'd bottled it completely. It was a chore, a punishment, and all around him he was beginning to see the mucky fingerprints on the whitewash, the puke in the gutters, and the mashed chips that littered the pavements. He thought about Lisa and how she'd aged about sixty years in the twenty they'd been here. She was sunbeaten, alcohol stretched. She kept herself in check with the makeup and the workout and the hairdos, but she was still a far cry from the soft, pale girl he'd once fingered in the back row of the Hackney Rio. He felt responsible. He felt as if he'd lied to her, that somewhere along the line he'd spun her the same cunt's yarn he'd been given about Marbella as heaven on earth, the promise that they'd never have to worry about money again.

He reached for his Bensons, sparked one.

He didn't worry about money. That much was true. Hadn't worried about money the whole time he'd lived here. But the other worries more than made up for it.

Because there were problems here, and they were multiplying at a rate of knots. Wasn't just this fucking matador that was giving him ball-ache, it was everyone else. There'd been talk of the Polish moving in round Puerto Banús; they'd bought themselves a boat and everything, one of them huge fuck-off yachts. Partied like it was 1999, and everyone knew the boat and everything on it—the girls, the champagne, enough blow to get you swimming to Africa—was snide. Whoever heard of a Pole who could afford a fucking yacht? Turned out they'd snuck it out from under some Russian, and if there was something the Russians hated more than being taken, it was being taken by the fucking Polish. Long and bloody history there, longer and bloodier than Tony had ever known. And so the Russians went in there, all guns, like a bunch of black ops fucking Navy SEALs. Killed everyone on the boat—not just the blokes but their bought-and-paid-for girlfriends, too—and cut the rope. The coast guard brought it back two days later. Tony and Liam had been out at one of the Puerto Banús bars when they saw it coming in. The one thing he remembered more than anything else was the blood on the hull. He still didn't know how blood had managed to get on the outside of the boat.

That was the Russians putting something personal to bed, but business wasn't that much different. When you lived in a poor country that long, you maybe got to thinking that you wanted everything yesterday, and you didn't give a fuck who you had to hurt to get it. Like the Russians weren't into the drugs in a big way, not yet. Their main trade was women—they brought these doped-up little runaways out to the motorway clubs and whiskerías, got them settled in there as satellites before they went in and demanded a piece of the action. One of Ollie's places that was used to launder, more than anything else, had been marked like that. They took in a new girl, she worked there for a couple of weeks, next thing they knew a couple of the biggest fucking Russians anyone ever saw— like pure fucking Ivan Drago types—wandered in and started giving orders on behalf of some bristly cunt called Antonin Turgenev. She was their girl, so it was their place. If there was any argument, they'd break arms. Maybe they'd mess up the girls. Maybe they'd get some disease-ridden Moroccan to go in there and spread his germs around. Anything to drive down the price.

Ollie sent Tony round to deal with it. He couldn't. It was already too late. And he wasn't about to get killed over a building full of slags.

It was common sense. Survival instinct. It wasn't that he'd taken a look at the Russians and turned on his heel without saying word number one, and the only person that said otherwise was a little fat French Algerian who'd been found in an abandoned and unfinished block of holiday flats with a small round hole in his skull.

Abdullah was an easy pop, though. And there'd been a personal reason for it, which made it easier.

And he wasn't the matador.

Tony flicked ash into the sink. He noticed his cigarette hand was shaking. If he'd been a superstitious bloke, he could've sworn that this Rafael Ortega was a ghost or something. He'd killed him—he was positive of it. He remembered it vividly. They'd picked him and Palmer up at the roadside café they'd thought was private and secure and then bundled them into the back of the car, drove them up to the mountains and tossed them a couple of shovels. It was hard work digging up there, especially when the sun was out, and Tony was fucked if he and Jason were going to do it. Course, they dragged arse about it, and Palmer talked the whole fucking time, telling them that what they were doing was a mistake, he could help them, all they had to do was put the gun away and they'd have a talk about it. Which meant that he only managed to get a couple of feet down before Tony popped him in the back of the head. Palmer's mouth was open and he made a little huck sound before his knees unlocked and he dropped straight into the hole. It was so clean that Tony did a little bow.

And then the other one, the matador, he'd stopped what he was doing. He stared at the dead man and his face was hard with fear.

Tony waved the gun at him. "Go on."

The matador didn't move. He muttered something in Spanish. Tony didn't know what it was. Sounded like he was cursing, but it could've been black magic given what came after.

Tony leveled the gun at him. "Go on, get on with it, Pedro."

The matador swore then. Lots of venom in it, every curse meant. So Tony shot him in the left side, clipped his ribs. The matador curled and turned, his mouth open and nothing but a groan coming out of it. That was more like it. You were supposed to go out crying, begging for your life. And to get them to that point, sometimes you had to remind them of what pain felt like. The matador struggled to stay upright. Tony and Jason watched him, waiting for him to fall.

He didn't. Sheer force of will kept him standing. More than that, he started to straighten up. Tony glanced across at Jason, and he was amazed.

No. That wouldn't do. No way was some poncey fucking bull-fighter going to make him look like a cunt. He stepped up and popped another into the dago's head. The matador dropped back, hit the ground, one leg over the side of the hole. Tony had to kick him into his grave before he and Jason started filling in the holes.

He didn't see him breathing. If he had, he would've finished the job. But the truth of it was he wanted to get out of there. He was embarrassed. He was supposed to show Jason how it was done. That was the reason the kid was there in the first place. And he'd fluffed it. The bastard had shown defiance. Even shooting him in the head had felt like a tantrum in retrospect. And when they'd buried the pair, Jason and Tony headed back to the car in silence.

There were plenty on Tony's tab, and not all of them had been shot. They'd been beaten, throttled, broken, stabbed, chucked off buildings and under moving vehicles. There had been accidents and emphatic messages. And not one of the bastards had developed a breathing habit afterward.

It was his first, and it was a show of weakness, the first crack in the ice. Nobody said anything, but he was sure the rest of the lads thought he'd lost his bottle. And it was times like this, when he didn't want to go back into the living room because he knew this old man was exactly like the bullfighter—he wouldn't go down, he wouldn't *admit* to the pain—that he thought maybe they were right.

He dropped his Bensons in the sink and closed his hand into a fist. It hurt.

They weren't right. It was a hiccup. That was all. The old man just hadn't felt enough pain yet. He pushed away from the sink and started pulling drawers. There'd be something in here somewhere he could use instead of his fists. And when he found it, he'd march back into that room and make sure the old man felt every last agonized moment of his short fucking life.

Eighteen

She led him to the sofa. He didn't want to go, but his head had
started to pound again and his legs didn't feel stable. When he
walked she noticed the rip in his trousers. "What happened?"

He sat on the sofa, which felt as if it grabbed him around the
waist as gravity pushed him into the cushion. The rip buckled to
show the wound, dressed and bandaged, a shock of white against
the dusty black of his trousers. He looked at it and blinked.

It took him a second to remember. "There was a bull."

"Did you speak to Al?"

The name rang a bell. He looked at her. "Al? Alejandro?"

"You were supposed to speak to him, remember? About the
money, and maybe training you again?"

"I don't remember that." His head hurt again, worse this time.
"When was I supposed to have done that?"

"Friday. You were supposed to talk to him about getting money
for us to leave. You said he would help you. But you left and you
didn't come back."

Friday? He ran a hand over his face. What day was it now,
Monday? The loss of a couple of days hadn't seemed so important
until now. He thought he remembered talking to Alejandro, and he
definitely remembered that there'd been a phone number on the
back of the corrida ticket. And there was something else, *someone*
else, a man in a gray suit, demanding money from him. A stab of

panic when he realized he was supposed to see him today. A loan shark? "How much do we need?"

"You said about six thousand for all three of us."

Six thousand. The amount was a red flag. He breathed out and closed his eyes.

"Are you okay?"

"Yes."

"You look terrible. You said they *shot* you?"

He opened his eyes. "Did I?"

"Just now." She got up. "I should phone for a doctor—"

"Don't." It was a harsh sound. The word echoed in his head. "I've already seen a doctor. It's fine." He moved and heard the rattle of pills in his pocket. He found them and brought them out. "I just need to take my medication, that's all."

"I'll get you some water."

"Don't need it." He dry-swallowed two of the pills and shook his head a little so they'd go down. He read the label then. They looked like painkillers. He hoped they were. He didn't know where he'd picked them up, even though it must have been recently. He replaced the bottle in his pocket and leaned forward.

Pilar returned to his side. She put her hand on his back. It was a light touch and he guessed it was supposed to be soothing, but it made him itchy instead. He moved away.

"Raf, tell me what's wrong. Are we leaving?"

"Yes, I should go."

"Where? And where have you been?"

He didn't know. All he knew was that there was nothing for him here. He didn't recognize the place or the people, even if they recognized him, even if they had defined him at one point in his life. He opened his eyes and looked at the floor. He couldn't look at her anymore, couldn't bear to see her watching him. She remembered him. Things had gone wrong. He had promised her something. "Did we split up?"

"I don't understand."

"Are we married?"

"Why are you…" She let out a sigh, but there was a break in it, a show of emotion. "Yes, we're married. You know that. We've been married for eleven years. You know that too."

"I don't remember."

"You never remembered the date, Raf, but you always remembered the event. What's the matter with you?"

"They shot me." The hand on his head moved to his mouth. He pulled on his bottom lip. Both the lip and his fingers trembled as a ball of pain throbbed in the middle of his throat. "There were men." He squinted. He could feel the images of the men become fuzzy around the edges, their faces already indistinct. He tried to concentrate on the important ones, the man in the white shirt, the one they called the gaffer. "They were English. They had guns. They knew." Another man, tall and smiling. The name disappeared, did a lap of his brain before it came back to his mouth three breaths late. "*Sancho*. Sancho took me away. I borrowed money from a loan shark. He wanted to hurt me. Sancho took me away, and then they took me to this other place." He shook his head. Sancho was a name more than a face now, a word more than a person. All that was left was a smile and the sound of laughter somewhere in the back of his mind. Everything else had become dark and numb. "I was at a place. There were women. Then there weren't. It was…there was a bull." Drifting again, and then a word floated by. "Ganadería."

"Where they breed the bulls?"

"Yes. They put me in the ring. The man in the white shirt was there. He was the boss. And I escaped, and then Alejandro found me, and then I came here."

"Does Al know you're here?"

Rafael shook his head. "I don't think so."

"Do you have his number? I should call him, let him know you're all right."

He rifled through his pockets, looking for the ticket, but it was gone. "I lost it." He leaned forward again. He wanted to get up, but he didn't have the energy. He couldn't remember the last time he'd eaten. His stomach made low gurgling noises.

"Did you speak to Palmer?"

"Who's Palmer?"

"The customs man. You said you needed to talk to him."

"When?"

"Before you left. You said you needed to talk to Al, and then you'd arrange to see Palmer. This was why we were leaving, Raf. You said you thought they knew about Palmer and you needed to call it off—"

"Shut up. Please." The pain in his head was worse now. It made him speak slowly and quietly. "I don't remember any of that. I don't remember you; I don't remember this place; I don't remember anything. It's all gone."

She studied him. He looked away. She stood up and left the room. A part of him wanted to call her back, but he didn't know her name anymore, and he didn't know what he could say to her. So he watched the black bugs swirl in front of his eyes, both hands up over his head, leaning forward and waiting for the painkillers to kick in.

There was the sound of a child roaring past the back window. He turned to see the boy running around with a toy gun. He was taking potshots at other cowboys, soldiers, aliens, dinosaurs, or whatever it was that he liked to kill. He rolled on the grass and then disappeared around the side of the villa.

She came back into the room, a piece of paper in one hand and a cordless phone in the other. She was dialing a number.

Rafael suddenly felt a twinge of fear. "What are you doing?"

"I'm calling them. They need to know?"

"Who?"

"The customs people." She showed him a flash of the paper. "Mr. Palmer needs to know what happened to you. What they did. He'll know what to do."

"Palmer? I don't—"

"It's okay, Raf. Don't worry. Everything's going to be all right. Mr. Palmer is the man from customs, from England. You talked to him sometimes about the work you did for the English." She frowned and looked at the display on the phone, checking it against the paper in her hand. "Every time they moved a large amount, you told him, and he would make a note of it."

"Large amount? Of what?"

"Drugs, Raf. Cannabis I think. You said it was something large."

"I was an informer?"

"Not always."

"Wait, put the phone down."

"They need to know."

"Please." A jolt in the temple. He closed his eyes, breathed through his mouth. "Please, just believe me. He won't pick up."

"Why not?"

He blinked. His eyes ached, pulsing in their sockets. He saw the dirt under his fingernails and caught a flash of a pale hand in the moonlight. He blinked again, and there were tears in his eyes. He sniffed and pushed at them with one hand. "They're coming here. They need to finish the job. If Sancho knew me, then he knows this place, and when they come looking for me, they'll come here." He cleared his throat. "You need to go. Take the boy and leave. Today. Now."

"Raf, the customs—"

"He's dead. They shot him. He's in the mountains." He stood up and rubbed at his face. "You need to leave. Go somewhere I wouldn't know about. I can't be trusted. My mind is all mixed up. I don't know what I could say to them, so..." He took the phone from her and threw it onto the sofa. "I'm sorry."

Heard himself saying it to Alejandro: "I'm sorry about the way things ended."

Saw Alejandro in a room that was dim, even though he knew it was daylight outside. He remembered rage blistering him, remembered leaving the room, remembered the afterimage of a man who looked at him as if he were something he'd scraped off his shoe. It was Alejandro, but it wasn't the same man who'd taken him in and called the doctor. And he didn't connect to Palmer or customs or any of the other side of it.

"I need to go."

His head hurt even more now. He fumbled out another couple of pills and swallowed them, or tried to. They wouldn't go down. He tilted his head back and swallowed again. One of them shifted, the other stayed put. When he breathed out, one of the pills bounced onto the floor. He moved to the nearest wall to steady himself. He heard the woman saying something, but she was far away. He told himself not to remember anymore. It hurt him now. Something told him that every salvaged memory pushed that nugget of metal farther toward its final, fatal resting place. It was irrational and frightening, but he couldn't shake it from his brain any more than he could the bullet. It was a scratched record, jumping and repeating, tormenting him until he couldn't breathe.

"Raf. Look at me."

When he looked at the woman again, she resembled an icon in church, her wide blue eyes pleading and shining with tears, the light haloing around the back of her head. He looked over her shoulder at the manicured back garden, saw her planting flowers, the red ones. And then there was the smell of those flowers, sweet and heady, mixing with that of freshly brewed coffee, and the warm feeling of skin on skin. He saw the view from their bedroom window on a bright spring morning. He saw the busy highway, cars zipping in both directions, a couple of modern apartment blocks that looked like two badly stacked towers of sugar cubes, and beyond them, glittering in the sun, the Mediterranean and the Strait and perhaps even farther beyond that, the rocky visage of Gibraltar itself off to the south.

He saw all that, and he knew his life here, and yet he didn't know her name.

He saw all that and felt it crowd his thoughts, and then a second after he saw it, it was gone.

"Raf."

He shook his head. He couldn't stay. There was no point.

"Please."

He pushed off the wall. He guessed that the large door up the steps was the way out, and so he set off in that direction. He heard quick footsteps behind him and felt a hand on his arm. He tried to shake it off, but it closed. She wouldn't let go. He turned to her—this woman with the tears in her eyes, the one asking him where he was going—and he pushed her away.

"You're not well, Raf. You need to sit down."

She was his wife. He remembered that much. There was a kid, too. "I have to go."

"Where?"

"I told you what to do."

"What about you?"

He didn't answer. He went up the steps. She made another grab for him, and he turned on her, slamming her back against the wall, knocking over the umbrella stand. He put one hand up over her throat, felt the warm pulse. He wanted to squeeze. It would be easier to do that. It almost seemed merciful.

"Leave. Take the kid and go."

He pushed away from her. She put a hand to her throat as he threw open the door.

"His name is Samuel. It was your father's name."

He left the house. It didn't matter what the kid was called. It didn't matter what his father was called. The kid wasn't his, the father wasn't his, the wife wasn't his. As far as he was concerned, they were all fictional, a family out of an advertisement, and he knew that as soon as she'd been out of sight for an hour, she'd be gone from his mind forever.

And despite the grinding in his chest, he knew that it was a good thing he didn't remember them, because they would only be a distraction, and he was running out of time.

Nineteen

They weren't professionals. They were street thugs. English pigs, Benalmádena corner trash with their accent that made it sound as if they were chewing something as they spoke. And they were squeamish into the bargain. The one called Tony was used to a little blood, but he wasn't used to Alejandro's smile, and Alejandro noticed that the younger one, Jason, turned a different shade of pale every time Tony threw a punch.

He smiled through it all. Alejandro thought Tony was aiming for his mouth, which confirmed how inexperienced these two were. What kind of man aimed at the one place where he knew the sharpest parts of the human body were housed? It made no sense. He showed his teeth, gave Tony a target. Still a few more to knock out.

Alejandro spat blood at Tony's shoes. He heard the blood spatter across books and opened his one good eye, the other swollen shut, and smiled once more.

"The fuck you smiling at?"

"How is your head?"

Another blow to the face and one more tooth gone. Something cracked in his jaw, too. Alejandro took his time coming out of that one, but when he did, he saw Tony massaging his fist.

"Fuck this." Tony was antsy, moving around. "Fuck this. Fuck *him*."

Jason said something, but Alejandro couldn't quite understand it. It was supposed to be soothing, whatever it was. It didn't work. Tony left the room. Alejandro heard him trashing the place, and then the sound of running water.

He was in the kitchen for a long time. So long that Jason didn't look comfortable anymore. He didn't like looking at Alejandro. Alejandro made a point of staring at him.

This is what you do, boy. This is your career now.

Finally, the young man seemed to grow restless enough to shout at Tony, who appeared from the hall like an explosion. Alejandro turned his head, saw something in Tony's hand and then felt the world dropping out as the chair fell back. It crashed into a pile of books, which turned the chair slightly and loosened the belt around his wrists. He tried to loosen it a little more, but Tony was on him, and whatever it was he'd been carrying was somewhere else now. He grabbed Alejandro's wrists and snapped the belt off, tossing it to one side and hauling Alejandro up by his arm. Alejandro stumbled as he tried to stand, his feet connecting with loose books and his head thrown into a spin by the sudden change in orientation. It took him a few steps to realize that he was being dragged toward the dining table where the laptop had been.

There it was, the thing that Tony had brought into the room.

Closer now, his eye focusing, Alejandro saw it was a hammer. He resisted, dug his heels into the floor, and an involuntary grunt forced its way out of him. He tried to twist his body away from Jason, tried to use his weight to bring Tony to the floor, but Tony was too strong, or he'd pivoted in such a way as to make Alejandro weak. Tony lifted him under the armpits and shoved him toward the dining table.

"Hold his fucking arm."

Jason grabbed Alejandro's right arm. Alejandro felt weak again. He closed his eye and his inner ear told him he was upside down. Liquid filled his throat. He swallowed it back. It burned.

"Bring his fucking hand here. Bring it here." Tony rapped the table with something hard—probably the end of the hammer. "Put it here."

Alejandro opened his eye. He was on his knees, half lying by the dining table, one arm held outstretched and taut by Jason, his hand out of sight. He felt the table under his fingers. He pictured his hand. It was pale and spattered with blood. It was someone else's hand. He stared at a pile of paperbacks that sat by the door to the hall. At the bottom of the pile was a French novel by a man who'd died young. It was slim and unassuming, and he remembered it was about a man who played the Good Samaritan and had his life destroyed because of it. It was fiction, but the incidents read like banal fact.

Tony's voice barking at him, "Where is he?"

Alejandro dropped his head. He summoned up the energy and breath to call Tony's mother a whore.

A blinding flash snapped his head back up, his little finger replaced by what felt like stripped wires, blazing with pain. He breathed in but refused to let the scream that rolled in his throat hitch a ride past his few remaining teeth. He hissed the breath, let the agony out like steam, his entire body knotted.

His head was light in weight and color. He saw nothing but white now, like morning sunshine. He heard birds and a breeze moving leaves.

"Forget the cape. You don't practice with the others."

A whine of a reply: "Why not?"

"Because they're amateurs. You study them, yes, but you don't practice with them. You practice with them, you pick up each other's mistakes, and I don't want you forgetting everything you learned with me just because some big-mouthed older boy told you to do it differently. You work with mediocrity, you *become* mediocrity. So no cape for you, not until I see that you're ready. First, you exercise."

There was a boy.

A pinch, a slap on the side of his swollen face, jarring him conscious. He saw the silhouette of one of the English. The smell told him it was Tony.

"Tell us where he is, mate, or I'll do another one."

"The matador?"

"Yes, the fucking matador."

"He is in the park, Señor."

"Park?"

"He is practicing his moves. Alone. No amateurs."

"The fuck is he talking about?"

"The exercises. Yes. They are important."

The exercises were important. They were also dull and the boy hated doing them, but he did them anyway because he was told to. No strength exercises. No push-ups, chin-ups, nothing that might overdevelop the arms, bind the muscles, or sacrifice flexibility for strength. Strength was not needed in the plaza. The toro was the strong one. And so the boy performed exercises to encourage litheness of the torso, neck, and back. He stretched; he loosened.

Sometimes it hurt, and sometimes he could see the boy trying not to cry.

Another blow, another flash of agony, and this time the scream caught Alejandro unawares and roared past his lips. He opened his mouth and saw a string of drool joining his bottom lip to his shoulder. He blew it away in a few pain-wracked breaths.

"That's more like it. Now where is he?"

"There were..."

"What?"

"Neck."

There were neck exercises. Revolve in a half circle, left to right, and then back again. Important to be loose in the neck, important to keep the toro in sight at all times. There were back exercises. The boy would touch his legs below the kneecaps, using only the motion of his shoulder and his waist. He learned to swing his shoulders in great, graceful arcs to the left and then to the right. This prepared him for cape work, specifically the *verónica*. Then he did knee bends to perfect his balance, waist bends with stiff knees to make the torso supple, sit-ups to strengthen the back and stomach. He made the boy—

Something nudged his ribs. He smelled cat litter and sweat.

"Wake up."

"Park."

He made the boy walk around the park, picking up imaginary leaves to prepare for the motion of the *trincherazo* with the muleta. He made him run forward and backward, then made him zigzag backward without bending his upper body.

Always grace. Always precision. Always true to the soul of the corrida.

A crack, and Alejandro's body jerked as if electrocuted. His hand was on fire and pinned to the table. His legs spasmed and shook in front of him, and he couldn't feel them move, heard his feet kicking the bare floor before he saw it. The pain in his hand now scampered with razor heels up his arm to his shoulder, where it dug deep into the bone and burrowed through the marrow and shook his entire arm in a violent rage. He breathed—he was still breathing—and it tickled his lungs. He coughed. His spit tasted like blood and had the slurry consistency of vomit.

"Haven't got all day, mate. And you're running out of fucking fingers."

"*El matador de* toros."

"The matador, yes."

"The killer of bulls."

"Where is he?"

"Rafael."

"Yes."

"Rafael Ortega."

"He is...standing."

Standing with his spine to a fence, his face smooth, his eyes narrowed at the sun that blazed and baked him as he practiced his verónicas, one after the other, hundreds of them. He wanted the cape; he got the cape, and he would be lost without the cape by the time training was over.

Alejandro, folded arms, watching from the shadows. "Keep your body straight."

"You what?"

"Extend your arms."

Another blow. Another crack, but a sound rather than a pain. He felt it, moved against it, but it was an irritation. The previous pain overwhelmed it. He was somewhere else, watching the boy.

Telling him now to run backward with the cape, learning *bregar*, hearing the objections.

"Why do I have to learn this? I'm a matador, not a banderillero."

"You're neither until your alternativa. And do you want to be a torero who knows less than one of his own cuadrilla? Listen to me: when you become a matador, you will know everything. You will place your own banderillas and you will shame the professionals. You will be called maestro."

The banderillas. The pain reminded him. After the picadors had gone to work on the toro, the banderilleros came into the plaza to place their pairs of tasseled darts. If the picadors hadn't done their job, the banderilleros would suffer first. They tested the bull's vision, how it hooked with its horns, how its short-distance charges worked. The banderillas hooked under the skin and bounced against the toro's hide, irritating it, and just like the pics, forcing its head down even more. It was also the part of the corrida that you saw the first true signs that the toro was thinking and realizing that the odds were stacked firmly against it.

And that was the tragedy of the corrida.

Death alone wasn't tragic. It was the simple entropy of cells. What made death tragic was the foreknowledge that it would happen, and being powerless to stop it. That was the prelude to the moment of truth, that split second in the third tercio when point met hide and when the mettle, ingenuity, and elegance of both man and bull were tested.

He had knowledge. That disease which pulsed and bred in his chest and liver, burrowing through tissue, rotting it from within. Each cough a constant, shuddering reminder of the cuadrilla that circled him, calling him, fluttering their capes, distracting him while someone else thrust the darts into him, each one making him weaker and sicker and slower. The prods, the tests, the blood, the chemicals. The remedies that were nothing more than expensive chemical ways to postpone the inevitable day when he lay birdlike and bony, as his skull rattled one last cough into a plastic mask.

"Rafael."

"Where?" The voice was English, hoarse, and ugly. "Hold him there. Hold him right fucking there."

He knew the voice. It belonged to the big one, the one who acted like a father to the child. The one who would disappoint eventually the way fathers always did.

The way they *almost* always did.

Episode Five

Twenty

His name was Alejandro Garcia.

If Rafael somehow forgot everything else, he told himself never to forget that name.

His name was Alejandro Garcia, and he was on the floor, his head in a halo of gore that had soaked through some paperback books and stained the floorboards. His jaw had been blown apart and another hole, no wider than his little finger, darkened the man's otherwise white hair. His shirt was open, the buttons scattered along with loose change. His undershirt, a white vest, was soaked with saliva-diluted blood and what looked like vomit. One of his hands had been pulped; the other provided a sickening contrast, lying pale and limp by his side.

Rafael approached the apoderado. He went to his knees and touched the man's face. It was cold. He turned and watched Alejandro's chest in the futile hope that it would move. It didn't. He stood up and saw the scuff marks on the dining room table, the chips taken out of the surface, and then saw what was left of the laptop in the corner of the room. His heart trembled and he felt dizzy. He sat on the couch. As he did so, he thought he saw Alejandro's mouth twitch, something moving the hairs of his mustache, thought he heard a groan. He went for the phone, found it on the table and looked for an address book. He found the name of a doctor and called the number. He turned and looked at the corpse on the floor.

The corpse?

No. Alejandro. His name was Alejandro something.

Alejandro Garcia.

Rafael let out a short breath. Already the name had started to lose its focus. He was beginning to drift again. He couldn't let that happen.

A woman's voice on the other end of the phone startled him. For a second, he forgot why he had the phone in his hand. "Hello?"

"Yes, may I help you?"

"Who is this?"

"This is Dr. Sanchez's office."

"Yes, the doctor. Is the doctor available?"

"I'm not sure. Who shall I say is calling?"

He swallowed. Blinked. "Alejandro."

"Alejandro…" Wanting a surname.

"I don't…" It began with a *G*. He wanted to cry. He had it a moment ago. He pushed paper on the table.

"Hello?"

There was a wallet lying open on the floor. There was a picture of the dead man in it. He grabbed it and read the name. "Alejandro Garcia."

A pause at the other end. He'd sounded too formal and too relieved.

His turn to say it: "Hello?"

"One moment, please."

"I don't have—"

She put him on hold. He should have called for an ambulance. He was sure he knew that number. It was an emergency number, he'd remembered it before—it had a two in it—but it wouldn't come to him now. He leaned against the table, his legs weak.

A man's voice came on the line. "Al?"

"No."

"Who is this?"

"You need to come and see him. He's not well. He's...I don't know if he's alive. They shot him. I'm sorry. It's my fault."

"Rafael?"

"Yes."

"Where are you, the apartment?"

"Yes."

"Have you called the police?"

"No." And he was scared. He didn't want to call the police. "He needs help."

"Stay where you are. I'll call an ambulance. Just stay there, okay?"

"Okay."

Then a dead line. He held the phone to his ear a while longer, his elbow locked in position. When the blood had leeched from his hand, he let the receiver drop to the floor. The clatter shook him out of a drift, and he suddenly couldn't remember who he was or what he was doing. And there was a dead man on the floor that he didn't recognize. He saw the phone and didn't remember who he'd been calling. He guessed the police or an ambulance.

"I'll call an ambulance."

Another jolt and he was back, shaking his head and trembling. He'd called the doctor. The doctor was sending an ambulance. The man on the floor was Alejandro Garcia. He was his apoderado. He meant a great deal to Rafael, the old Rafael, the one who'd lived before him. The one who knew who he was.

And they had killed him.

Wait.

Rafael found a notepad in his back pocket. He flipped over a page with an address on it as he walked to the sofa.

He started writing. He had to remember as much as possible. He had to get it written down so he wouldn't forget again.

He wrote, and the light in the room appeared to brighten to a painful glare.

He stopped. His head hurt too much. He ripped off a sheet, folded the paper and pushed it into this pocket. It would have to do. Because he was beginning to remember much more of the past, while the present shifted out of focus. And he knew that if he stopped for a moment, then he could lose his thread and the next thing he'd know he'd be like Alejandro. Something nagged at him to say that he'd already *been* Alejandro in a past life, two bullets in him and dead to the world.

Rafael stood. His legs were watery. He wasn't well. He needed to lie down. They were sending an ambulance. The doctor had said so. He could wait. He went out into the hall, holding on to the wall for support, and then went through to the bedroom. It was dim in here and his eyes felt better. It felt like home in here. It felt safe. He went to the bed and dropped onto it. A breeze came in through the open window, bringing with it the smell of the sea and, from some-where farther away, the smell of pine needles and earth. He looked up and saw a trincherazo and *puntilla* hanging on the far wall.

His eyes drifted out of focus. And then he was in the dark.

A thud brought him back.

He opened his eyes to gloom, his body trapped in a sheet. The room smelled like an abattoir. He struggled out of the sheet and tossed it to one side. He swung his legs out of bed, leaned forward as a dizzy spell threw his brain around.

It was still daylight outside. He was dressed in a suit, one of the trouser legs ripped at the thigh. It stank. *He* stank. His head hurt, felt stuffed. He couldn't shake it loose to think properly, felt himself fall into a stare that rooted him to the bed.

Wait.

His name was Rafael.

That was it. His mind swarmed with images, but most were blurred, distorted, and quick to vanish.

The thud again, now a knocking sound, fist on wood. On the opposite wall hung a sword and dagger. He launched himself from the bed and grabbed the dagger. The sword above it would be no good—too thin, too unwieldy. He moved to the bedroom door with the dagger in his hand and pulled the door slightly ajar. He was in an apartment—he could see the kitchen and bathroom doors open, so he knew he wasn't in a house—but it didn't look familiar. He decided that he couldn't have slept very long judging by the fatigue that lingered in his limbs. Was it his apartment? He doubted it. The smell in here wasn't his, and his first instinct upon waking was panic, like he wasn't supposed to be there. Then again, the dagger fit comfortably in his hand, so he guessed that either it belonged to him or he'd used one very similar before.

Another knock at the front door. More noise behind it. Hushed talking and then something operating on the lock. The front door opened slowly. A policeman appeared in the gap. He was young and long and white. He looked frightened, and as he stepped into the hall, the gun in his hand did little to change Rafael's first impression. The muzzle trembled in the policeman's grip. First time he'd drawn, perhaps. Another policeman came in behind him. He was slightly older, dusted gray at the temples, taller than the other policeman and more obviously in control. This policeman spoke, his voice a bass note as he identified them and asked if there was anybody home. The young policeman headed toward an open door out of Rafael's line of sight, the older policeman following.

Both disappeared. Rafael switched sides. Saw the open door to what looked like a living room.

He heard someone stumble and retch. The young policeman came out of the room backward, guided by his partner. He had one gloved hand over his mouth. The glove was wet. His gun hand swung loose at his side. Rafael heard the other policeman mutter something, followed by the squeak, squelch, and static of a radio.

Something cold tweaked at the back of his mind.

The young policeman leaned against a wall. He was paler than before.

He'd seen a dead body. There was a dead body in the living room. And the dead body was someone called Alejandro Garcia.

Rafael moved behind the door as the pale policeman crossed in front of it. He saw the policeman push open the bathroom door. A brief check, and then he moved on to the kitchen. From there, he turned to the bedroom. Rafael slipped away from the door as it opened. He braced himself against a chest of drawers that creaked as he leaned, watched the open door. The gun appeared in the gap, followed by the policeman's hand, followed by his wrist. As soon as the elbow made an appearance, Rafael shouldered the open door. The policeman shouted, his arm caught between door and jamb. The gun went off. Splinters burst from the floor. Rafael grabbed the policeman and pulled him into the room, swinging him round before he let him tumble back toward the bed. Rafael sprinted out of the bedroom. He heard another shot clip the wall to his left and launched himself at the front door, yanking it shut as the young policeman squeezed off another round, a shower of splinters exploding out of the wood.

Rafael put a hand on the railing, felt it quiver under his palm as he vaulted over onto the stairs. He caught the bottom step and rolled onto the landing. He grunted, struggled to his feet and hauled himself to the second flight of stairs, taking them at speed, his feet a blur. There were footsteps above him, shouts. Rafael jumped the last few steps, landed on a weak ankle that put his cheek to the floor in an instant, the impact snapping his jaw close on part of his cheek. He tasted blood, spat it out, shook off the pain and lurched toward the front doors, pulling them open with one hand, the other white around the dagger.

Fresh air. Bright light. He couldn't see.

He turned to the left, put his shoulder to the wall, using it as a guide as he tried to blink away the glare. He hobbled as quickly as he could, still that taste of blood in his mouth, his ankle burning with every step, other pain awakened and snatching at his thigh, his side, and his head. He looked at the ground, blinking. His vision stuttered back, and he glanced over his shoulder. An empty police car stood outside the building. He sped up, turned the first corner he found and ducked into the shadows.

He felt around in his pockets, found a wallet. His name was Rafael, he was positive, but the wallet held credit and debit cards in the name of Alejandro Garcia.

The dead man.

There was no photo identification. Rafael couldn't remember what the dead man was supposed to look like. There was money in the billfold—thirty-five euros. A press card with Alejandro's name on it and contact number. Some receipts. A picture of La Macarena. He closed the wallet and stuffed it back into his pocket, which held something else.

A piece of paper, crumpled. There was writing on it, scribbled in haste.

He focused on it, read it once. Then read it again.

And grew colder with each sentence.

TERCIO DE MATAR

Twenty-One

His world smelled of manure and hay and wet leather.

He was nervous. There were voices and shouts all around him, but he couldn't understand what they were saying. He knew they'd been shouting at him for hours now, here in the dark, and he wished they would stop. Somewhere farther off he heard another noise; it sounded like music. He moved his head. It felt heavy, but his neck felt strong enough to hold it upright.

There was another noise up ahead, and it angered him. Movement out the corner of his eye angered him even more. He turned toward it and ran. Determined he'd hurt it somehow, kill it for being so close to him, such a shock to the system. He ran up what was now a narrow concrete corridor, toward white sand ahead. He knew sand. He liked sand. It reminded him of when he was younger.

He burst out and straight across a wide circle of sand to what felt like an explosion of sound and movement. He whirled around, looking for the original source of movement, but it had gone. He whirled again. He needed comfort. He wanted to be back in the dark. It was too open out here. Too many things moved. They confused him. They irritated him. He wanted to be somewhere else.

He turned back to where he'd come from, but the door was closed. It was hot out here. He didn't know what he had to—

A movement. Over there. A large one. Something flapping. He eyed it. Saw it move again, taunting him, and then he charged. He felt something brush his head, and then it became air, and he was confronted with more white sand and light and noise. He stopped, turned. Saw the movement and went for it again, and again it disappeared from his view.

There were other movements now, other creatures in the circle. And these ones he knew. He recognized them. These were horses. They had men on them. A man on a horse was a threat. He remembered them from when he was younger too, and how they used to ride around and taunt him and prod him with the sticks, just like the ones they had now. He geared up and ran for one of the horses, connecting sharply, and used all his strength and weight to try and push it over, knowing that if he pushed it over, he could kill it. And then there was a jutting pain in the back of his neck, and he kept pushing but the pain got worse, but he kept on pushing until the pain came a second time, and there was a lot of noise, and then he moved away from the horse. The man on top kicked at the sides and pulled the horse away just as something fluttered over his nose, and he whirled round to catch it, dipping his head to one side. He missed, slowed to a halt. Saw another horse. There were two riders. The other horse would be weaker. Something told him that was the case. He charged the other horse. Again pushed hard, again felt that stabbing pain in the back of his neck that didn't so much hurt as weaken. Blood running over his back, he backed away and tried to angle his head for maximum damage, but the horse didn't so much as whinny.

Another flourish over the snout and he whirled round, saw a flash of something sparkly, a man on his feet, dancing out to one side, and then he couldn't see him anymore.

He stopped, breathing hard. Blood dripped onto the sand. He turned. There were men out here, but they were hiding somewhere.

He had recognized the men. He had recognized them as the creatures that sometimes came out to the fields at night and tried to dazzle him the same way they were trying to now out here in the noisy place.

A blast of something. A long noise.

He turned his back to the door where he'd come in, and then turned again so he'd face it. He walked back over there. It was safe there; he felt safe there. He'd stay there as long as he could.

Movement.

One of the men. Running. He turned and charged. The man was there; he was there; right in his sights, right off there, and he would get it in a minute, but then the man disappeared and something burned him right where he was wounded before, something else slapping his hide in the back. He turned, his head spinning, his back aching, to see more movement ahead. He barely paused for breath before he charged again. He couldn't afford to slow down, not when there were so many of them. Again, the man disappeared, and again his back burned. He stopped, his tongue out. Breathing hard. It was hot out here.

"Hey."

A sound.

"Hey. Hey, toro, hey."

He turned to the sound. Another man. He looked different than the other two. He held two sticks in his hand. There was no shield with him this time. He was a man alone and running toward him. He breathed out once harshly through his nose and then charged the man.

He was there, right there, right in his sights.

And yet again the man disappeared. And there was a lancing pain right between his shoulder blades. He stopped abruptly and twisted his head, felt something connect and pushed the advantage, but the advantage disappeared just as the ambient noise became deafening.

He moved around back to the door where he'd come in. He was tired. He was bleeding. He couldn't catch his breath.

Another blast of noise. He shook his head.

The man. The one who'd disappeared the last time, came out in front of him, way far away. He had a small thing in one hand.

"Hey."

Making that noise again.

"Hey, *hey!*"

He charged, his heart pounding, his lungs on fire, his back in tatters. The man disappeared. He wanted to bellow in frustration, but he didn't have the breath to do it. He turned and the saw the movement again, followed it with his head, determined to keep it in view, perhaps get a little closer to it so he could hook it with his head and then trample and hook the rest. He got closer. He hooked. The movement went again. The man was there somewhere, and he became determined to get the man. But every time he thought he had him, he couldn't focus.

The movement disappeared, and there was a colossal roar from somewhere above him. He was dazed, staggering a little. He tried to go back to his safe spot, but the man wouldn't let him. He turned his back, but the man was there, off to one side. He wanted to kill the man, but the man wouldn't let him do it. He would never be close enough, never *stay* close enough for him to be able to hook into him the way he needed to.

And then it was silent. He was alone. He turned from his safe spot.

"Hey."

Saw the man. There was something in his hand, long and thin and shining.

"Hey, toro, hey."

He saw the fluttering thing in the man's other hand. He saw the shining thing pointing at him. He felt the claustrophobic silence.

"Hey."

He followed the man as he approached. He felt the rage build up inside him, uncontrollable, primal, and dark. There was nothing he wanted to do more than kill this man. There was nothing he could understand more than wanting to charge. He was bleeding and tired and desperate, but when the man came closer, he knew he would stay where he was and he'd have a chance to hook him in the belly.

"Hey."

He charged. And he saw the man arch.

He felt the breeze that made him blink. Hooked at the man, caught nothing but more air.

Then a sharp bolt of pain in his back, shooting through into his chest. A bubbling in his lungs, froth popping at his lips. He tried to find the man, but the pain blinded him. All he saw were large flashing things now, as if the man had multiplied and each was testing him. He panicked, turned, groaned in frustration. It hurt to speak. It hurt to breathe.

He looked around for the man, tried to turn, and his legs gave out from under him.

He hit the sand and then jerked awake.

Someone saying, "Señor?"

Rafael was on a bed. He was naked, his body laced with scars. He looked at the door. The voice came from behind it. "Señor, I can leave your clothes by your door, if you would prefer."

"Yes, please."

There was the sound of something wrapped in plastic hitting the floor outside his room. He blinked and sat upright. He had been lying on a bed, on top of a stiff quilt cover, which was a washed-out version of the deep red on the walls. There was a table and a full-length mirror opposite, and a small flat-screen television fixed to a bracket in the corner. The air-conditioner choked and whirred. A couple next door argued about something in a language he didn't understand.

He was tired, but he'd slept. He guessed he was in a hotel, but he didn't remember checking in. He moved to the door and checked the peephole. There was nobody in the corridor. He unlocked and opened the door, and something moved against it at the bottom.

A clear plastic bag. A label that read GARCIA. He picked up the bag and closed the door. A pair of suit trousers with a rip in the thigh, mended with no real enthusiasm, a white shirt, some undergarments, all freshly laundered. He laid out the clothes on the bed.

He had laid out his clothes like this before. It felt natural. A hotel room, sometimes a suite, the smell of tobacco, hair oil, and soap in the air. There were normally at least five or six men in the room, all of them with cigarettes or cigars in their mouths, drinks in their hands, most of their faces indistinguishable from the smoke that eddied the air in front of them.

Alejandro was there. So was Sancho.

The room fell silent as Rafael emerged from the bathroom, a towel around his waist. The mood of the room was dictated by him. If he joked, they joked. If he was silent, they wouldn't say a word.

His hair was combed and oiled, his body clean and smooth. He smoked a cigarette as the moisture evaporated from his skin and then dismissed everyone but Astrubal, his *mozo de espadas*, a hunchback with light blue eyes, dark skin, and a thick gray-and-white bristle that occupied the bottom half of his face. He was the only man allowed to help Rafael with his *traje de luces*, and Rafael always thought of the hunchback as a mute—in thirteen years of dressing, the man hadn't uttered a word. Whenever he needed to communicate, it was a series of grunts, clicks, and gestures, a shorthand that appeared to suit the ritual.

First came the pink stockings, two pairs, each smoothed up and over the calf and secured with elastic garters. Then he would tape his genitals to his dress thigh before he pulled on the knee-length underpants. Some toreros were known to bulk out with handkerchiefs at this point, but Rafael wasn't one of them. Astrubal brought over the first part of the suit, the *taleguilla*, a pair of silk britches that went from nipple to knee and that were so tight Rafael had to be helped into them in short, halting movements. Once in, the trousers were fastened just below the knee. Rafael held the lace with one finger as Astrubal tied the knots, one precisely positioned on the outside of each leg. As he slipped his feet into a pair of rubber-soled shoes, Astrubal would attach the *coleta* to the back of his head so it lay like a small ponytail down the back of his neck.

Then came the shirt, white and ruffled, and the braces pulled over that, and then the thin black tie that would be secured to his shirt, courtesy of Astrubal, with a single stitch. Following that was the sash, wound tightly around Rafael's waist, which secured the taleguilla. Astrubal looked him over then, clicked and nodded, and went to fetch his *chaquetilla*, the stiff, heavily embroidered silk jacket that felt like armor plating, even though it afforded him no protection in the plaza. At the shoulders, the jacket was fastened again by laces and topped with ornate epaulettes.

Finally, Rafael put on the black *montera*, adjusting the hat so it was on straight, and then stood in front of Astrubal for final inspection. Astrubal stepped back, scanned him from head to foot, then stepped forward and yanked on Rafael's jacket, jolting him in his suit. Then he prepared Rafael's ceremonial cape, his *capote de paseo*, which would be wrapped around his arm like a sling on his first parade into the plaza. Rafael's was particular to him. It bore large red roses which offset the red and gold of his chaquetilla and recalled the same flowers on Antonio Ordoñez's capote de paseo.

He approached his portable shrine. Pictures of La Macarena, the Virgin Mother, Jesus Christ, the saints, a worn picture of his mother. He kissed his thumb and pressed each photo in turn. He said a prayer—"I ask for your forgiveness for my human weakness"—and then lit a candle, which would stay lit until he returned to the room.

There was a candle burning now, a small tea light. Rafael stood in front of the full-length mirror, his image flickering. He wore the laundered clothes, carried the dagger in his right hand. It felt at home there. Somewhere in the back of his mind, he heard a paso doble.

He folded the piece of paper that he'd found on the table and that indicated exactly what he had to do, and then placed it into his back pocket. Then he walked to the door, pulled it open. A breeze blew out the candle.

He paused in the darkness, then left the room and went looking for the Casa de Verónica.

Twenty-Two

Rafael watched the café from across the street, only a few meters from where the taxi had dropped him off. It was easy to find places if you could afford a cab and, thanks to Alejandro, he could.

The café didn't look at all familiar, but Sancho was. Just like the note described—tall, dark haired, well dressed, perpetually grinning and smoking French cigarettes that were white filtered and came in a pack the size of a dresser drawer. The car was as the note described too—a white Land Rover, parked in an alley a five-minute walk from the café. The car sported temporary windows and bullet holes in the bodywork. Rafael had examined it up close and found it smelled of shampoo and something else, something rotten. Sancho was a vain man. He couldn't be seen in a battered car like that, but he didn't have any other transport, so he'd parked it out of the way.

He could have waited by the Land Rover, but he wanted to make sure that Sancho didn't leave with anyone. The note told him that he smiled at women. If that was the case, he might accidentally score and chance a taxi rather than take his car. That wouldn't do. He would have to break them up before they got too far. He hoped it wouldn't come to that. His thoughts were too bloody to deal with innocent people.

As it turned out, Sancho left with another man. The other man was short and dark skinned. He looked like an Arab or a

Moroccan. His hair was plastered back away from his face, and he was clearly drunk. They were walking as they hit the street, and then they split, Sancho heading in the direction of his car, the other man staggering off the opposite way. Rafael waited, then crossed the road, following Sancho at a distance. Then, when he was sure that Sancho was on his way back to the car, he took a shortcut around the block to where the Land Rover was parked. He waited in the darkness, his breathing low and steady, watching for Sancho.

Sure enough, after a minute or two, Sancho arrived at the mouth of the alley. He hummed to himself, his car keys dancing in one hand.

He cheeped off the alarm, then unlocked the car. When he opened the driver's-side door, Rafael ran at him. Sancho turned at the sound, couldn't see; one hand came up to protect himself as Rafael grabbed him by the shirt front and slammed him back against the side of the Land Rover. He bounced once, the keys flying out of his hand, and then Rafael swung him into the alley wall. Sancho hit the wall with his head and doubled up, dizzy and stumbling. Rafael shoved him toward a cluster of bins, where he lost his balance and dropped into a nest of black plastic bags. He kicked out, tried to get upright. He looked like a doomed insect.

And then, all at once, the energy drained out of him. He pulled out his wallet and held it out to Rafael, his other hand covering his head.

"Take it. Take what you want."

Rafael's shadow fell across Sancho. He saw the wet twinkle of an eye behind Sancho's arm.

"Please."

He was a coward. There was no fight in him. There never had been.

Rafael reached forward and grabbed Sancho by the shirt, bursting one of the plastic bags with his foot as he hauled Sancho to his feet and shoved him against the alley wall. The collision thumped the air out of his lungs with a muffled *huh*. Only then did Sancho see Rafael properly, and his expression went from fearful to terrified to conniving. He blinked, his mouth open, nothing but small clicking noises emerging from the back of his throat, the hard drive in his head struggling to come up with a decent story.

"Shh." Rafael kept his voice low. "Listen to me. Don't say anything. I know what you did. You know what you did."

"Please." Sancho found his voice, and it was shrill. "I didn't mean to—"

"Shh. I told you." Rafael pulled the dagger from the back of his trousers and pressed the tip against Sancho's lower gut. "We both know what you did. But you need to answer some questions. I need the whole story, okay?"

Sancho nodded and stared.

"Why did they try to kill me?"

"You talked."

"To who?"

"English customs."

"What did I say?"

"I don't know. They think you told them routes, drops, things like that."

"How did they know?"

Sancho glanced at the dagger, then showed his bottom teeth. "You were obvious about it. You were trying to skip out. They could smell it."

"Who are they?"

"They?"

He pressed the dagger into flesh.

Sancho gasped. "Frank Graham. Ollie Graham."

"Ollie is the gaffer, yes? Who's Frank?"

"Ollie's father. I never saw him. He's the real boss. Ollie takes care of the business, but Frank is the one who tells him what to do."

"What business?"

"Are you fucking kidding?"

The dagger broke the material and then broke skin.

"Jesus, *God*..." Sancho moved under Rafael's arm. "He's a middleman. They arc. They buy cannabis from the Moroccans and then they ship it to England. And they own hotels, bars, a ganadería—"

"He is a criminal."

"Yes."

"And I worked for him."

"Yes."

"What did I do?"

"I don't know. I think you drove. The way they talked about you, sounded like you were a driver." His voice jumped when he realized the answer wasn't good enough. "I got you in, Raf. I made introductions. You *wanted* in, so I got you in. I'm on the outside, though, I didn't...I don't know anything. I don't want to know. I just put people with people. I'm not involved. Nobody fucking tells me anything. Whatever you did, whatever you told customs, y'know, I'm good with that, I'm fine. I don't judge you for it. You did what you had to do. You had your reasons, right? You're a good man, you were probably doing the right thing. I don't know. But I swear, Raf, I didn't have anything to do with it. I didn't know about the mountains, man."

"You did. At the whorehouse. You knew about it then."

Sancho glanced around him. Panic in his face, a shudder in his jaw. He shifted under the blade, drew more blood, and then froze, pinned to the wall. "I had to."

"You had to?"

"It was for your own good. The way you were, they would have found you anyway. And I mean, what were you doing? You were talking about Alejandro—he couldn't help you. You were talking about your *family*. What would've happened if you'd gone back to Pilar? You would have put her and Sam in danger. I couldn't let you do that. And at least, right, if it was me controlling things, if

I delivered you, then there'd be a chance that I could plead your case, right? I stood up for you. I told them. I said you didn't remember anything, and they would've believed me if you hadn't done all that shit with the bull—"

"They put me in there to die. I didn't know what I was doing."

"I know that, but they're *English*, Raf. They don't know torero from tit fucking. You were supposed to be scared. That was all. Ollie's a joker. He likes to see men scared. He likes to show you who's boss. He did it to *scare* you. Christ, you know what he's like, you—"

"No, I don't."

Sancho's face tightened. "Listen to me, I saved your fucking life, all right? If it wasn't for me, Javier would've cut you up in the toilets and left you for dead. I got you out of that; I took care of you. I always took care of you. Whatever you needed, I got for you. I did *right* by you, *always*. If you remembered anything about the old life, you'd know that."

Rafael glanced at the mouth of the alley as a couple passed. They hadn't looked to their right, which was good. Sancho hadn't seen them either, which was better. "Frank Graham is the boss?"

"Yes."

"Where is he?"

"I don't know. He doesn't live at the ganadería. I think he has a villa in the hills, but I don't know where it is."

"Bullshit."

"I don't know; I swear to God." His eyes were watery. "When the fuck do I go there? I told you, Raf, I'm nobody, I'm on the outside. The English don't trust me. I'm just *useful* to them, I'm not a part of anything." He was nodding now, apparently oblivious to the pain in his stomach. "Ring any bells?" His bottom lip trembled and he sneered to kill the movement. "I don't know where it is. I was never invited. You'd have to ask one of the English. They're up there all the fucking time."

"Where do I find one?"

"Anywhere you want. They own the coast."

"Where tonight?" He removed the dagger and pressed it into Sancho's other side, where the nerves still worked.

"Anywhere, I told you. The Water Line, the Red Lion, Flying Dutchman, Flanagans."

"Are those bars?"

"*Pubs.*" Sancho spat the English word as if it were rancid. "You want to check the Water Line. That's where you'll find some of the seconds."

"Where is it?"

"On the beach. But take my advice and forget about it. Just disappear."

"I can't."

"It's the only way. They own the police, Raf. They own the local government. You can't hurt them. You can't even talk to them."

Rafael felt tired. He lowered the dagger and stepped back. "Your wallet and your car keys."

"Listen to me, Raf—"

"Wallet. Car keys."

Sancho put his wallet in Rafael's free hand. He gestured at the ground. "I don't have the keys. I think I dropped them, but take them, I don't care. Take whatever you need, okay?" He nodded at the wallet. "There's still a bit of money in there and I won't call in the cards for a couple of days, all right? Give you a head start so you can get to Portugal or France. I won't say anything to the Grahams, I promise." He smiled. "I always looked out for you, Raf. Really I did. We were brothers."

Rafael felt a tremble inside his chest, but his hands remained still. He breathed out, put the wallet in his back pocket. He saw the car keys shining on the ground by the car. He waved the dagger at Sancho. "Turn around."

"What?"

"Face the wall."

Sancho did as he was told. As soon as he saw brick, he started speaking again. "You're a good man, Raf. You always were. I'm sorry for introducing you to all this, I really am. If I'd known it was all going to turn out like this, I would have warned you, kept you away. I would've told you the old man was right, you should've stuck with the toros." He sighed. He was smiling. He shook his head. "But it is what it is. For what it's worth, amigo, I'm glad you're leaving. I never wanted to see you die, and you're not a killer."

"A matador."

"A matador de toros, Raf. Not a killer of men. You're too good for that."

"You think so?"

"I know so."

"Huh."

Sancho saw the blade glitter out in front of him. He opened his mouth but the dagger killed the scream, the blade dipping in behind the windpipe and then through and out. Blood sprayed the wall in a fine arc. Rafael stepped back, the dagger held at arm's length, his back straight and his chin raised. Sancho made a wet sound and stumbled face-first into the wall. Rafael stepped back a little farther. Sancho slid down the brick, his legs folding underneath him, one hand up to his throat. He turned as he dropped. His shirt made a noise like ripping paper as it scraped down the wall. His hand was slick and black with blood by the time he reached the ground, his eyes intent on Rafael.

Rafael watched him goldfish until Sancho's eyes lost focus and his hand slipped from his open throat to his bloody chest. He waited a moment longer, watching for light or signs of movement, but there was nothing. He crouched and wiped the dagger on Sancho's shirt, retrieved the car keys and got behind the wheel of the

Land Rover. He started the engine and adjusted the mirror. He saw a thin spray of blood on his face and wiped it off with the back of his hand.

He hoped that the others wouldn't be as messy. There was only so much blood a man could take.

Twenty-Three

"You all right, babes?"

Lisa touched Tony's arm, brought his attention back to the room. It was dimly lit, warm colored, sweaty, and loud. He smelled the black currant on her breath, the strong scent of the rum that went with it. She was looking at him, expecting an answer, so he gave her a smile and a shake of the head, and soon the ambient noise of the pub swallowed him again. Lawrence was there, bandaged under his chinos and telling the long, loud story of how he'd managed to get himself gored that afternoon, or at least the version of the story that he was permitted to tell, which didn't include an amnesiac matador pulling a fast one on them. This was the one where they were all up at the ranch and someone thought it'd be a good idea to let out one of Ollie's bulls to give it a cape and that. Jill rolled her eyes at that, shared a disgusted look with Lisa, like *aren't men idiots?*

"They're this special breed. Miura. And they're nasty bastards. I mean, you know that look what Cooper gets when he sees a cat? That kind of, that…" Lawrence attempted to look like his Rottweiler focusing on a cat. "I'm gonna fucking *hurt* you. Like that. Except it's attached to a great big fuck-off animal with great big fuck-off horns." He raised both eyebrows, nodded at Tony. "Tell you, one of those bastards comes at you, you better get out of the way."

"Except you didn't." Tony sipped his beer.

"Except I didn't."

"Because you're a fat bastard."

Jill slapped Lawrence's shoulder. "I told him he should lose weight. I did."

"She did. She said I should lose weight because otherwise I'd get fucking gored." He nodded. "Her exact words."

Another slap of the shoulder. "Shut up, you."

Tony smiled but didn't join in the laughter. He excused himself from the table, said he was going out for a smoke. Somewhere in the place they were playing Adele, which was as good a reason as any for walking out. The music was like ground glass in his ears, just like the shit craic that passed for light conversation these days. It was Lawrence talking about his near-death experience, Max and his apartment block up in the Blanca where the holiday tenants were "fucking animals, honest to God," or how they all thought Scott was a fucking arse bandit because he never went out on the pull with the younger lads like Liam and Chris, or Doug the Geezer's missus Lorraine talking about how he got drunk and fell asleep on the beach and got himself burned all over—"Tell you, it's been a nightmare. He's been shitting rusty water for three days and he still can't wear clothes."

Or, above all that, talking about the Jubilee. Did Tony and Lisa see it on the telly, the big show? Wasn't it lovely? Did Her Majesty proud, didn't they? And was everyone going up to the villa tomorrow for the big lunch? Then Max said that he was looking forward to getting hammered in the gaffer's house, but his missus was having none of it, because the kids were going to be there, and he wasn't going to show her up like he did at Gemma's tenth birthday party. That turned the conversation on to alcohol and they all talked about how much they drank on a daily, weekly, monthly basis; and it was all bollocks, every last word of it, because they only counted spirits, only counted the times they got off their faces, and you only needed to look at them to know that they went to bed sober maybe one night of the week.

It grated on him. It made him raw. And so he had to leave the table.

He went out to the terrace, where he lit a Benson and checked his mobile for messages.

Still nothing. That wasn't good.

By the time they left the old man's apartment, it had been getting on for five o'clock. He had to head home and get showered and dressed for the night out, but he told Jason to hang back in the Mazda and give him a ring if the rabbit came back. He went home, drank a Red Bull, got in the shower, and when he came out, his mobile was ringing. The rabbit had showed up.

"How's he looking?"

"Like shit."

"All right, keep an eye on him. If he leaves, follow him and give us another ring, all right?" Checking his watch to make sure he still had enough time to pop over there and finish this before it was time for the pub. Because he knew this was important, but he didn't relish the idea of an all-night nag from Lisa, either. "You can handle this, Jase. Counting on you, son."

He disconnected, got dressed. The mobile went off again.

"The police are here."

"How many?"

"Just the one car."

Like a fucking miracle, like God had sent some other poor bastards to do the dirty work for once.

"You want me to stay or what?" Jason sounded nervous. He'd never really encountered the Spanish filth before, didn't know how to play them even when he knew they were on the same side. Hadn't been that long ago he'd wanted to give one of them a dig, for crying out loud. "I mean, I can follow them—"

"You said he's in a state?"

"Yeah."

"Then leave it. Go home. He's not going to give a couple of armed police any trouble, not if he knows what's good for him. I'll follow up with Manuel."

And that was the plan in a nutshell. Let the Spanish coppers either shoot the rabbit for trying to resist or else take him into custody. If he got shot, the job was sorted. If he didn't, he'd call Manuel and get them to hold the rabbit in a cell until he could get out of the pub. That wouldn't be too hard for them, either. Tony assumed they'd have the rabbit on a murder suss at least. So there was no way he'd be out in less than twenty-four hours, and if he clammed up, they could ship him off to prison, no bother—fuckers over here could hold you for two years without a charge. All Tony needed to do was get the confirmation from Manuel, and Bob's your auntie's common-law husband.

Except he'd already left two messages for Manuel, and the greasy little shitbag had yet to call him back, which set all sorts of alarm bells ringing.

He blew smoke and leaned against the railing, watching the people walk on the beach. The usual red-faced tourists and linen-clad pensioners were out in force. The Spanish didn't come out this early—they were night owls—and if they did come out at all, they'd come out in Puerto Banús. This stretch of the beach was 100 percent British. Pubs as far as the eye could see, outdoor terraces and café-style seating, lots of expats thinking they were being all fucking cosmopolitan because they were drinking San Miguel instead of Carling.

His shirt kept sticking to his skin. He pulled at it. He felt fat and warm. He checked his mobile again.

Still nothing.

Things were going to shit; he could feel it. Manuel might have been a prize arsehole but he knew on which side his bread was buttered, and he knew better than to fuck about too much with the

Grahams. He called Manuel's mobile again, and it went straight to voice mail. He thought about disconnecting, but then a surge of frustration made him speak. "Manuel, it's Tony. I know you've got a fella there called Rafael Ortega? Picked him up this afternoon. Listen, give us a ring back and let us know what the situation is with him, will you? He's the rabbit you let slip the other day. Be terrible if I had to tell my gaffer you did it twice in one week, eh? You know the number, son. Give it a ring."

He disconnected and noticed his hand was trembling. He put it down to anger, but he knew it wasn't. He questioned what he'd just said, whether it had been too much information for a voice mail that anyone could listen to. He let out a breath, but there was no smoke attached to it.

Getting para. Getting scared. Losing your bottle.

He stuffed the mobile into his pocket.

He hadn't lost his bottle. He was fine. It was just—like he said before, just like he said before—it was just *fatigue* making him shake, clouding his mind, making him nervous. And if he was absolutely honest with himself, the old man had thrown him off a bit.

There, he'd admitted it.

The defiance the old bastard had shown was one thing. He hadn't expected that. Old men crumpled quickly once they remembered what real pain felt like. He also hadn't expected the old man's attitude to piss him off so much. It was like he knew that Tony's nerve was going, and he leaned on it. Truth be told, it made Tony lose his composure a little bit—that and the tiredness, of course—and that was why he'd gone to work on the old man's fingers. He wanted to hurt the old bastard, really fucking wreck him, but maybe he'd gone too far, because all he did after the first finger was burble on about a kid in a park. It was a lapse in judgment. Just like the first bullet was a lapse in concentration. He'd almost told Jason to finish the old man off. It would've taken the heat off him and blooded the boy at the same time, but in the end he couldn't do it. Because that would have been an admission of failure, and Tony didn't do stuff like that.

So he'd shot the old man again himself. And there was a part of him that still wondered if the old man was dead when they left the apartment.

He sucked on the filter, blew smoke impatiently. Of course he was dead. They'd carpeted the place with his brain.

Still, he checked the mobile once more. And still there was nothing.

"Tony, you coming back in or what?"

Lisa appeared at his side. She put her arms around his waist. His damp shirt stuck to his skin. He smoked the edge of the filter and ditched the Benson. "Yeah, I'm coming."

"You thinking?"

"Yeah."

"Work?"

He nodded.

"They're still talking about the Jubilee in there."

"Still?"

"Doing my head in. Do we have to go?"

"Lisa—"

"I know. I'm just kidding. Kind of." She moved in closed behind him, rested her head on his shoulder. "You're not working tonight, are you?"

He thought about Manuel and Jason. He thought about the rabbit and felt himself getting worked up again. "No. I'm half-pissed already."

"Then come on and get whole pissed. Take the night off. We've got Kirsty looking after the kids until ten, and they'll be in bed when we get home." She eased round in front of him, smiling. One of her hands strayed to his belt. In the light, she looked soft and pale again. "Okay?"

He nodded.

She gave him a wide, white, youthful grin that kick-started his circulation. "Attaboy."

Lisa led him back toward the pub, the sea a white noise that signaled nothing, the music on the loudspeakers a white noise that signaled even less, and Tony's mind staggered into a drunken blank. He let himself be carried away on the tides of banal chatter and cheap jokes and tried not to think too much about the silent mobile in his pocket or Sancho's Land Rover, which was parked halfway up the street.

Twenty-Four

Rafael watched the one he remembered as Tony go back into the bar, a woman hanging off him. He waited and watched. Soon, the fat man came out. He remembered the fat man. He wore a pair of light-colored trousers that looked bulky on one thigh, and a blue shirt, open three buttons from the throat, under a jacket that matched the trouser in color and in bulk, a lump of what could've been a holster or an oversized wallet just under the fat man's heart. Even at this distance, the man's clothes looked as if they resented his size, straining at the seams, even more so when he leaned against the terrace. He rolled a cigar between his fingers as he touched a flaming match to one end, puffing great clouds of smoke that forced a cough out of the man next to him and, as he turned, detours out of anyone passing by. This was the one who'd been gored. Rafael remembered the shape and heft of him, remembered thinking that the fat man was too large and slow a target to miss.

He still was. From the slight sway in his walk, Rafael guessed the man was drunk, a guess confirmed when he watched the fat man miss his mouth with the cigar. Rafael flipped open the glove compartment and retrieved the small, steel-finish pistol he'd discovered earlier. It held six shots and disappeared into his hand, but it looked clean and serviceable. He doubted it had ever been used—from what he remembered of Sancho, he was the kind of man who'd rather gab his way out of a bad situation than shoot.

He shook off the memory. The piece of paper warned him about that. And as long as the gun looked the part, it would do.

Rafael started the engine. He let the Land Rover roll slowly toward the pub. Just then, a plump little apple of a woman appeared behind the fat man and tugged on his sleeve. Rafael slowed the car to a stop. The fat man's wife—she couldn't be anything else—said something to the fat man that made him look indignant, then put upon. She pointed at the street, and he pointed at the bar. There was a discussion that went on for three minutes by the dashboard clock and that ended with the wife waving at someone in the bar and hustling her fat husband away from the terrace. Her face was the same color as the roses on her dress, and she looked as if she were telling her husband a particularly long and personally upsetting story, while the fat man sucked blankly on his cigar and limped along behind.

Rafael hadn't figured on a couple, but this was the best opportunity he'd get. He opened and closed his fingers around the pistol and eased his foot against the accelerator as the couple turned onto the street and continued away from him. The Land Rover was distinctive enough for the fat man to recognize, and it was dark enough that he wouldn't ask himself who was driving. Rafael tailed the couple for about twenty meters before they turned into a street, and he turned with them, buzzing down the passenger window at the same time. He revved the engine. The fat man looked round, saw the car.

Rafael kept his voice neutral and his face slightly lowered. "Ollie wants to see you."

"Me?" No other questions, no who-the-fuck-are-yous. Too drunk, too stupid, or too dark to recognize Rafael in the shadows.

Just as he'd hoped. "Yes, you."

The fat man looked to his wife for support. She peered into the car. Rafael felt his fingers tighten around the pistol. He glanced in the side mirror. There were too many people around. His voice hardened. "Now. You want to keep the gaffer waiting?"

"No. I suppose not." The fat man moved toward the car, put his hand on the door.

His wife's face crumpled and became darker in color. "You're not going?"

"I have to, love. It's work."

She pointed back the way they'd come. "Then he can get one of the others in there to go along, can't he?" She squinted at him. "Can't you?"

"They are coming too."

"You see?" The fat man shrugged. He moved in front of the passenger-side door, blocking Rafael's view of the wife, and hers of him. He pictured raising the gun and squeezing the trigger, a couple of small shots piercing the fat man's back, and then hitting the gas as the wife screeched the buildings down around her.

But he couldn't do that. The only thing the fat man had done was pick bad friends, an accusation that could've also been leveled at Rafael, if the piece of paper was to be believed. The fat man had information, and that was enough to keep him alive for now.

"Tick tock." Rafael revved the engine. "Time to go."

"I need to go, love."

"What am I supposed to do?"

"Here, look, get a cab, all right?" The fat man fumbled with money.

Rafael looked in the rearview mirror. There were more people approaching, definitely English from the lobster complexion and the lack of coordination. He hoped they weren't the fat man's friends, hoped the wife wouldn't say anything to them, because if she did, then he would have to take off and regroup. One of the men behind the Land Rover shouted something. Rafael looked at the fat man, who was too busy giving his wife the cab fare and excuses to bother with the shouts of another drunk expat.

"I'm sorry, love, all right? I'll be home when I can." The fat man opened the passenger door, his back still to Rafael. "Don't wait up, all right?"

"Yeah, all right." She sighed. It was an irritated sound. "You be careful, Lawrence."

"I will." He eased into the passenger seat and pulled the door closed.

Rafael leaned on the accelerator, and the Land Rover lurched forward. Lawrence put both hands on the dashboard to brace himself and swore at the same time. Rafael turned the wheel and accelerated further. He glanced in the rearview and saw Lawrence's dumpy wife watch them leave with a confused expression on her face.

She wasn't the only one. "What the fuck d'you think you're playing at, Sancho?"

Rafael jammed the muzzle of the pistol into what he guessed was either Lawrence's scrotum or the roll of fat that protected it.

Lawrence saw the gun, looked up at Rafael, and then froze as the situation became clear and the alcohol leached from his system.

Rafael glanced at him, then back at the road. "You move, I shoot. Do you understand?"

The fat man's voice was thin. "Yes."

He was carrying a weapon, but he wouldn't make the move. He knew better than to provoke a man with a gun pointed at his balls. He'd lose his cojones before he touched his jacket. He was old, slow, and injured. So he huffed out a sigh and attempted to tighten his face enough so that his bottom lip didn't tremble, but the quiver in his double chin gave him away.

"Your name is Lawrence?"

"Yes."

"Okay, Lawrence, if you tell me what I need to know, I will not hurt you." Rafael turned the Land Rover up a backstreet that overlooked waste ground, padlocked dumpsters, and an old VW van. He killed the engine and shifted in his seat. The fat man didn't move. "Put your gun on the dashboard, please."

"I don't have a gun."

"I am not stupid, Lawrence. You of all people should know that. You have a gun. Put it on the dashboard, please. One hand. Slowly."

Lawrence's face shifted in waves and he raised one hand from the dashboard, opening his fingers and then slowly bringing the hand round to the lump in his jacket. Rafael dug his pistol farther into the soft folds of flesh under Lawrence's belt. Lawrence froze.

"I said slowly."

Lawrence nodded, moved slower as he reached into his jacket and brought out a small revolver. He gently laid the gun on the dashboard and held up both hands. "There. Take it."

Rafael leaned forward and pushed the pistol into Lawrence as he grabbed the revolver. Lawrence flinched and let out a grunt that ended on a squeak and appeared to make his whole body shiver. He was frightened. That was good. It would make everything easier. Rafael tested the weight of the revolver in his hand. It was heavy. It would probably kick like a mule, and he probably wouldn't be able to hit anything with it. He removed the pistol from Lawrence's underbelly and shoved it into his trouser pocket. The fat man visibly relaxed.

Rafael continued to inspect the revolver. "You work for Ollie Graham, yes?"

As questions went, it clearly wasn't the one that Lawrence had been expecting. He could barely keep the contempt from his voice. "You know I fucking do."

"Where is he?"

"I don't know."

"He is not at home?"

"The fuck do I know?" He moved his shoulders. "All right, he's at home."

"You know that?"

"It's plausible."

"Where is his home?"

Lawrence turned a little in his seat. Rafael lifted the revolver.

"Show me where his home is."

Lawrence stared at him. He was less frightened now. He knew that Rafael couldn't remember. "I don't know."

"It was not a question."

"I don't know which place he's at, do I?"

"The ranch. The ganadería—where is that?"

"I don't know."

"You were there today."

"In the *day*time, yeah. But it's black as fuck out there. I'm not going to be able to show you fuck all, mate."

"What is the address?"

"It doesn't have one."

Rafael looked at the revolver.

"No, I mean it. It's a fucking ranch in the middle of nowhere, isn't it?"

A place found more by intuition than direction. They could drive around the countryside all night and they wouldn't see anything that wasn't within a hundred meters or so. Rafael let out a breath and lowered the gun. He leaned against the driver's door and looked out of the side window.

He turned and opened his mouth to speak. "Okay, Lawrence—"

There was a creak of the seat, a rush of air as the passenger door flew open, and Lawrence was out of the car and trying to run. He hadn't closed the passenger door properly. He was already planning his escape then. Which was disappointing, because it meant that Lawrence was fat *and* stupid.

Rafael got out of the car. He heard Lawrence's scuffed, limping footsteps as he attempted to run. Lawrence cried out for help. Rafael aimed the revolver at Lawrence's good leg and fired. There was an explosion that made Rafael blink, and he heard Lawrence's muted scream above the ringing in his ears. The fat man had pitched forward, a mess of blood just under the back of his knee. Rafael waggled a finger in his ear—the gunshot had been louder than expected. The recoil made his wrist ache.

Something crackled and broke in his ear, and his hearing returned, bringing with it a high-pitched ringing sound.

Lawrence wasn't screaming anymore. Now he sobbed into the grit and made scratching noises as he tried to crawl away. Rafael watched him until the ringing in his ears had disappeared and Lawrence had bled and weakened enough to make moving him a nonviolent prospect. Then Rafael returned to the Land Rover and opened the back.

Episode Six

Twenty-Five

Tony had to admit it wasn't every day you got to celebrate something like the Diamond Jubilee. Once every thirty-five years, as that smart arse Max put it. Otherwise, you had your St. George's Day and every couple of years you had your Euro Cup or your World Cup, and they'd all celebrate for the short time that England was actually involved, normally stinking up the pitch the whole fucking time, and then there'd be the longer after-session to commiserate with others on their homeland's apparent inability to field a team of anyone other than arse-faced spastics. And if Spain was in there—as it typically was, seeing as Spain was a country that knew its football—then they'd support it for as long as it took.

But the Diamond Jubilee—that was something special, because that was a party up at Ollie's villa, which had views out across the coast and was big enough to accommodate every one of his employees and their families. It was one big happy company outing, a chance for Ollie to show off and for his dad to get out and about.

After all, the way the rumors went, Frank Graham wasn't long for this world.

Once upon a time he'd worn sharp and packed sharper. He was a man who'd made his money on the backs of a million scratching junkies and who'd parlayed that dirty cash into the big holiday apartment boom of the mid-1980s, which he'd then apparently further parlayed into regular shipments of African weed, choosing to live out his later years in comparative safety. He'd been a big man back in the day, crowning six four and barrel chested. Now his legs were spindly, blue veined, and always awkwardly arranged, and the shirts he would've once used as hankies now hung off him. Ollie liked to dress the old man in bright colors. It was supposed to be fun, but anyone who'd had the dubious pleasure of dealing with Frank Graham back in the day would've had trouble finding the man's Hawaii look anything but sarcastic. Nobody said anything, but the sick look on the old man's face coupled with Ollie's obvious enjoyment spoke volumes.

Right now the Grahams were still asleep. The only people moving on the villa grounds were employees. The place stood like a large white horseshoe, surrounded by trees on all sides and gated, up on the edge of the hills that overlooked Marbella and the coast. They called it the Villa Del Barón—as if anyone living under its roof would have ties to nobility—and there were currently five people up and about. There was the maid, Carmelita, who was said to dirty the sheets as much as she cleaned them. Then there was Liam, the ex-boxer from Staines, who was out the back by the pool and the gardenias; and Big Chris, who was down by the gates talking to Tony and Max and sipping take-out coffee. Tony and Max weren't needed up at the house just yet, and it was better to hang out around the gates than inside. They couldn't smoke in the villa; it was always freakishly cold; and there was the chance you'd accidentally bump into the old man, which was always bad news. Nobody left a conversation with Frank Graham without wanting to butt up against a radiator for a while.

Max was busy examining Big Chris's gun. He'd wanted one of the little Czech submachine guns for a while, ever since he fired a Škorpion on a firing range over in Tenerife; and he was gabbing on about it while Tony tramped gravel, smoked his Regal, and tried to ignore his hangover and the fact that Manuel still hadn't fucking called.

Instead, Jill rang Tony's mobile and asked him in a trembling voice if Lawrence had arrived at the villa.

"No, Jill. I haven't seen him since last night. Is he not with you, then?"

"He went off with that lad Sancho last night."

"Ah well, then he's probably fine. Probably just got pissed up and he's asleep somewhere. I wouldn't worry about it."

"He said it was business."

Tony smiled. Wasn't the first time someone had used business as an excuse to pull an all-nighter. "Oh right. Okay, well, we haven't seen him up here yet, but I'll keep an eye out, all right?"

"Okay." She didn't sound convinced.

"You're coming up to the villa, yeah?"

"Yes."

"I'll see you then, then."

She hung up, and Tony disconnected. Wasn't like Lawrence to fuck about like that, especially not with Sancho. As far as Tony knew, they didn't really get on. Lawrence wasn't fond of the Spanish, and he always referred to Sancho as "that little brown poof."

"What's that?" Max had looked up from the gun.

"Jill. Says Lawrence hasn't been home yet."

"Russians sold him into slavery."

Tony smiled. Whenever they were late, it was always the Russians' fault. The Russians kidnapped my wife; the Russians ambushed me on the way out to my car; I didn't get much sleep last night because a Russian assassin tried to garrote me and the wife. They were the boogeymen, but they were always "they." No matter how much you wanted to joke, you never mentioned an individual name, especially not Turgenev's. That had a way of killing any joke stone dead.

"What would they want with Lawrence?"

"Some lads pay extra for a bigger man."

Big Chris pulled a face. "You're not fucking right, you."

"What?"

"That's the first thing that came into your head, was it?"

"I'm telling you, it happens. It's *specific*—"

"Very fucking specific."

"But there's some fellas like a bit of meat on their sex slaves."

"Says the happily married father of two."

Max smiled. "I'm just saying, different strokes for different folks."

"You keep your fucking strokes away from me." Big Chris took his gun back. "Oi-oi, speak of the devil."

Tony turned. It wasn't Lawrence; it was Scott's Merc appearing at the foot of the driveway. It was a new model, black, with tinted windows. Scott was a single bloke, what Tony's mum would've called a "confirmed bachelor" and what everyone else round here called an arse bandit. Not that Scott's sexuality really bothered Tony or the rest of them that much. They envied the fucker's disposable income than anything else. He wasn't tied down with a wife and kids; he could afford a brand-new Merc with gangster trimmings. And so even though they didn't mean it, the lads tended to refer to Scott as an arse rapist rather than a gay gentleman. The three men watched as the Merc shuddered to a stop in front of the gates.

The driver's window buzzed down. Scott looked at them. He was blond, styled, young, and slender. "Ollie up yet?"

Tony shook his head.

"I need to see him."

"You'll have to wait."

"It's urgent."

Tony glanced at his watch. "It'll have to wait."

"Sancho's dead."

There was a pause while the men took that in. Tony frowned. "Where'd you hear that?"

"I think I better talk to Ollie."

"No, Scott, you'll talk to me." Tony dropped his cigarette. "It's the Jubilee, mate. Ollie's all keyed up for that, so you need to be sure it's something worth distracting him for, know what I mean?"

"He's *dead*."

"So he's going to have questions, isn't he? And those questions better be answered quick-fucking-smart if you're dragging him out of his pit. What happened?"

"He was robbed. At least, that's what the police are saying. His throat was cut."

"Could be a robbery."

"Could be, yeah. Or it could be someone did him and then took his wallet to make it *look* like a robbery."

"You been over to the comisaría, then?"

"Yeah."

"Well, what're they doing about it?"

"What do you think they're doing about it? When given a choice of two, they always go for fuck all, don't they? It's open and shut—"

"All right." Tony waved at him to calm down. "Don't get yourself worked up."

"He was known, wasn't he? The police aren't going to dig any more than they have to, are they?"

Another wave as Tony took out his phone and dialed Lawrence. One thing at a time.

"It's probably nothing." Max shook his head. "Probably the lad just got unlucky and pissed off the wrong bloke. You know what these Latin types are like. Very emotional."

Scott frowned at him. "You think that's plausible?"

"Shh." The phone connected, and then the call went to Lawrence's voice mail. "Fuck's sake."

"What is it?"

"Voice mail. Lawrence turned his phone off."

"Lawrence?" Scott looked confused. "We were talking about Sancho—"

"And Sancho picked him up last night, didn't he? Just got off the phone to Jill. She said Sancho came by, picked up Lawrence and that was the last she saw of him."

Max laughed. "You don't think Lawrence had anything to do with it, do you?"

"No." Tony felt for his cigarettes and lit another. He wiped his nose and walked to the side of the drive, staring off behind Scott's Merc. It was a long way down to the main road, and this was the only way up to the villa unless you wanted to run through the trees. One of the reasons the Grahams bought the place was its position. It was their citadel. Nothing was getting up here without their knowledge.

"Tony?" Max's voice. "What d'you think we should do?"

He turned. All eyes on him. He was senior man, and in the absence of anyone with the surname Graham, he was the one they'd listen to. It was a rare moment of power, but Tony didn't want it. He didn't want any of this, because it was "damned if you do and damned if you don't."

Fuck it.

"All right, call up to the villa, Chris, will you? Better be on the safe side."

Twenty-Six

The room was cold, damp, and green. A strip ran along all four walls at waist height. It was an alarm. A table and two chairs stood in the middle of the room, and in one corner of the ceiling a camera gazed down at them, its one black eye cold and implacable.

Rafael was leaning over the table, his head low. He was shattered and dirty, his face raw with tears, and his head whirling with the possibilities of prison abroad. He was in England, but only just—stopped at the ferry gate and taken to one side. Patted down and searched, asked questions about the load, where he'd picked it up from, who'd packed it, who he was driving for, all the rest of it. And then they put him in this room. He could still smell the rain on his clothes, the exhaust fumes, the overnight sweat, and the belch in his throat from that petrol station *croque-monsieur*. He let his chin rest against the metal tabletop and stared at a stain on the far wall.

There was another man in the room with him. The other man was portly, round of gut and head. He wore a cheap suit—they all wore cheap suits round here—and sported mismatched socks in scuffed shoes. His face was smooth, his hands small and knotted in his lap. He watched Rafael now, just as he'd watched him for the last two hours. Waiting for Rafael to answer his last question. Not pushing, playing patient, and waiting him out. He had all the time in the world, he'd said. Nothing to get away for. The longer Rafael took, the better it was for him—he'd put in for overtime and coin it—so he didn't care if he had to stay here all night. "Fact is, Rafael, my old son, we have you bang to rights. You don't get to feign innocence here. So the only question is, how long do we have to wait before you roll?"

Without food or drink, without a toilet break, without so much as another word, it took five hours. Rafael felt the stress roll into a ball that expanded inside his head until the pressure was too much. He raised his head and fixed the man with a stare. "What happens to me if I tell you?"

"I told you that."

"Tell me again."

"We talk, Rafael. That's all we do. If you have something to exchange, we look to exchange, but I'm not offering up nothing until we get something from you first. And if you don't talk, that's fine. I can wait."

"Frank Graham."

"A name. Could be anyone."

"You know Frank Graham."

"I know *a* Frank Graham."

"He is a drug runner. I work for him. I work for Ollie Graham, his son."

"And what can you tell me about these people, Rafael?"

"Anything you want."

The man smiled. He could see the desperation. He could see the family back in Marbella, the fear of prison, the man recognizing when he'd hit rock bottom. No doubt he'd seen it hundreds of times before, and he'd used it to his advantage every time.

And the time with Rafael was no different.

"Tell me about Frank Graham."

He did. Frank Graham was the old man. He was never seen. Some people said he was ill; others said he was too important to show his face in public in case someone took it upon themselves to put a bullet in it.

"What about Ollie Graham?"

Ollie Graham was the gaffer. He was the day-to-day boss. He ran the business.

"The load there, under the oranges—"

"That is their business, yes."

Cannabis, with occasional side trips into coke and synthetics, but not often enough to count on. A marathon run from Morocco to Hackney; they kept the runs large and well protected.

Palmer smiled. "Most of the time."

Most of the time. They were quiet about their disputes, and if things got a little too noisy, they had enough tame police to smooth it over.

"Inside men, eh?" Palmer shook his head sadly. "What a terrible state of affairs. And the Spanish police are normally so bloody *upright*."

Rafael was given a number and a name. The number belonged to a mobile phone, the name, Gavin Palmer, was obviously false. The man in the cheap suit was to be Rafael's contact. He was based in Málaga, a little way up the coast, and as far as Rafael knew, he was responsible for the ongoing operation against a few specific drug smugglers in the south of Spain. Frank and Ollie Graham were near the bottom of his priority list and only really present because of Frank's past criminal life. Just like the Spanish police, British customs were more interested in the trafficking of coke and cigarettes than they were in cannabis. But Palmer wasn't the kind of man who turned his nose up at free information and a willing informant. And so Rafael was tasked with monthly reports, punctuated with major updates whenever there was a shipment of any size. They didn't do anything to the Grahams, they just monitored, and it got to the point that Rafael wasn't even sure if Palmer was customs or not.

And then they found out.

Rafael didn't remember how. A monthly meeting. Perhaps someone had seen them out at one of the rest stops out on the motorway, even though they always picked them at random. Sometimes luck was like that. Mala suerte.

No. Not mala suerte. No such thing. He'd wanted to get caught. He'd wanted to leave. He'd wanted something to force either a change of life or its premature end. He'd lost his nerve before, with the bulls. And then he'd lost his nerve again, with the business. He wanted to be punished. It was the only logical reason. Just like Alejandro used to say, a man held his own fate in both hands. What happened was his choice, filtered through the will of God. Or maybe it was supposed to be the other way around. He couldn't remember.

Palmer was trying to get him to stay when the two men arrived. The older one, Tone, had called him by his name. And when Palmer tried to make his excuses, he was press-ganged into following.

And then the desert and the mountains.

He opened his eyes now to the same. Wondered what time it was. The sky had gone from black to brilliant blue. There was a pueblo off in the distance, a rough cluster of buildings, and the odd car; but there was nobody walking around.

It was still early, and Rafael was remembering.

The piece of paper told him not to. The piece of paper told him to kill any memories before he got too caught up. Because every time he remembered something old, something from the past life, he came out of it discombobulated, grasping at the present with a blank mind and a quivering guilt.

The past tried to suck him in now. If it succeeded, he would die—he knew that much, knew it without the scrawl on the piece of paper to tell him so.

The piece of paper told him everything. His name was Rafael Ortega. He used to be a matador, but he worked for a man named Frank Graham and his son, Ollie. They had tried to kill him. They might still kill his wife and child. They *did* kill his apoderado. The only way to stop them was to take the dagger to them. The piece of paper told him to focus on that above all else. If he faltered, he would fall into memory. If he fell into memory, he would die.

The chances were he'd die anyway. But he refused to go quietly, and he refused to let anyone get hurt because of him, especially those people he might have loved once.

He looked in the rearview mirror. Lawrence lay in the back of the Land Rover, breathing heavily. Machismo was a loose fit on Lawrence, and yet he'd tried to man his way through. But Rafael had taken a leaf out of Palmer's book—this was why he'd started to remember the man—and sat silently and patiently and waited for the fat man to talk. With gentle persistence and time on his side, Rafael had managed to erode the fat man's bluster until he showed himself as the raw wound he really was, old and frightened and in considerable pain, his bravado shuddering into sobs, the information running as freely as the tears from his eyes.

Rafael smoked French cigarettes as he listened, making the odd note. The piece of paper was right—his short-term memory was on the slide. The present stayed with him for minutes, but if he was going to make it through this, he'd have to hold on to it a little harder, otherwise it would continue to exist in flashes of information that didn't quite knit into a narrative. The piece of paper held the salient points and told him to be vigilant.

He sloshed the water around the bottom of the bottle, then threw it over Lawrence. He flinched and coughed.

"Wake up. Time to talk."

Lawrence looked around the inside of the Land Rover as if he wasn't sure where he was. Once he remembered, a pained expression creased his face and he lowered his head.

"Your boss. You were going to tell me where he is."

"I can't."

"You told me about the villa."

It was in the hills above Marbella. Secluded, accessed by one two-mile private road and a set of security gates that were manned by armed guards. In the villa were more guards—at least two at any given time. They were also armed.

Maybe today would be different. Maybe it wouldn't.

"Tell me about today."

"They're having a party for the Jubilee. Having all the families round."

"They are armed today?"

"Probably."

Rafael tossed the empty bottle out of the window and let the breeze clear out the sweaty funk that had thickened the air in the car over the last hour or so. "Are they expecting you to attend?"

"Yes."

"Will they be looking for you if you do not?"

"Yeah. My wife's probably already called the police."

"Good." Rafael took the fat man's phone from the dashboard. "You have fine friends, Lawrence. Only one missed call and no message." He looked at Lawrence in the mirror. "Do you think they will miss you?"

Lawrence didn't answer. He tried to roll over, but his bulk and the pain kept him on his front. He breathed out a long, slow groan.

"You know where the villa is."

"No."

"How else would you attend the party? You will tell me where the villa is."

"I can't do that."

Rafael stared at the back of his head, then nodded as if he understood. He got out of the Land Rover. His feet felt good against the ground, and he stretched his legs a little as he walked round to the back of the car. He flicked the cigarette as far as he could and watched it bounce into some dry-looking bushes. He pulled open the back door. Lawrence tried to turn and look up but couldn't see much beyond his shoulder. Rafael grabbed Lawrence's legs and pulled, dragging him across the carpet in the back of the Land Rover and making the fat man screech and thrash, until he dropped out of the back of the car. He landed on his face, nose first, and when Rafael dropped the man's legs, he saw the blood. Lawrence twisted in the dirt, face bloody, his eyes rolling, his chest moving as if he was in the middle of an asthma attack.

"Wait."

"No."

Rafael stepped over him and returned to the driver's seat.

"Wait!"

He started the engine. The radio came on, some obnoxious dance music that Rafael killed after a few frowning seconds. As soon as the music died, he heard the screaming pleas for him to *wait, please, just hold on a minute, you don't have to do this.*

Rafael let the engine idle. He checked the mirror. Lawrence was only partially visible on the ground, but his entire body was tense with the effort of shouting. If they weren't in the middle of nowhere, he might have been worried about being heard. Instead, he let the engine run for a while longer before he finally got out of the car.

"Talk."

"Please don't leave me here."

"You will show me where the villa is."

"Yes. Okay. Sorry. Please." Lawrence stared at him upside down. Tears ran sideways over and into his ears. His mouth hung open, strung with spittle. "I'll tell you whatever you need to know."

Rafael regarded the fat man and thought about the effort required to get him back into the Land Rover. Perhaps he could leave him here, try to find the place on his own. Lawrence had said it was in the mountains overlooking Marbella. There couldn't be that many villas in that particular situation.

But then, why waste time looking for a maybe when he had a guide to the definite right here? So he hauled Lawrence back into the Land Rover, making sure to keep his body as far away from the fat man's bloodied clothes as possible. He hoisted Lawrence into a sitting position against the tinted back windows and then slammed the boot.

They drove for an hour before Lawrence appeared to know where they were. He tried to get Rafael to drive into Marbella but was refused. A busy town center and a fat man with lungs like Lawrence, and there'd be trouble. Rafael wished that Lawrence wouldn't keep thinking he was stupid. It irritated him.

"It is in the hills, Lawrence. That was what you told me. Concentrate."

He did. No more tricks, no more escape attempts, even though he knew what would likely happen the moment they arrived. He directed Rafael out to the highway again, and then the longer way round to a set of tree-lined hills with a few white specks visible at the top. "Up there."

They passed by the entrance to the private road, then Rafael brought the Land Rover back the way they'd come and found a turnoff farther on down the way. Rafael pulled the Land Rover into the turnoff and switched off the engine. The two men sat listening to the trees moving all around them.

"What time are they supposed to arrive?"

"Noon."

Rafael checked his watch. It was ten thirty now.

He nodded, let Lawrence breathe for half an hour longer, until he was settled and safe and complacent, and then he turned in his seat and put a bullet in the fat man's right eye.

Twenty-Seven

Ten thirty in the morning, and Ollie had been awake for about an hour longer than he'd wanted. He stood at the breakfast bar in his large, pristine kitchen poking at a half grapefruit with a silver spoon. He wore a thin, Chinese-looking dressing gown that brushed his knees and a T-shirt from the Warner Brothers theme park in Valdemoro. Looked as if Bugs Bunny was waiting for the embroidered dragon to speak.

"So what you telling me, Scott?" Ollie put some grapefruit in his mouth and his nose wrinkled. "Ugh, Jesus Christ. Good for your heart, rotten in your mouth. Who eats this for breakfast?"

Scott looked across at Tony, who looked away. No help.

"Well?"

Scott shrugged. "Some people like it. An acquired taste—"

"No, what's your fucking news, Scott?"

"Oh. I don't really know. I mean, it was Tony who thought we should tell you."

"Tell me what?"

"Someone killed Sancho."

"Sancho?"

"Sancho Rios."

"The sleazy twat, right? Yeah, I remember him." Ollie nodded. He dug the spoon into a bowl of sugar and dumped some onto the grapefruit. "And what does that have to do with me?"

"Well, I thought it might be trouble." Scott cleared his throat. "Perhaps the start of something." Another glance at Tony. "I mean, we all know how things have been—"

"No, we don't." Ollie pointed the spoon at Scott. "*You* don't, I know that much. You don't have a clue. You shouldn't anyway." He nodded at Tony. "What do you think?"

"I think there are explanations. I think Sancho Rios was a piece of shit and that he hung out with other pieces of shit, and maybe one of them took a knife to him. There's that scalper"—he clicked his fingers, trying to remember the name of the guy in the gray suit, the Spanish Tony Curtis wannabe—"*Javier*. That guy."

"Do I know him?"

"Don't think so. He's small time. He's a scalper mostly, does a bit of peseta loan sharking. Fingers in pies, but no threat, not to us. Thing is, he acts like an Italian. Very emotional, carries a blade, and the last I heard, him and Sancho weren't on good terms. I wouldn't be surprised if they'd had a meeting up and a falling out and emotions ran a bit high. Next thing you know, someone's got a breathing hole where his Adam's apple used to be."

"You think that, do you?" Ollie's cheeks sucked in with another bite of grapefruit, his left eye twitching a little.

"I think it's a possibility."

"Any other possibilities?"

"Nothing concrete."

"But?" Ollie waited for Tony to continue and then waved the spoon. "You have ideas. Let's hear 'em."

"Lawrence hasn't come in yet. And as much as he's a slow bugger, he's never been late a day in his life. Plus we had his missus calling up for him. Seems he went off with Sancho last night and he hasn't been home yet. Now I don't think Lawrence had anything to do with Sancho, but it's still not right. They never spent any time together before, so there's no reason why they'd pal around now. Lawrence is more likely to chase a fucking buffet than a bird, and like I said, he's never late. Got his mobile switched off too, which is something else he never does."

"So what's the story now? Someone did the Spaniard and then—what?—took Lawrence hostage or something?" Ollie looked at the men gathered in his kitchen and shook his head, smiling. "Well, it's new, I'll give you that. Christ knows we've heard enough fucking threats recently."

"If Turgenev wanted to send us a message, Ollie, then Sancho would be an easy target."

"No."

"I know it's not a popular suggestion, Ollie—"

"It's a paranoid suggestion, Tony."

"Okay, maybe, but I'd rather be paranoid and wrong than complacent and dead."

Ollie pushed the grapefruit away and clattered the spoon into the bowl. He sighed and turned on his stool. Behind him, the kitchen opened into a dining area that was festooned with Union Jack bunting, the table already set for the big roast dinner. They had an HD projector set up and ready with the stream from the BBC iPlayer of the Jubilee celebrations from the day before. He seemed to weigh up the decorations as if he was thinking of tearing them down. "All right. Sancho Rios was bent as a dog's hind leg, wasn't he?"

"Yeah."

"So if it wasn't someone else, it would've been us doing the dig later on."

"Probably."

"He knew the rabbit, didn't he? The matador?"

Tony forced a shrug. He didn't need this coming back to bite him in the arse, not until he'd heard from Manuel or, more likely, Jason. He'd called Jason earlier on, told him to get himself down to the police station and ask for Rafael Ortega by name. He'd yet to hear back. "I think so. They weren't close or anything, though."

"Okay, so right, the police want to call it a robbery?" He looked at Scott.

Scott nodded. "That's the official line."

"Let them have it. Move on." Ollie looked at the watch on the inside of his wrist. "As for Lawrence, it's still early yet. This might be the one time he's hungover and tardy, and I don't need you lot shitting kittens over it." He slid off the stool and led the way through the dining room. "Listen, today isn't about being frightened. It's a celebration—not just the fucking Jubilee, but of everything we've accomplished out here. We've made it ours. You should be proud of yourselves." He smiled, stopped by the large French doors that led outside to the enclosed backyard and swimming pool. "Besides, if that cunt Turgenev decides to make today the day he loses the fucking plot and comes after me, he'll have a house full of men with semiautomatic weapons to deal with, won't he?"

He slapped Tony's arm and then pushed out into the backyard.

Yeah, he had a house full of men with semiautomatic weapons. But that house would also be full of those men's families. "Ollie—"

"Don't worry about it." Ollie stopped by one of the loungers and sat down. "Go and get your broods up here. We'll get the dinner on, have a nice time of it."

Tony didn't move. Ollie gave him a look.

"Seriously. On you go."

And on he went, with Scott by his side. Carmelita came out of one of the bedrooms that smelled like stale sweat and shouted at Ollie for not finishing his grapefruit.

Scott chirped up as soon as they hit the open air. "You think it's something, don't you?"

Tony lit a cigarette and barely had the first drag in his lungs before he blew it out. He ran a finger under his nose and looked around to make sure nobody was watching. "I'm not sure. Better we keep an eye out, eh? Last thing we fucking need is to be caught short out here."

Max approached from the main gates. "What happened?"

"Nothing. Ollie doesn't want to know about it. Thinks we're all para."

"Sancho's still dead, mind."

"I know that."

"You don't think it's our Russian pal, though, do you?"

Tony shrugged. "I don't know who it is, or if it's anyone." He shook his head. "Could be the Russians, I don't know. Does it matter?" He pulled his mobile and checked for messages. There was nothing. "Lawrence hasn't called back."

Max frowned. "Anything you want me to do?"

"Yeah, keep an eye out. Ollie wants this to be happy families; he can have it, but it doesn't mean we can't be careful."

Tony moved back to the gates, leaving Scott looking around and trying not to show it. The bloke was well meaning, but there wasn't an aggressive bone in his body. He'd be fucking useless in a square go. And as the rest of them arrived at the villa, Tony started to think that if it all kicked off, they'd be well up the fucking creek.

First to arrive were Max's wife and daughter. Max took his missus off to one side and looked as if he was explaining the situation. His daughter went straight in, and Tony heard Carmelita spoiling her rotten. Then there was Barry and Scotch Alec, a couple of young wide lads with tribal bands and close-cropped hair who both smelled like a fucking brewery and whose movements and attitudes suggested that they were still half-pissed from the night before. They didn't have any families, but they'd brought a pair of orange-tanned and barely dressed girlfriends along with them instead. Tony told them about Lawrence and Sancho and asked if they were carrying. Both shook their heads. Tony told them to go and pick something up from the wine cellar. Big Chris's family was next; closely followed by Doug the Geezer, Lorraine, and their three boys; and Liam's young wife, Corrine, and their baby girl, who had a name Tony could never remember that had too many vowels in it. Soon the villa was thick with chatter and laugh-ter and it was knocking on noon. Tony saw Lisa's car pulling in front of the villa, the courtyard already gleaming with a variety of well-waxed people-carriers and low-slung sports cars. He excused himself from a conversation with Max and trotted out to meet her. He smiled at the kids, and they went in to play with the others. He watched them go, one hand on Lisa's arm.

She looked worried. "What's the matter?"

He looked over her shoulder. "Do us a favor and lay off the wine, all right?"

The worry turned into a frown. "What's that supposed to mean?"

"We had a bit of trouble this morning, that's what it means. If it all kicks off, I want to make sure you're going to be sharp, you get me?"

"Kicks off?"

He put a finger on his lips. "Not so loud, all right? It's not com-mon knowledge, and Ollie wants us to keep it quiet—"

She was quieter now, but no less insistent. "What d'you mean 'kick off,' though?"

"Someone got killed last night."

"Who?"

"Nobody you know. Nobody important. But I don't want us to get complacent." He smiled and opened his hands. "Listen, noth-ing's going to happen probably. But if it does, I want us looked after."

"Okay."

He smiled wider, touched her face. "Okay?"

She nodded. "You're carrying?"

"Always, love."

She poked him in the middle of the chest. "Never off duty."

"Never."

"You coming in?"

"Got something to do first." He nodded at the door. "I'll see you in a bit."

She kissed him and headed into the villa. He stood watching her and wondered if she'd manage to keep her mouth shut. Probably would. Probably nothing to worry about, but he didn't want Ollie hearing that it was his missus who spread the goss that took the buzz off the party. But Tony couldn't keep his mind from wandering to the what-ifs. Fact of the matter was they were overdue a show of force, and early signs pointed to today as the day. As much as Ollie thought they were safe, most of the blokes were like Scotch Alec and Barry—they were unarmed and they'd probably be a bit lagered up by midafternoon. They were sitting ducks if Turgenev wanted to make his move.

But he couldn't keep thinking like that. He'd warned his wife and told the single blokes to tool up on the sly, which reminded him...He called Jason. It went to voice mail and the moment it did, Tony felt a sickening chill. Jason wasn't the kind of lad to turn off his mobile, just like Lawrence wasn't the kind of bloke to be late to a free lunch. And where was Jill? Even if Lawrence hadn't turned up, Tony expected Jill to have called back by now.

His mobile rang. The display read LAWRENCE.

He connected the call. "Lawrence, where the fuck are you, mate?"

The voice that answered didn't belong to Lawrence, but it was still familiar. "This is Tony?"

"Who is this?"

"He is at the end of your road."

"You what?"

"The white Land Rover, Tony. You will find him in the back."

"Who the fuck is this?"

The call disconnected. The caller didn't sound Russian, but the way his ears were buzzing right now, he couldn't exactly remember what kind of accent he had either. He certainly hadn't been English. Tony went into the villa and grabbed Scott from the hall.

"What you doing?" Scott took one look at his face and his mouth snapped shut.

"Outside." They went outside. "You armed, Scott?"

"In the car. What happened?"

"Just got a call from someone who says they know where Lawrence is."

"Where?"

"The end of the road."

Scott took a second before he appeared to understand. "What, this road? Here?"

"I need you to go down and have a look."

Scott shook his head. "I can't do that."

"You're going to have to, mate. I can't leave here, just in case."

"Why me?"

"Because you're the only fucker in grabbing distance who doesn't have a wife, kids, or a fucking girlfriend in there."

Scott's face opened with indignation. "What, so I'm expendable?"

"I didn't fucking say that, did I? I just mean if you leave the party for a little while, nobody's going to be asking where you are. Except me. You've got my number. Give us a ring when you get down there."

"You could come with me."

"Got my family to look after, mate."

"Yeah, but—"

"Listen, Scott, don't be a selfish cunt all your life. Get your arse down to the end of the road and see if Lawrence is down there, see what kind of state he's in, and give us a ring. It's a piece of piss. Just do it." He turned to walk away, then stopped and nodded at Scott. "*Now*, Scott. Before I lose my fucking temper with you."

Scott looked around him, then walked off to his brand-new Merc with its tinted windows and top-of-the-line stereo system and all mod cons, and Tony couldn't help but think that Scott would've swapped all that for a nagging wife and screaming kids right about now.

Twenty-Eight

He'd watched the cars slow and indicate as they turned up toward the private road. There were family cars, SUVs, and people carriers. There were a variety of children, many different ages, clogging the backseats, harassed and pale-looking men behind the steering wheels, and their cheaply glamorous women next to them. A couple of the men arrived with girlfriends who looked older than the middle-aged wives he'd just seen. It had taken him all his concentration to count the number of men who had driven up to the villa, and the last number he could remember was five or six, but he knew that there were more men up there, because of the families that arrived driven by the wives. So nine or ten men, and the two Grahams, most likely armed.

If he'd had any sense he would have waited until the night before he made his move, waited until they were all drunk and half-asleep before firing that first shot. But his head hurt and his mind wandered, and both told him that he didn't have the time to waste waiting for the perfect opportunity.

He stood now in the trees behind the Land Rover, as still as possible. He had smoked the last of Sancho's cigarettes a few minutes ago, but his brain cried out for another. He wasn't nervous, but there was an energy that would spill into a tremble if he didn't continue to control it.

Lawrence was laid out in the back of the Land Rover. He hadn't smelled very good when he was alive and now he was positively rank. Rafael had dropped all the windows to allow for a draft. It meant he could smell the fat man's dead stench from his position in the trees, mingling with the smoke from the fire.

He had taken the dagger to one of Lawrence's sleeves, then dropped the strip of material into the petrol tank, fed it down until it was soaked through, and then did the same with the other end. Then he used the lighter on the wet ends and threw it into the back of the Land Rover. One end of the sleeve landed next to Lawrence's leg, the other up by the side of his shirt, and the breeze took the flames from sleeve to trouser in seconds. Once the cheap material of his shirt took, the flames blossomed over Lawrence's belly and there was a slight smell of pork in the air to go with the smoke and crackling.

It was then that Rafael called Tony and told him where he could find his fat friend.

He waited, forcing himself to count to a hundred, more to keep his mind from slipping into the past than anything else. When he heard the sound of an approaching car, he had just counted off eighty-seven.

The car was a Mercedes, glossy and black all over. Even the windscreen appeared to be tinted. It turned out of the private road and stuttered, the car itself almost rearing back in horror at the sight of the burning Land Rover. Rafael saw brake lights and the figure behind the wheel shift a little as if it wasn't sure what to do next. Then a young man, slim and well dressed, got out of the car, a mobile phone to his ear. He was talking, but Rafael couldn't hear what he was saying. The man approached the Land Rover warily, as if he expected the car to explode at any moment. A child brought up on cheap straight-to-video action movies, no doubt.

"…don't know, Tony. I mean, I can't *see*, can I? It's all smoke."

Rafael watched the man get closer to the car. The man squinted through the smoke, trying to avoid it as he leaned to one side. It was then that he must have caught sight of Lawrence in the back, because he recoiled and a grunt of surprise jumped from his throat.

Someone at the other end must have said something. The man opened his mouth to reply but waited for them to stop talking first. "Yeah, he's here. He's out here. I think they shot him. There's blood on the inside of the…Yeah, and he's on fire now." A brief pause and a look of incredulity. "Yes, he's dead. Of course he's fucking dead…Well, it was a stupid fucking question, wasn't it?" A shake of the head and the man's bottom lip rolled upward as he turned away from the car. He looked as if he was going to be sick. Trying to catch his breath, leaning forward as he listened to Tony.

Rafael moved in the woods, raised the revolver. Pointed it at the back of the man's head.

"Okay." The man straightened up. "You're going to tell Ollie?"

A pause. Rafael moved out of the woods now. A sudden movement from the man and he'd shoot. Anything else and he'd work with it.

"You have to tell him, Tony."

The man turned back to the Land Rover and saw Rafael. He opened his mouth, his eyes wide.

"Oh—"

Rafael shook his head, mimed a chop across his throat with his free hand.

The man appeared to regain his composure, speaking into the phone as if nothing had happened. "No, yeah, I'll come back up. No problem. See you."

The man disconnected the call. The phone shook in his hand.

Rafael gestured to the Mercedes. "You drive."

He followed the man to the car and tapped him on the shoulder. The man turned. Rafael put his hand on the door.

"When I tap, we open."

And when he tapped, they opened the doors and got into the car at the same time, Rafael with the revolver trained at the back of the man's head. The man kept his hands in the air until Rafael told him to shut his door.

The man glanced at him in the rearview mirror. "What do you want?"

"Go."

"Where?"

"To the villa. And move the mirror. Do not look at me."

The man moved the mirror.

Rafael pressed the barrel of the revolver into the back of the man's neck. "Now drive."

The man put the car into gear. He reversed a little way from the Land Rover, then turned right, back onto the private road. The brown hair at the back of his neck was dark and matted with sweat. When he spoke, his attempt at outward calm was mitigated by the tremor in his voice. "You don't sound Russian. Don't look Russian, either." He sniffed. "So I'm guessing this has got nothing to do with Turgenev, am I right? So this is some kind of personal thing. I know you killed Lawrence, but what about Sancho? You kill him, too?"

Rafael remained quiet. He watched the sweat on the man's neck, with occasional glances out through the side windows at the rumbling scenery. The car moved slowly. The man was careful not to go too fast just in case of bumps, obviously. He cared about his own life. That was a good sign. It meant he was thinking.

"Okay, I'm just going to put it out there. What you're doing, if it's personal, then there's something you should probably know. If there's someone up at that villa you want to hurt, you need to know that all his mates are there today, and their families are with them. And these lads, they'll do anything to protect their families. They won't think twice about shooting you in the face if you get anywhere near them. So what I'm saying is, you might want to rethink your current plan, because there's no way you're going to be able to storm in there with your six-shooter there and take out more than the plaster on the walls before they bring you down. The best thing you could do is let me stop the car, and then you can do one. I'm not saying that you *shouldn't* do whatever it is you want to do, but I'm saying there's probably a better time for it, you get me? Yeah?" The engine growl lowered, the car slowing as it jumped over a bump in the road. "So I'll just pull over and you can—"

"Drive." Rafael jabbed the gun into the back of the man's neck hard enough to knock his head forward. The front sight left a red mark, scraped a small strip of skin raw.

"Drive. Right." The man swallowed. "I'm just saying, I don't want you to think that this is the only course of action."

"You do not want to die?"

"No, I don't want to die."

"Then do as I say."

Up ahead, Rafael saw two figures. Both carried weapons.

The man saw them too. "What d'you want me to do?"

"Slow down." Rafael moved back in his seat, removing the revolver from the back of the man's neck and getting settled farther down. He could see through the back and front windows but was satisfied that nobody would be able to see in. "I still have the gun on you. Understand that."

"Okay."

"See what they want."

Rafael kept the gun trained on the back of the man's head as the car slowed to a stop by the two men.

The man buzzed down the window. "All right, Chris?"

Chris approached the driver's side. There was a small machine gun in his hands and a radio on his hip. He was a large, square man, had a military air and a spongy midriff. He looked worried. "You see Lawrence?"

"Yeah, he's down there."

"How bad is it?"

"He's dead."

Chris wet his lips. He leaned a hand on the roof of the Mercedes and showed a large, dark sweat patch under one arm. "How are you?"

Scott's smile was tight when he turned to answer. His hand moved from the steering wheel. "I'm fine. I should probably see Tony, though."

His hand moved again. A muscle twitch, just out of sight, a tremor from his hand through to his shoulder. Rafael moved in the backseat. Scott was moving something on the steering column. It made a faint clicking sound.

The headlights.

"All right, then. He's waiting for you up at the villa." Chris stepped away from the car. His gaze went from Scott to the tinted back window and then he gave an almost imperceptible nod to his colleague on the other side of the car as his hand went back to the machine gun.

Rafael pulled the trigger first. Scott's head exploded, snapped forward, stippled the windscreen with blood, brain, and skull. The shot deafened Rafael, shocked the two men outside into a freeze.

Rafael kicked the door open on the back driver's side.

The movement grabbed Chris's attention. He peppered the door with bullets as Rafael hauled himself across the backseat in the opposite direction. He saw the other man raise his gun, saw the revolver sight pass in front of the man's chest, and squeezed the trigger, the tinted window spider-webbing on impact. There was a jagged report. The high whine replaced Rafael's hearing again. The man dropped to the ground, a pink mist hanging in the air for a second before dispersing. Rafael pulled himself out of the car and onto the ground. He dropped and rolled, looked under the car, saw feet and pulled the trigger again and again. A bullet caught Chris's shin and Chris dropped to the ground. The revolver clicked empty. Rafael pulled himself upright and behind the back tire just before it exploded and wilted as Chris let off one more burst. Rafael felt a burn in his leg, saw blood.

The whine in his ears crackled into normal hearing, or close enough. He heard Chris breathing heavily, heard the scuff of trainer against ground and glanced around the side of the car to see him pulling himself to his feet. Rafael tossed the empty revolver and pulled Sancho's pistol. He heard Chris move away from the car, coming round the side. A volley of bullets tore up the trunk. Rafael sprung from the back tire and ran, head down, to the front of the car. The bullets kept coming, stamping the bodywork, punching through the windows and snatching up dirt at Rafael's feet until he felt one connect and put him off-balance. He yelled and made a grab for the bonnet, bounced once, then dropped to the ground.

He rolled again, kicked up dirt and dust. He saw Chris start to limp around the side of the car and then unloaded Sancho's pistol into the first moving target he had, his eyes screwed shut as he let out a throat-ripping yell.

Then it all stopped. Silence for a few seconds. He opened his eyes to a small dust storm in front of him. He dropped the empty pistol on the ground and pulled himself back along the dirt. There was that sound of heavy breathing again, but it was wetter this time.

He crawled over to the other man and grabbed his machine gun, then got to his feet, the gun pointed in the direction of the sound.

He limped round the side of the Mercedes, gun up and ready, to discover Chris on his side, facing away from him. The machine gun lay off to one side. Something hitched in the man's lungs and then gurgled as he exhaled. Rafael watched him as he drew up to the driver's-side door. Chris tried to move, but he was too weak.

Rafael watched him flail for a moment then turned away. He wasn't worth the ammunition.

Rafael grabbed Scott by the shoulder and pulled him, then let him tumble out of the Mercedes. He got behind the wheel and leaned on the accelerator. The car jumped forward and some of the windscreen shook out of the frame. He knocked the rest away with the butt of the gun and accelerated.

Up ahead, he could see the villa's gleaming alabaster behind the heavy black gates. He pulled his seat belt across just before the collision, which took one gate off its hinges and sent a screech of metal against metal through the whole car. Rafael opened his eyes to see the car wedged between the gate and the post. He kicked open the passenger-side door and got out. There were shouts from inside the villa.

Rafael ran to the tree line. Somewhere close he thought he could hear a baby crying.

Episode Seven

Twenty-Nine

Scott hadn't sounded right, which was why Tony sent Big Chris and Barry down to intercept him before he got anywhere near the villa. He was glad, too, because that gunfire was all the confirmation he needed that something had gone completely fucking pear shaped. He ran to the windows in the front living room, saw Scott's Merc wedged sideways in the front gates. No way to get anyone out unless they brought down the whole fucking fence.

He went back into the villa, ran to the kitchen. In the dining area that stretched out to the backyard, everyone was gathered round the table for roast and a show but had frozen at the sound of the guns. Ollie was the first out of his seat, marching toward Tony. He didn't say anything until he was within grabbing distance, then he put a hand on Tony's shoulder and ushered him out of the kitchen while he gestured for the men to follow.

"Fuck's going on, Tone?"

"I don't know. Turgenev?"

"You're having a laugh."

Scotch Alec closed the door to the kitchen. Five men with Tony in the hallway now, and they were all looking at him. "I don't know what it is, but I know Scott's Merc is blocking the gates out there, and whoever it was managed to get past two blokes with machine guns, so if that sounds like having a laugh, Ollie…"

"Fuck's sake."

"We need to shift the families."

"Why?"

"You've got an open back way there, Ollie." Tony pointed at a far door. "What's that? Game room?"

"Yes."

"It's an inner room. No windows. We need to get the families in there. Max and Doug, you go and get them in there, all right?" He nodded at the kitchen door. "*Now*, fellas."

Max and Doug ran off to the kitchen. As soon as the door opened, there was a rising tide of shouted questions and crying children. Scotch Alec and Liam were already carrying, but Tony suddenly felt light. "Anyone got an extra on them?"

Liam pulled out a revolver and handed it to Tony.

The families started to filter out from the kitchen. When Lisa appeared, she frowned a question at Tony. He nodded at her, and she hugged Aiden and Hayley to her as they fell back into the stream of people headed for the game room. Doug brought up the rear. His sunburn red turned a pale pink, and his Adam's apple danced in his throat.

"Doug, you stay in there with them. You carrying?"

"No."

"Fuck's sake. Here." Tony handed him the revolver. He'd have to pop down to the wine cellar. "Look after them, all right? Don't open that fucking door for anyone until I tell you, okay?"

Doug looked at the revolver. He was old, thin, hadn't been a major part of the business for ten years or more. The sight of a gun in his hands didn't exactly fill Tony full of confidence, but he was more use in there than he would be outside.

Tony slapped him on the shoulder. "You'll be all right, Doug. Just try to keep them calm."

Doug followed the last kid, a small blond lad who belonged to Big Chris, into the game room and closed the door. Tony led the way into the kitchen and told Alec and Liam to watch out the back. "If they're coming in, they'll come in there and try to drive us out the front. Me and Max need guns, so we're going down the cellar. Any problems, give us a shout."

"You do what you need to do." Ollie made for the back bedrooms.

"Where you going?"

"I'm looking after Dad."

"You need a weapon, Ollie."

"I'm sorted. It's all right."

"We need you out here."

"And he needs me in there, doesn't he?" He pointed at the door to Frank Graham's bedroom. "No disrespect or anything, but he's worth more than all your kids combined, so don't forget who you're fucking working for here, Tone. You and the lads sort this out, I'll make sure you're well rewarded." He moved away toward his father's bedroom.

"Ollie—"

"I'm serious, Tony. Sort it." He disappeared into his father's room, slamming the door behind him.

Max puffed his cheeks. "All for one, eh?"

"Fuck it." Tony turned away. "Come on."

They jogged into the kitchen and through to the utility room and the door that led to the wine cellar. Tony tugged on a light cord and fluorescents came on below. Max closed the door behind them as they descended the narrow staircase to the wine cellar. It was a low-ceilinged room, stacked with crates and wine racks. In one of the crates was a selection of machine guns and pistols collected over the years. These were throwaways, one-hit wonders, and Tony wasn't sure most of them still shot straight, but he wasn't in a position to be too picky. He blew the dust off a revolver and loaded it.

Max hoisted a machine gun to his shoulder. "Tell me the truth. How many people d'you think's out there?"

"I don't know."

"Ballpark."

"I didn't see anyone. All I saw was the car. If I was pressed, I'd say *one*."

Max shook his head. "One man doesn't kill three and do this much fucking damage."

"He does if he's determined."

Max slung the machine gun over his shoulder and picked up a pistol. He checked the ammo, then chambered a round. "If it's one, then it should be a piece of piss, shouldn't it?"

"Yeah."

A burst of gunfire upstairs; sounded like it came from out back. As they climbed the steps again, there was a scream; sounded like Alec. He was shouting for help.

Another burst cut him short.

Tony ran through the kitchen to the dining area and pressed himself up against the far wall.

Alec was down, sprawled over a sun lounger. His legs were spread, one knee bent, and he was hanging off the lounger with his head back and mouth open. The bullets that had cut him short had almost cut him in two. The back of his head was only an inch or so away from the ground. His gun lay about three feet away from his outstretched hand. Liam was in the swimming pool. What looked like a lifejacket of blood billowed up around his neck. There was no sign of a struggle, no sign of anyone else's presence. If Tony didn't know better, he'd think that Alec and Liam had shot each other. Max appeared at the opposite wall.

Tony adjusted his grip on his gun. "What d'you think?"

"I think we're fucked. I think we need to get out of here, man. Grab the girls and the kids and go."

"We can't do that."

"Course we can. Life's too bastard short." Max looked out at the backyard. "Getting shorter by the second an' all. Listen, Ollie's a daft cunt, and we're even dafter cunts for working for him. I didn't pick any fights with the fucking Russians, did I? No, I just did what I had to do to make a bit of money for my family." He looked back toward the hallway. "And he's just done one, hasn't he? So I'm telling you, mate, the best way for us is the Russian way, fucking offski, know what I mean?"

"Wait, Max."

But he was already running back toward the hallway. Tony followed, meant to stop him, but as soon as he left the kitchen, the idea left his head. Max was right. There was no loyalty here, not anymore, not when your family was at risk. Ollie'd fucked off and now so had Max, and everyone else was dead.

His phone rang. He fumbled it out of his pocket. The display read JASON.

As he connected the call there was another gunshot. It echoed through the villa, joining the screams from the game room.

He didn't say anything, couldn't find the words, his breath caught like a ball in his throat.

"Tony, you there?"

Tony nodded slowly, then realized he couldn't be seen. His voice came out in a whisper. "Yeah."

He saw something on the floor at the end of the hallway. Blood, pooling and spreading out across the tile. The light changed, a shadow moved.

"Just come out of the police station. Finally got to see someone—they keep you waiting for fucking ever in those places, don't they?"

"Yes."

The shadow grew larger. Tony saw a foot appear, then a leg.

"He's not there. I asked for Manuel, Manuel wasn't there. Had to do some digging around myself, found out they didn't pick him up. They tried to."

"He got away."

The matador emerged from around the corner. Slowly, as if he was in pain, his arm up and a revolver pointed right at Tony's head. It was almost a relief to see the bastard. It meant there was only one man, after all.

It also meant it was personal.

"Yeah, they lost him. Sorry, Tony."

"It's okay. Don't worry about it."

The matador stood. Watched him. Blood and dirt all over his white shirt. He was pale, probably injured, bleeding out. Part of his right shoe had been blown open.

Jason sounded as if he was driving. "How is it up there?"

"Oh, you know, the usual carnage." He cleared his throat. "Do me a favor, Jason, will you? Go and check out the manager's apartment again."

"Why?"

"Because he might come back."

"He won't, though."

The matador made a signal to kill the call.

"Don't come up to the villa. I'm telling you, don't come near the place. Seriously."

"What's up?"

Tony stared at the matador. He stepped closer. "Ollie's on the fucking warpath. Listen, just go down to the apartment. I'll see you there, okay?"

"Yeah, all right."

Jason disconnected. Tony kept the phone to his ear. He swallowed. He wouldn't beg, wouldn't go out crying. Even if the matador tortured him, he wouldn't go out like that. He still had his fucking bottle, even if everyone else had lost theirs.

"You are finished?"

"Looks like it."

"Then put your phone on the floor, please." The matador gestured to Tony's other hand. "The gun, too."

Tony did as he was told, slowly crouching and placing his gun and the phone on the floor in front of him, like they were an offering.

It wasn't Antonin Turgenev, wasn't the fucking Russians. Ollie and Frank Graham weren't important enough to warrant Turgenev's attention. The rumors were just their bullshit way of making their own little circle seem so important. And when you were a part of that circle, it was like wearing blinkers. Couldn't see anything beyond the end of your own arm, beyond your immediate experience. The Grahams were small fry to anyone outside of that circle. They would be crushed, Tony knew that, but it wouldn't be a huge decisive attack. There would be no drama from the Russians. It would be a simple case of mopping up whatever stains were left after the Grahams fucked up their own household. There was no immediate hurry, because the Grahams never posed any immediate threat.

And now, looking at one determined man with half a fucking brain, Tony understood why.

"Where is Frank Graham?"

"I don't know. Probably in the panic room."

"Panic room?"

"A special room. Locked from the inside. There's a code you need—"

"Do you know it?"

Of course he did, but he didn't say so. He swallowed. "You'll never get to him."

"Show me the room."

"It won't matter."

"Now. Show me."

Tony walked toward the matador, his hands up and his palms open. The closer he got, the worse the matador looked and smelled. It had been a long couple of days. He wondered how the fucker had managed to get away from the cops, and then he hoped that Jason did what he was told. The matador backed away as Tony headed for Frank Graham's bedroom. Tony glanced down when he saw the blood on the floor. Max's head was more hole than flesh. Must've caught it point blank.

He stopped in front of the bedroom door.

"In there?"

Tony nodded.

"Open it."

He opened the door. A single bed stood against the far wall. A window looked out onto a small walled garden on the side of the villa. There were white and yellow flowers, climbing greenery, and a bird table and bath. There was a small desk in the room, a television set, and a lingering smell of infirmity. A double wardrobe stood against a wall. Above the wardrobe was a small camera. Tony stopped in front of it and looked up at the lens.

The entrance was through the wardrobe. Anyone with eyes could see it—the door was flush to the floor and the rails and clothes that hung from them lay now in a pile. Another door stood silent and impervious like the entrance to some Narnian prison. A keypad was on the wall next to the door.

"Can he hear me?"

"I don't know."

The matador backed up and looked at the camera. Tony heard movement inside the panic room. They were in there, both of them. Something about the sound made Tony's lip curl.

"I have seen the families."

Tony swallowed. He looked at the keypad.

"You will open the door or I will kill them, one by one."

"It won't work, I'm telling you." Tony turned. "He doesn't have any family out here."

"I was not talking to him, Tony."

Thirty

They had been easy, these men. Like bulls charging at every movement, whirling at the slightest thing, easily maneuvered and easily slaughtered. When they were frightened, they went wild. When Rafael was frightened, his movements became minimal and measured. It was his one true advantage over them, and he had moved like a ghost, his feet light against the tile. He was wounded, yes. There had been the lucky bullets that tore into his shoe and made him leave a weak blood trail everywhere he went. There was the pain in his thigh, the blood already dried against his leg; his side, where the stitches had split; and his head—no longer bleeding, no longer aching, but frightening Rafael with the lack of pain, the numbness that spread into his mind, calling him on to remember the past when he needed to stay sharply in the present, even if he wasn't entirely sure why he was there anymore.

He pointed the gun at the back of the man's head. This man was named Tony. He remembered Tony. He was the one he'd called earlier on, tried to bring down to the end of the road to see Lawrence; the one who'd sent the young man—Scott?—down to do his dirty work instead. And outside of the two men behind this door and whoever was in the family room, it was just Tony and Rafael now.

"You know the code."

"I don't."

"I will kill you, Tony, and then I will kill your family."

"You'll kill me anyway."

"Not necessarily."

He had thought about shooting him the moment the door was open, but it didn't seem right. The man had surrendered immediately. He wasn't like the rest.

"I am tired, Señor. I want this to be finished."

Tony gave him a sidelong glance. Saw that he meant it, that there was a chance for escape. He stepped up to the keypad, his mouth open as if he wasn't sure which numbers to press.

"Is there a problem?"

"I can't remember."

"Think."

"I can't."

"Remember."

"I'm too fuckin' *scared*, all right?"

"Okay."

Tony blinked furiously. He touched the sweat on his face, his hand shaking. He swallowed.

Then he hit two buttons in quick succession, following it with three more.

On the final key press, there was a grating beep somewhere behind the wall and the door unlocked.

"Open it."

Tony put a hand on the door and pushed as hard as he could. The door swung inward. Rafael put a hand on his shoulder. He was about to tell him to go and see his family when a terrible roar hurled the Englishman backward, leaving only a bloody mist and the smell of smoke. Tony collided with Rafael, the pair of them stumbling backward into the bedroom and landing in a heap on the floor. Rafael shoved Tony off him and rolled as another explosion tore up the floor he'd just vacated. The Englishman was dead, his stomach and lower chest a glistening pulp. A bloody bile-like substance oozed from the side of his mouth.

Rafael kicked back across the floor to the nearest wall. He shook a finger in his ear, his hearing gone again. He concentrated, tried to hear. An empty sound. Hollow. A cracked metal weapon. Judging by the mess it had made of Tony, it was a shotgun. And the pause now, the commotion inside the small room next door, that pointed to a double-barreled shotgun. Given the standard of weapon he'd already seen—all cheap automatics and rusty old revolvers—that was a credible assumption to make. Which meant that his opportunity to take advantage of a reload was now gone.

The man in the panic room was speaking, but Rafael couldn't hear what was being said, the tone and volume too low to be heard. Sounded like those films of Americans who spoke in tongues and threw themselves around on the floor of their church. He checked his own gun, found he was down to two bullets. Tony had left his weapon in the hallway, so there was no use risking a quick search of the corpse. He still had the dagger in the back of his trousers, but he needed to be close enough to use it.

Rafael pushed back against the wall, rose to his feet, and looked around the room. He wiped his nose on the back of his hand.

Something flashed in his peripheral vision. He blinked, and the room changed. It became strange. He didn't know where he was. Saw the gun in his hand and the blood on his shirt, the dead man in front of him, and heard the other one shouting.

"You hear that, you fucking cunt? That's what you're going to get!"

The voice was familiar. His heart raced. The voice was familiar, and its familiarity was frightening.

Think. Remember.

Another flash, another blink, and he remembered. A double-barreled shotgun. The man in there had a double-barreled shotgun. He needed to get the man to fire twice in quick succession;

then he'd be able to take a chance. He shouted from the side of the door. "What is your name?"

There was silence. He heard a cough, or it could have been laughter; he didn't know for sure.

"You know my name. Everyone knows my fucking name."

"You are the gaffer, yes?" The name came to him then. "Ollie Graham."

That same sound, definitely laughter. "Who the fuck are *you*?"

He glanced at the revolver. "My name is Rafael Ortega."

The laughter, building into full-blown hysteria. "Oh Jesus Christ, are you fucking *kidding* me? Seriously? The fucking *bull-fighter*?"

"Yes."

"You hear that, Dad? It's the fucking bullfighter."

There was another sound, a wheeze. Rafael guessed it was the father.

"What do you want, Rafael Ortega?" The sound of movement in the room. Someone standing up, preparing for something. "You want your old job back, son? How about this, instead of driving, how about we get you on the fucking muscle? Thought you were an army of Russians coming to get us, so I think you've got some talent in that regard. What do you say?"

"You tried to kill me."

"Did nothing of the sort, Rafael. That wasn't me. That was Tony."

"Tony?"

More laughter. "The silly cunt on the floor out there."

Rafael looked at the dead man, searching for something familiar. There was another flash off to one side, and he felt tired. He was in the backseat of a car with a man named Palmer. A young man drove, the other man watched them from the front passenger seat, a gun in his hand. They drove for a long time, and the man in the front passenger seat—this Tony—asked them both vague questions, making time, which neither man answered. They drove out to the mountains—he remembered the sweetness of the air, the salt taste underneath, the sea breeze flowing up off the Med below—and then Tony told them to get out and dig...

Stop. Focus.

His head hurt. He put a hand to it. He was bleeding.

"...pain in the arse, and you know what, Dad? You were absolutely right. Should've put this one in the ground a long time before. Hasn't changed, either. He's still a fucking pain in the arse. You're a fucking ghost, mate, did you know that? You shouldn't be walking around. Tony shot you in the fucking skull. You should be as dead as him right now, and you know it. But never mind, son. You just stick your head round that door, and I'll sort that out for you."

A shotgun. Double-barreled. Remembering. Two shots.

Rafael picked up the bedside lamp, yanked it so the plug jerked out of the socket. He hefted the lamp in one hand, felt its weight. Looked at the open door. He braced himself. He wouldn't get another chance at this.

He ran for the door, turned and threw the lamp at the first figure he saw. A snapshot of the room—two men, one standing, one sitting—and then the first blast. The lamp shattered. Another blast quickly followed, splintering the wardrobe door as Rafael hit the other side.

That was it. That was two.

He turned back to the panic room, the revolver up and aimed.

A third blast punched him out, twisted his body off to the side and made him fire wild. The revolver bucked in his grip twice before the hammer clicked on empty and he hit the floor on his back.

The floor whirled around him. He didn't know which way to crawl.

He coughed, and the movement sent a wrecking ball through his lungs. He scrabbled at the floor, trying to pull himself out of

Ollie's line of sight. The dead gun still filled his palm, and he tossed it to one side. Tears in his eyes from the pain and the smoke and the knowledge that he'd misread the situation. It hadn't been a double-barrel, it was a pump-action, and of course there'd been more than two shots.

He crawled to the corner of the bedroom and slumped back against the wall. Blood slicked the tatters of his shirt on his left side. The pain in his side had gone from ache to agony with a single shot. His lungs screamed when he breathed. There wasn't just one wound now, there were many, all clustered around his ribs and stomach, all of them bleeding profusely. He put a hand to the wounds but only succeeded in stoking the fire that spread up the left side of his body. He put the hand to the wall, left a bloody smear as he leaned himself upright, kicking out with weak legs until he was on his feet. His head was spinning, his hearing shot, his mouth already thick with his own blood. He leaned against the wall, then the wardrobe, reaching for the dagger in his back with his free hand.

He couldn't stop now. He had to finish this. He'd lost his nerve too many times before to quit again now.

Rafael felt along the side of the wardrobe with his one free hand, leaning his right shoulder against the wood. Four steps to the gap, and then he waited, listening.

There was movement in the room, but it didn't sound the way it had before.

Rafael leaned around the corner, ready to pull his head back in case they fired again.

They didn't.

Ollie looked as if he was trying to make snow angels on the floor. He had a hole instead of a nose, and another instead of a throat. Blood on the floor around him, some more spray on the wall behind. Rafael watched him, moving his hand around the grip of the dagger like a heartbeat as he tried to keep his arm from going completely numb. Then Ollie stopped moving, and a clicking noise escaped the wound in his throat.

Rafael leaned against the doorway. The back wall of the panic room was shelving, bottled water, medical supplies, energy bars, and a bank of monitors. In the top left monitor, Rafael saw himself. He smiled. It meant he was still standing.

An old man stared at him from his wheelchair. He wore a brightly colored shirt with images of palm trees, beaches, and umbrella drinks all over it. It was spattered with blood. His eyes were wild, and he moved his lips in a parody of speech, trying to summon up saliva. He clutched what looked like an electric shaver in one hand. At first Rafael though it was a stun gun, but when the old man moved it to the puckered scar in his throat, he realized that it was a voice box.

The old man buzzed a curse that sounded like a dying radio. Rafael pushed away from the wall and entered the room. The curses became more extreme, cluttered with more static. Rafael slapped the gadget from the old man's hand. It bounced off the wall and landed by Ollie's head.

"Your name is Frank Graham."

The old man moved his lips. His nostrils had flared.

"You wanted to kill me."

Rafael leaned on the wheelchair, the dagger hand on the arm of the chair, the other holding the back of the seat. He breathed heavily, painfully, the effort threatening to put him on his knees. He looked closely at Frank, saw the veins in the whites of his eyes, the twitching pupils. They looked like horse eyes, startled and dumb.

"You wanted to kill me. I do not care why. Whatever it was, it was a bad reason. It was a stupid reason. I know it was this, because the decision was made by a bad and stupid man."

Frank breathed out through his nostrils, a snort of contempt. His hands shook against the arms of his wheelchair.

"You think you are powerful, because you have had men tell you so all your life. And maybe you have hurt weaker men to demonstrate your power, but you have bought or buried your obstacles because you know in your heart..." He pressed the point of the dagger into Frank's chest, felt the old man flinch under the blade. "You know in your heart that you are more manso than man. You shiver in your *querencia*; you paw at the sand and make a show, but you have no nobility, no value. When we kill a good, brave bull, he is given his *vuelta*, and the mules drag his carcass around the ring in a lap of honor. You are not worth the flow of the cape or the blood spilled for you. You are not worth the violence or the pain. And you know this, Señor. In your heart, you know this."

Rafael broke away to look at the floor for a moment, a wave of nausea crashing through him. He didn't have much time. He pushed away from the wheelchair with one hand, let the other guide him round to the back. He moved one hand up over the old man's head, grabbed a fistful of white hair. It was soft, like a baby's. There was some resistance, but it was weak. The old man shook in his chair. His breathing became noisier. There was a creaking sound somewhere down by the wheels.

"So you know, Señor, I do not do this because you are a threat. I do this as mercy."

The old man made a gasping noise as Rafael pushed his head forward.

"*Olé.*"

Rafael slammed the dagger into the base of the old man's neck. The old man opened his mouth. A breath whistled through the hole in his throat. His hands became white claws digging into the armrests. Blood welled up around the hilt of the dagger. When Rafael let go of the old man's head, it dropped to his chest with a click as his dentures came together. A dark stain appeared on the old man's shorts.

Rafael pushed away from the wheelchair, turning it slightly as he staggered toward the nearest wall. The floor tilted on him. He dropped the dagger and braced himself with both hands. His head ached again, and when he touched the wound he saw that he was bleeding, new blood on top of the dried already staining his fingers. He slid against the wall, threw a hand out to grab the doorjamb, and then hauled himself into the bedroom and then the hall.

It was cold. He leaned against the nearest wall and looked at the tile. A ghostly reflection looked back.

He heard movement in front of him.

Across the way, a door stood open and an old man, thin and trembling, held a pistol that looked as if it would break his wrists on the first shot. Rafael smiled at him, one hand pressed to the wound in his side, the other held up in mock surrender.

The old man swallowed. His mouth trembled. He lowered the gun.

A woman appeared at his side. She was blonde, might have been attractive a few decades ago. "Doug, what are you doing?"

Rafael moved from the wall. He headed for the front door.

"Fucking *shoot* him, Doug."

He staggered a few steps, then leaned on the front door, where he turned to see the woman reaching for the old man's gun. Behind them, he could see a small boy, blond like his mother, five or six years old, staring at him with large blue eyes.

He looked familiar, but he couldn't think why.

VUELTA

Marbella was a beautiful town.

It basked in the afternoon sun, the water reflecting a clear blue sky. If you squinted just so, or if your vision had been clouded with blood loss, and the numbness that you felt spreading through your limbs didn't stop you from feeling the warmth of the sun on your face, then you might believe that this was heaven.

And then you'd hear them. The English.

The bars along the beach were packed with expats. They were drinking hard to celebrate some event in a country they'd long since fled. They were a nation of patriots only when they were a couple of thousand miles away, and the Spaniards indulged them because of their money.

The money was everything, after all. It was what had turned Marbella into what you saw around you, and the money came from the English. They brought the money, the money built the hotels, created an industry, turned a fishing village into a full-blown resort where everyone had to speak English over their native tongue or else be branded arrogant. Because the expats didn't want to learn Spanish, or at least nothing beyond a few phrases to bark in a restaurant, or at a doctor when their diabetes was playing up, or when the local authorities wanted to charge them additional fees for building their holiday homes on prohibited land. And even then, the most serious issues were taken care of by their embassy representatives, the expat equivalent of mummy and daddy.

But there was still something about the place that drew Rafael back even though he was dusty, bloody, and close to collapse.

It was the sea. He was glad to see the sea. He remembered the sea. He remembered playing on the beach. He was remembering a lot more now; memories came to him in a rush of information and emotion, and he allowed it to happen. It numbed him as he staggered through the sweaty crowds, bracing his carcass against fat English women who screamed and clung to their fatter English husbands, their floral prints smeared with Spanish *sangre*. He heard someone suggest they call an ambulance or the police or something like that, only for someone else to say that it was none of their business. You know what the fucking Spaniards are like. Always up to something seedy. It was probably some kind of gang thing, right?

Rafael smiled and walked on. He couldn't stop, not now, not until he reached the sand. He felt his way now, using buildings and the odd person as a guide. He was bolstered by the buildings and pushed by the people, and still he walked, one foot in front of the other and sometimes off to the side, but always moving.

He reached the edge of concrete and tumbled down onto the sand, where he lay on his back, his arms out at his side, and stared at the sky.

Clouds scudded above. Seagulls circled. They looked like vultures.

"Señor, would you like to buy a flower?"

He saw a baggy old woman with a bunch of wilted marigolds in one hand. She moved down onto the beach with tiny steps and then sat on the sand next to him.

"I'm sorry, Señora, I don't have any money."

"I know. Neither do I." She smiled at him, showed white, perfect teeth. "I think we're the only ones, though."

"Maybe."

"This is a place of great riches, did you know that? Here, Puerto Banús, Estepona. People are very rich here. They own several homes; they have large yachts; they have large cars. I don't much like boats, Señor, but the *cars*. Beautiful cars. You could live in the cars. Did you know that El Cuñadísimo used to live in Marbella, Señor? Yes, he lived here in his declining years. He was a survivor, Señor. He lived past a hundred, can you imagine? Franco's brother-in-law, his right-hand man, a bloody man, a dangerous man, and all is supposed to be forgotten, yes?"

He smiled. "You remind me of someone."

"Someone clever, I think. Someone *wise*." She tapped the side of her head. "Yes, I remember, Señor."

"He remembered too."

"Everyone else likes to forget, but I like to remember. You should have seen his car. A beautiful car. One you could live in. One your entire family could live in."

"I have a family."

"Of course you do."

"I have a wife and son. They're beautiful."

"It was a Mercedes. I don't know the name of the car, the type, but I know it was a Mercedes. A big one. It was as black as night. As black as that man's soul. He had a chauffeur. The chauffeur drove him down here to the beach every morning. The car would pull up, that lovely huge car, and then the chauffeur would get out and open the door for El Cuñadísimo."

She let out a disgusted breath. Her top lip was curled up to one nostril and her eyes had half closed.

"You should have seen him, Señor. He was rich. Wealthy. Old-fashioned. In my day, and in his day, people would find him distinguished. He wore a tie with a tiepin. He carried a walking stick. If you didn't know who he was, if you didn't recognize him, then you might think that he was just another old man with money. And even if you did recognize him, perhaps you would rather forget. But not me, Señor. I did not forget. I remembered him. I remembered what he did, what he was responsible for. That man, Señor, he and his brother-in-law, they killed many, many innocent people. And yet there he was, must have been a hundred years old, fit and healthy and his conscience was undisturbed. I couldn't believe it. He should have been *haunted*, but he was acquitted, Señor. We allowed him to walk free because of our absent minds."

Another huff. Her voice cracked when she spoke again.

"But I did not forget. I saw him one morning. He was smiling, looking out to sea. He was on his walk. I went to him with my marigolds and I asked him if he wanted to buy a flower and then I spat in his face."

She fell quiet, remembering. The noise from the bar faded. Rafael heard the sea and the gulls above him.

"His chauffeur hit me in the stomach, threw me down. I bled inside. I was very sick. But I didn't forget. I still don't."

He closed his eyes.

He saw himself in his mind's eye. He was talking to Alejandro, asking him about Mexico and South America. He wanted to start again; he was desperate, but he knew that Alejandro wouldn't be able to help him, not really. He lost his temper, stormed out of the café, walking into the heat of the afternoon and cursing himself for trying to reconnect with the old bastard but knowing that Alejandro saw through him, that something had died the moment he turned his back on the plaza, that he had been ruined by his work for the Grahams. And he had been close to breaking down with Alejandro, close to tears, admitting his hubris and greed had brought him to this. But there had still been enough pride to smother true repentance.

And so he went to Javier. He saw himself now in the Casa de Verónica, sharing a few glasses of cheap wine and telling dirty jokes until it was time to steer the conversation toward money. And then he lowered his voice and asked, very humbly, for six thousand euros. A little problem with the planning rights on a holiday home up near Málaga. He had the money, but he wasn't liquid. Javier understood, didn't he?

Of course he did.

He saw himself with the six thousand euros that he'd borrowed off Javier, hiding it in Pilar's jewelry box. He thought about leaving a note but then decided against it. He would be home again soon enough. All he had to do was meet Palmer for one last time, give him the information, and then come home. He would have a few days to sort everything out—Palmer had promised him they would move quickly, and Ollie Graham wouldn't have time to ask questions when they did.

But they'd found him out on the coast road, at the petrol station, him and Palmer. There were two of them, Tony and Jason, who bundled Palmer and him into the back of a car, a Mazda—he remembered the car, because he'd seen it on his walk back into Marbella just now, and maybe he'd seen the boy behind the wheel too. Then they drove him up to the mountains, emptied his pockets, forced him to dig. Palmer talked and cried. Rafael remembered being glad of Palmer's tears. It meant he was stronger than the customs man, and it gave him the courage to turn on Tony after they'd shot Palmer in the back of the head. It gave him the strength to catch both bullets and survive.

They were all dead. Pilar and Samuel would have money to leave if they wanted. If they didn't, then they would be safe. There was nobody left to hurt them, except the old man who couldn't even hold his pistol high enough to aim and perhaps the boy who'd passed him in the Mazda. But then Rafael had left a strong enough tableau to make thoughts of revenge seem ridiculous.

He breathed out.

"I remember."

"Yes, Señor. You remember. You don't forget, like everyone else. It's good to remember."

He was back in the plaza then, on his knees, the toro smell in his nostrils as the bull sailed past his ear before it rumbled into the middle of the sand. He saw himself stand with a flourish, resplendent in his traje de luces, and the crowd exploded with cheers and applause as he turned to cape the bull, close enough to feel the animal's breath on his leg as it passed. And with each pass he heard the *diana*, the paso dobles looping with every pass he produced, the bull moving with him, attached to him by some unseen force, while the crowd screamed olé.

And he found himself then in his faena, faced with the bull, pic'ed and decorated with banderillas but still strong and willing. And he caped the bull again, brought it close until they almost moved as one, joined at the hip and cape. There was magic here; there was life. And as he moved away to prepare for the final blow, the moment of truth, sword in hand, he glanced across at the barriers and saw Alejandro watching him with tears in his eyes.

He smiled at Alejandro, then focused on the bull.

Both man and animal charged at the same time, came together at once. The sword slipped in to the hilt. The bull staggered and dropped.

"I remember."

He turned to the plaza audience as they brought out the handkerchiefs that demanded he be awarded both ears, a tangible eruption of emotion that hit him hard, made him blink, made him tired.

He opened his eyes and heard the sea now, like applause.

He saw the sun, and it looked like twenty-five thousand white handkerchiefs fluttering his triumph.

And he smiled as he faded into the white.

Acknowledgments

Great big sloppy thanks must go to:

Everyone at T&M and Amazon, especially Andy Bartlett and Jacque Ben-Zekry, both of whom have impeccable taste that will be vindicated by the colossal sales of this book. Ahem.

Those brave souls Marcus Trower and Rebecca Friedman who proofread *Matador* so you don't have to. Bless yer eyes, and I promise to invest in a Chicago and MW one day. (note from proofreaders: should be *Chicago* and *M-W*)

John Rector, matchmaker extraordinaire. Hope I didn't ruin your rep.

Marc Gerald, who never met a contract he couldn't tweak, and Sasha Raskin, who never met a publisher she couldn't make pay.

Allan Guthrie and Vince Keenan, who both read *Matador* when it was wheezing and deformed, and helped nurse it back to health.

Finito de Córdoba, Morante de la Puebla and El Juli, for providing the inspiration in the first place.

A.L. Kennedy, Edward Lewine and John McCormick, for providing a comprehensive reading list.

Anyone who bought the serial and liked it enough to review. Yeah, I'm watching you. *All* of you.

The Natural Brunette, who remains the only person I really want to impress.

About The Author

Ray Banks shares his birthday with Chuck Barris and Curtis Mayfield, and he came screeching into the world on the same day that Roberto Rossellini took his leave. His past careers include gigs as a wedding singer, double-glazing salesman, croupier, dole monkey, and multiple turns as a disgruntled temp. Now he writes novels (eight so far, including *Dead Money*, *Sucker Punch*, and *Beast of Burden*) as well as novellas and a seemingly endless list of short stories. He spends his days holed up somewhere in Edinburgh, Scotland.

Kindle *Serials*

This book was originally released in episodes as a Kindle Serial. Kindle Serials launched in 2012 as a new way to experience serialized books. Kindle Serials allow readers to enjoy the story as the author creates it, purchasing once and receiving all existing episodes immediately, followed by future episodes as they are published. To find out more about Kindle Serials and to see the current selection of Serials titles, visit www.amazon.com/kindleserials.

23704553R00147

Made in the USA
Charleston, SC
30 October 2013